THE MISBEHAVING
DEAD

Edited by

Jack Burgos

The Misbehaving Dead

A Murder of Storytellers, LLC

Tulsa, Oklahoma

Edited by Jack Burgos

Cover Illustration by George Cotronis

A Murder of Storytellers, LLC
P.O. Box 700391
Tulsa, Ok 74170
www.AMurderOfStorytellers.com

This is a work of fiction. Names, characters, businesses, places, events, and incidents are either the products of the author's imagination or used in a fictitious manner. Any resemblance to actual persons, living or dead, or actual events is purely coincidental.

ISBN: 0-9986512-8-1
ISBN-13: 978-0-9986512-8-6

To those who have passed from this world into the great unknown beyond the threshold of death: please, don't ever come back.

CONTENTS

ENCEPHALOSHROOMS
by Adrian Ludens

Her customers craved a fix and Mara did her best to make sure her supply kept pace with the growing demand. It was nerve-racking, demanding, and deadly work but she was driven and determined to survive.

Mara crouched, concealed and waiting, with her finger on the trigger. A trickle of perspiration began a maddening insect-like crawl down her neck. She ignored the urge to move and waited for her target to step close enough for a sure shot. The zombie lurched past her as the bait squealed and strained at its bonds. She'd been three years into her neurosurgical residency when the zombie outbreak had altered the world. In moments like these, her experience steadied her hands. At the last possible moment, she squeezed her rifle's trigger. She saw a blossom of something that resembled raspberry jam seeping down the back of her prey's neck. It was, by some quirk of fate, near the same spot sweat still tickled Mara's neck.

The zombie collapsed. Mara scrambled to the fallen zombie, focused on getting it off the street and into the safety of her workshop before she encountered anyone. She crouched beside the zombie. The bullet slug had shattered two neck vertebrae and severed the spinal cord. It gazed up, paralyzed. A few inches higher and she'd have wasted a bullet.

Someone groaned. It wasn't the zombie.

"Shit." Mara looked up at the bait. The man she'd gagged and trussed to the splintered wooden light pole jerked his body within the confines of the ropes. He'd been one of those irritating bleeding hearts who insisted zombies deserved limited rights as citizens and should be confined to secured areas, but under no circumstances be killed. She endeavored to see things from this point of view but couldn't. Not that she'd tried too hard; zombies had killed her husband and daughter.

The bait's bulging eyes seemed even less human than the zombie's as he fought to break free. Mara mentally chastised herself for botching the job. Hunted relentlessly by armed bands of survivors, zombie numbers had dwindled as a result. The hunters didn't realize the zombies' secret potential. As far as Mara knew, she was the only person to have discovered the value in harvesting from incapacitated zombies. She made her living off the recently resurrected. Thanks to their contributions, she could almost say she thrived.

But now she had a loose end. Mara usually waited, letting the zombie bite and infect the blood of the bait first. *Then* she made the paralyzing neck shot, dragged her prey to safety, and returned to free the newly-turned. Kill a zombie; create a zombie—that was her motto in what she had dubbed this Crave New World.

But today she'd let herself get careless. She'd screwed up. Royally. She sighed, knowing she couldn't let him go.

The bait met her gaze, accusation in his eyes. He tried again to cry for help but the gag she'd stuffed in his mouth rendered his words inaudible. Mara chambered another round and shouldered her rifle.

This time the slug tore straight through the brain, leaving behind it a path of irreparable destruction. *Like the zombie outbreak itself,* she realized.

The report from the shot echoed once and faded. The tang of gunpowder lingered much longer.

☠☠☠

"Mommy, will you keep me safe?"

Dark circles hung like nesting bats beneath Skylar's eyes. Her six-year-old daughter sat on their couch with her knees beneath her chin, hands clasped protectively across her shins.

"Of course I will, honey." Mara took inventory of their jugs of filtered water and cans of food. She thought they had enough vegetables, but the shortage of fruit concerned her. If they had to stay locked down for longer than two or three weeks...

"What about Daddy?"

"What, honey?" She'd heard her daughter's question but automatically stalled.

"Where *is* Daddy? Did something bad happen to him?"

Keith had worked as a camera operator for one of the three local TV news teams. He'd been one of the first people in the city to encounter the city's earliest large assemblage of zombies. He and his assigned reporter had gotten a better camera shot than their competitors but had paid for it with their lives.

"Yes, but it's going to be okay because he's with Jesus now."

"In Heaven?" Skylar picked at a hangnail. Mara looked closer and realized her daughter had bitten all her nails to the quick.

"That's right."

"Why can't Jesus come down here and help us? Everything will be all right in Heaven while he's gone."

"He'll be around when you need him most," Mara lied. "As long as you believe."

⚘⚘⚘

Mara loaded the incapacitated zombie into her battered but functional wheelbarrow and steered down an alley toward her current safe haven.

She'd selected a location close to the home she had fled and not yet revisited. She wasn't sure she could face the memories head-on and had forfeited all her earthly possessions as a result. Instead she'd set up her base of operations in a ground level apartment adjacent to downtown.

She encountered no one on the return expedition, and for this, she felt thankful. Had she run into one of the gun nuts, she'd likely have gotten nothing more than a high five for eliminating another zombie, but in their enthusiasm, they often asked too many prying questions. A zombie rights activist, on the other hand, might accost her—not physically but with words. They often gathered to chant and carry signs with slogans like "Zombie lives matter," "Shame on Zombie Killers," and her personal favorite, "Jesus: the Original Zombie."

The zombie's eyes rolled in their sockets as she wheeled him into her workshop area. Whether he felt angry, afraid, or simply craved sustenance, Mara couldn't say. She paused to lock and bar the door. Then she dumped the zombie onto a rocker recliner and eased the blood-drenched back of the chair to a 45-degree angle. She fired up a generator she'd salvaged from an abandoned auto body shop and dragged a wooden straight-backed chair behind the recliner.

Mara plugged her most cherished possession into the generator. She'd stolen a cranial bone saw from a mortuary. Like the auto body shop, the mortuary had been abandoned, but it hadn't been entirely empty. Though any cadavers lying on the prep room's embalming table when they reanimated were long gone, she heard several zombies still locked inside the coolers pounding on their trays. She'd listened to the sounds as she'd gathered all the tools she thought necessary for her survival then fled the building, heart pounding.

3

In the months that passed Mara became adept at capturing and harvesting zombies, just as Indian snake charmers know how to handle cobras.

☠☠☠

The man standing just inside her door acted skittish and overcompensated by running his mouth.

"Have you ever tried your own stuff? You must have. It's the best— better than anything."

Mara didn't reply. Instead she gave her customer what she hoped passed for a warm smile. They'd completed their transaction: a Rolex for her and something that resembled a dead night crawler cut into pieces and stored in a plastic sandwich bag for him. Now she wanted him gone. He stank of flop sweat and unwashed feet.

The man dragged one hand through his greasy hair and giggled, chirpy and porpoise-like. Mara wondered how much longer before he cracked. Suicides now outnumbered confirmed zombie kills, according to the crackly AM radio broadcasts she picked up during her all-too-frequent sleepless nights.

"I tried a lot of stuff in the old days." The man giggled again. It was a sound tinged with madness and sorrow. "I made a lot of money in the stock market and really took advantage, y'know? Coke, mushrooms, heroin, even mescaline; but this stuff beats it all. It's mind-blowing, like having an orgy up in Heaven with a bunch of hot angels."

Mara mumbled her vague assent. She'd never tried her wares, but she'd heard similar colorful analogies. One professorial man had explained, "It is like introducing absinthe directly into the bloodstream, yet there is no hangover whatsoever; only a feeling of disappointment when the euphoria fades." A barefoot, dreadlocked woman had confided, "It's pure bliss. After I eat one of your 'shrooms, I feel like my brain is drizzled with THC gravy." Mara mentally filed these descriptions and had even used them on occasion with prospective customers. She had to admit "like an orgy with angels" had a certain allure to it.

"It's an escape from the hell this world has become," the former stockbroker said. He raked his fingers through his hair again. Mara wondered how soon he'd start balding if the gesture became a habit. Not that it mattered; she didn't think he'd tough it out much longer. Most of her customers seemed to be that way. Turning to drugs to escape the horrors of the real world was only a temporary coping method. She guessed most of them either ran afoul of zombies or took their own lives, swallowed up in tar pits of hopelessness and despair.

"What is it exactly?" The man's eyes glittered. "Shrooms, right? But laced with something."

Mara had no intention of giving her secret away. "You deserve a break. You *need* this," she urged. "You have a chance to soar up above this rotten world for a while."

The man gave her a look of surprise. "Yes…yes I do." He turned toward the door. Now that he'd been reminded of the gift in his hands, he seemed anxious to be gone, and for that, Mara felt thankful. What would she say if he'd pressed her? She knew someday she'd have to defend her secret. She kept a loaded handgun among other precautions against this eventuality.

"Make sure you go somewhere safe."

"Of course. Always." He left her apartment at a brisk walk and Mara chained and barred the door behind him. The warning had become her standard disclaimer. Mara concluded that some of her customers had died while taking the drug based on the uncomfortable fact that none of her customers returned more than twice despite their praise. She didn't think it possible to overdose, but surmised the out-of-body experiences left users in such a helpless state that some had been attacked and killed by zombies without ever being aware of the impending danger.

※ ※ ※

Zombies craved brains. So did the living.

After making this discovery, Mara had managed to live well—at least by modern standards. The world had changed. Though money had become obsolete, many still clung to it, stubbornly waiting for the day when things would go back to normal. Mara knew that day would never come.

She played all sides. She found this to be the best way to survive. Mara traded for goods and services, and kept herself on friendly terms with all factions, yet insulated herself against potential attack.

Life was good, but there was so much death. Mara, always a realist, knew that death was inevitable, as was suffering, hardship, pain, and grief.

She grieved the deaths of her husband and daughter. She still grieved the deaths of her parents, though they'd passed on long before the zombie outbreaks.

But she did not grieve the deaths of the others. The ones she killed were necessary for her own survival. Death was a bitter pill, one she swallowed out of necessity every day.

Only nagging memories of her daughter truly troubled her. She envisioned Skylar swinging at the park; stuffing popcorn into her mouth at the movies; drawing pictures at the dining room table.

In every one of Mara's memories of her daughter, Sky looked up and

5

asked, "Why did you lie to me, Mommy? Jesus wasn't there when I needed him. And you left me. Why did you let the zombies find me?"

☠☠☠

"Skylar, come here. Right now!"

Her daughter ignored her command. "I want Daddy!"

Zombies roamed downstairs. Mara had counted at least six of them as they burst through their home's front door and into the living room. Mara had raced upstairs to Skylar's room, knowing that more zombies would likely follow the first contingent. If she and Sky climbed down the vine trellis while the invaders shambled below, she thought they could lock themselves in the garden shed or the garage until the zombies grew restless and left the neighborhood.

But Skylar wasn't cooperating.

"Sky, get out of the closet. They're coming upstairs!" Mara cast a frantic glance over her shoulder. She could see the shadow of a pair of filthy bare feet through the crack between her daughter's bedroom door and the floor. The figure began pounding on the door. Mara's heartbeat seemed to match the pounding's tempo and urgency.

"We have to *go*!" Mara's voice cracked on the last word. Four years of undergraduate school followed by four years of medical school meant nothing to the zombies. Three years into her residency all hell had broken lose. What good was being a neurosurgeon when just finding food, water, and shelter had become nearly impossible tasks?

The pounding became incessant and the door began to splinter on its hinges; other zombies had joined the barrage. Her years lost on a now-worthless degree weren't even the worst of it. The worst, Mara realized, was that after Sky had been born, finishing medical school and starting her residency had kept her away from home. Skylar had grown up very much Daddy's Girl. It had never bothered Mara—until now.

"Sky, baby, you have to listen to Mommy. Daddy's not here and we have to leave..."

"I only want Daddy to carry me!"

Sky's words, though muffled by the hanging clothes, wounded Mara. She knew she couldn't afford to wait any longer. She crawled on her hands and knees into the dark depths of the closet. Sky screamed and kicked out, mashing Mara's nose against her face. Fireworks filled her field of vision and she withdrew. Liquefied copper seemed to be melting down the back of her throat. She gagged and spat blood.

The door exploded inward and a trio of zombies stumbled into the room. Panicked, Mara reached far into the closet and seized her daughter's

16

foot. She yanked, turned, and dove for the window as desiccated hands clutched at her clothing and hair.

Mara forgot about the trellis. In a moment of raw terror she kicked off against the windowsill and dove onto the roof of the garden shed.

She awoke in the weak gray light of the pre-dawn sky lying in relative safety above the reach of any zombies. Her nose throbbed and the tissue and nerves surrounding her left shoulder howled their dismay. She assumed she'd dislocated it in the fall. The pain from something else hurt worse however. In her right hand Mara clutched one of Skylar's shoes.

Mara heard the woman's screams and crept to her door, her rifle ready. Through the peephole she recognized her latest customer. *So much for getting somewhere safe before you got your fix,* she thought. She threw open her door and shot a look in both directions. Seeing no zombies, and no apparent danger, she hurried over and crouched beside the writhing woman.

"Dear God! Kill me!" The woman shook as if suffering a seizure. Saliva dribbled from her mouth onto the filthy hallway carpet.

"What's wrong?" Mara looked the woman over but refrained from touching her. "Where does it hurt?"

"In my soul!" The woman's eyes bulged from their sockets. Her hands shook. "So much pain, so much sorrow."

"From what? I don't understand."

"What the fuck did you give me?" Her customer moaned. "I feel pain, isolation, regret. I ca-ah-ah-ah-ah—" Mara guessed the woman had suffered a psychotic break. Blood vessels had burst in her eyes, creating bloody red clouds that encroached on the blue skies of her irises. Her pupils had become pinpricks.

Mara stood, realizing her assumptions had been wrong. She'd thought zombie attacks and suicides accounted for her customers not returning. Now the truth stared her in the face; many of her clients had suffered bad trips. Her harvested tissue provided a temporary ascent to ecstasy—or an unbearable descent into agony. Unfortunately, she had no way of knowing which experience awaited the user.

In a rare act of mercy, Mara aimed and pulled the trigger. Then she slung the rifle onto her back. Her ears rang from the report as she dragged the dead woman by her wrists down the hallway and out into the alley for disposal.

7

Two weeks and three successful zombie kills later, Mara crouched in an alley behind an overflowing dumpster. She watched a band of survivors march past, patrolling the streets. They were all armed, and she knew if they encountered any zombies, they'd shoot to kill without hesitation.

And they'll make a mess of things while doing it, Mara thought. In most cases after these groups made kills, she couldn't salvage anything from the cadavers. The brains had to be removed intact.

Mara visualized her harvesting process. She used the cranial saw to remove the top half of each zombie's skull. Then she severed the brain stem at the base of the skull. She removed the entire brain, flipped it upside down, and removed the temporal lobe. This allowed her to access the much narrower limbic lobe. This she always extracted with utmost care. In life the limbic lobe regulated emotions. And according to her customers, in death—or undeath—it contained a lifetime of happiness in concentrated form. She hung the harvested lobes on a rustic wooden clothes-drying rack until they dehydrated. There was a method to it, like drying fruit or smoking jerky.

Much to her frustration, bullet slugs—and even the occasional crowbar or baseball bat—did too much damage to zombies' brains. Out of necessity, she hunted alone. Mara wished these roving bands would find somewhere else to stomp around. They inhibited her livelihood. She watched in silence as this latest group trailed away down the street and disappeared around a corner. Her eyes slid to the other end of the block in search of prey.

A door opened in her subconscious and a mental image came to her with such force that she fell back on the dirty concrete, stunned. Pain lanced up from her tailbone, but she pushed the feeling away. She'd visualized a revolving door. A man and zombie chased each other in an endless circle. The man fled the zombie, yes. But the man could also represent one of her customers seeking escape from real world troubles. And what helped him escape? Zombie brains, specifically the limbic lobes.

The zombie, in turn, chased the man. Everyone knew the undead craved brains, but no one knew why. Could it be for the same reason? Mara trembled with excitement. Did zombies instinctively try to escape their futile existence by ingesting new memories and emotions found in the brains of their victims?

Mara rose to her feet, intent on returning to her workshop to consider this new idea further. She turned and stopped cold, confronted by a nightmare she never thought possible.

While Mara ruminated, a zombie had shambled to within arm's length. It stood there, glowering up at her through milky eyes. Half of its face had been torn away. Dried gore had congealed around the zombie's gaping maw. A once-pink t-shirt was now torn, grimy, and encrusted in dried blood. The zombie's fingernails had all sheared off, leaving bony stubs protruding from filthy, desiccated fingers.

Still, Mara thought she recognized those fingers, the nails chewed away by a scared little girl huddled on a sofa and asking about her daddy and about Jesus. Mara glanced down and confirmed her fear.

The diminutive zombie still wore one tattered shoe.

Tears blurring her vision, Mara knelt and held her arms open as Skylar stepped closer.

⚘⚘⚘

Time crawled, a snail laboring through molasses. Seconds passed like minutes, minutes felt like hours, and days masqueraded as weeks. Mara lived her life in a haze, hunting zombies on autopilot, and dispensing doses of ecstasy—or insanity—with curt brevity.

Embracing her daughter, only to betray her with the twist of a blade had been the hardest thing she'd ever done. But the decision she had made next had pushed her resolve further than she had ever thought possible. She needed to see, needed to *know*. And the only way to know was to experience the memories herself.

Mara had brought Skylar home in the wheelbarrow and eased her into the recliner in the workshop. Skylar had looked tiny nestled in the recliner. Mara had stroked her daughter's cheeks, no longer fearful of being bit and infected. Violent sobs shook her until her tear ducts gave up, unable to keep pace with her guilt and sorrow. At last, Mara had plugged the cranial saw into the generator and sat down to her task.

Bone dust and the odor of burned hair had permeated the room by the time she'd finished. Mara had removed her daughter's brain, extracted the limbic lobe and had left it hanging in the drying room apart from the others.

That had been a month prior.

Now Mara sat alone in the same bloodstained recliner; a dealer about to sample her product for the first and last time. She fingered the dried brain matter, so mushroom-like in texture. It looked and felt enough like hallucinogenic fungi that she understood how so many of her clients could have missed the truth. Or perhaps, deep down, some of them had known but had not wanted to acknowledge the inconvenient reality.

"They're encephaloshrooms," Mara muttered. "That's marketing gold." She laughed without mirth.

In carrying out the details of the sentence she'd handed down upon herself, Mara had intentionally left her door unlocked; if someone living came to rob her, so be it. If one of the undead intruded upon her while the drug swept her away, so be that as well. She had made her peace with both possibilities.

Right now only one thing mattered. Mara needed to see herself through her daughter's eyes. She'd witness what kind of life Skylar had lived. Had she been happy or miserable? Had she felt loved or ignored? Mara would experience it firsthand in one concentrated dose. But would the revelation bring her jubilation or retribution?

Mara pressed the dried shred of brain onto her tongue like a communion wafer and closed her eyes. She chewed, swallowed, and attempted to prepare herself for whatever came next.

THE EDGE OF THE DOCK

by Shannon Iwanski

Before you ask, yes, this is all there is.

You find her standing at the end of a weather-beaten dock. Silver-blue mist swirls around her ankles and obscures the hem of her dress. Dark stains cascade downward from the once-green material. You momentarily have the silly thought that it looks like chocolate syrup splashed onto her in a Rorschach pattern, but you know that it's blood.

You call her name, "Missy!" but she doesn't move. It's so cold out that every frosty exhalation adds to the miasma surrounding the tiny woodland lake hidden away near the center of the uncharted forest. Except someone had to have known about this place, once upon a time, because there *is* a dock jutting out into the onyx water.

You shake your head, clearing it of the intrusive thoughts, and remember the cold. So cold that Missy should be shivering. She should be shaking, especially barefoot on icy wood. But she stands there. A statue staring out over the mirror surface of water. At least, you think she's staring. You can only see the wet, tangled mass of curly brown hair draped over her shoulders and down her back.

Your first step onto the dock is tentative, quiet, almost sneaky. It still sounds like a platoon of soldiers marching through a landmine-riddled war zone. You stop and still your breathing. Missy doesn't move. In the distance, a fish leaps into the air, unseen by you, and splashes back into the water. Glancing in that direction, you watch the ripples until they all subside. Still Missy doesn't move. Still you try to regulate your breathing.

Your next two steps aren't as loud as the first two, but as you move from boards over land to boards over water, the hollow thumping of your steps carries into the distance. You create your own ripples from the vibrations of your steps. On the fourth board, you nearly fall onto your face. A red-tinted puddle of water, mixed with the mist and frost, causes you to lose traction. Your arms windmill in the air, and just when you think that all hope is lost, that you're going to see what lies beneath the surface of the pond in the middle of nowhere, you right yourself. You center yourself and breathe a cleansing breath of relief.

Missy sighs as you try to gather the courage to keep walking toward her. Still, she doesn't move. The sound hangs in the air for such a brief time that you can almost convince yourself that you imagined it. Careful of the hazards at your feet, but still not wanting to take your gaze from Missy's back, you take a step onto the fifth plank, the sixth. The seventh looms before you. If you take it, you only have half a dozen more before you can reach out and touch Missy.

She begins to lift her arms. They arc outward and upward, drawing with them the wet, clinging fabric of her dress sleeves. Blood splotches the material in tiny dots that look like filled-in bullseyes. Targets for your attention. There are so many of them. They're so close together that they could almost form a morbid dot-to-dot of "what the hell happened?" You brave the seventh plank. Missy calls your name. You freeze.

"I'm here." The words are needless, but you say them anyway. Her voice cannot be allowed to hang in the air. Your name is putrid and foul on her lips, in the dank atmosphere above the pond. You say, "I'm here" again, when she doesn't respond, but it does no good. She's stopped talking. You call her name again, but she pays no attention to it.

You chance the eighth plank. Missy stops the slow-motion ascent of her arms. They jut straight out from her body. Blood drips from her fingers. Tiny ripples form on the right side of the dock. Crimson splashes onto the plank beneath Missy's feet and then drip, drip, drips into the pond. Dark shapes dart just beneath the surface, feasting on the life sacrifice.

"Missy, come back from the edge." The words are ominous. You didn't mean them that way, but you shiver when you realize the implication. You move to the ninth plank. A slight squeaking noise, like rubber ground against an unyielding surface, sends a flock of birds on the distant shore into the sky. You didn't realize until their movement caught your attention, but the sky is grey and fading to black.

"Don't look," Missy says. You want to ask, "Don't look at what?" but then the squeak repeats itself, and you can feel the vibrations through the wood. You have to know what's back there. Inch by inch you turn your head. In your peripheral vision, you see a black shape morph from obscure lump to refined mass. Missy tells you again not to look. Before you can clearly see what is behind you, Missy grasps you by the chin and turns your head back toward her, toward the edge of the dock.

She stands on the tenth plank, her back still to you. Her grip on your face tightens almost imperceptively before she releases you and moves her arm back to perpendicular. Still you cannot see her face, and you wonder how she was able to reach back and stop you from seeing what awaits at the other edge of the dock.

"I saw the surface and what lies beyond." Her words are a whisper, yet they are enunciated and succinct, like the words of a competitor in an elocution contest.

"What is behind me?" You don't want to know, but not knowing is more than you can bear. If you don't find out, no matter what Missy does, no matter if she strips the flesh from your face, you will look. You *will* look.

"There is nothing."

"Why won't you look at me? Why won't you tell me the truth?"

"Do you want to know? Do you want to see?"

"Yes!" The word tears itself from your throat so forcefully that blood follows it. It leaves flecks across Missy's back, in her hair. It adds to the targets on her sleeves. You fall to your knees. Blood drips from your lips onto your chin and then into the water through a space between the planks.

"There is nothing."

You turn your head. The sky has gone black. Fireflies dance along the edge of the pond, forming a glowing circle that dances back and forth, up and down like a psychedelic roller coaster.

Missy giggles. Her arms thrust backward, and she grabs onto you, embraces you in an impossible hug. You feel a damp spot forming on the front of your shirt. "I told you there was nothing." She leans toward the side. You struggle. Mist covers the dock completely, and now you feel warmth leeching from your feet, your ankles, your legs. "I told you there was nothing."

You're leaning farther out over the water, almost forty-five degrees. What is Missy doing? What is beneath the surface?

The water kisses your skin with a thousand biting blades. You feel every molecule pressing against the surface of your flesh, burrowing in, through, and out. The water turns darker, like chocolate syrup. Your lungs burn. There is no air. No escape. Missy won't let go, and you feel her dragging you down farther. The pond shouldn't be this deep, but it's deeper than the ocean. Deeper than imagination.

Your vision begins to match the darkness. You inhale, and the water fills your lungs. When you reach the point of no return, the point where you should be seeing the white light, Missy whispers, "I told you there was nothing."

SISTERS OF MIDNIGHT

by Kim Munsamy

Pigtails bouncing above stalks of wheat, Elyse ran through the field.

She stumbled, fell, and covered her mouth. Tears slipped down her face as she tried to capture her laughter. Her sisters, Sindel and Juliet, ran past her. They were covered in mud and called out her name. They cooed to her, but she knew better. If she gave herself up now, they would tickle her until she succumbed.

Elyse could hear more laughter. She peeked through the sheaves and saw her parents on the hill. They looked so beautiful to her. Her father, an ancient oak tree with kind sunshine eyes. Her mother, a petite angel with soft curls. Both beautiful and a contrast to the man who stood over them. His name was Herbert. He appeared ordinary, but there was nothing that could disguise the deformity of his mind. Herbert was her uncle, a man who dedicated his time to the collection of wealth. Elyse was the only one who could coax him out of his office. She was his weakness and his good.

Something touched her leg. She nearly screamed but stopped when she saw the creature. It was a rat. There was blood all over it and incisions the width and breadth of a large dog's teeth. The rat looked up at her. Herbert believed that animals were soulless. He believed it vehemently and preached it with the same vigor. Yet, as Elyse looked at the rat, she thought it kind and sorrowful. She cried when it keeled over at her feet.

Elyse looked around but could not see her sisters. They told her, warned her, that she should not do it without them. Making a choice, she took the rat into her hands and blew her breath onto its face. The hot wind crinkled its whiskers, scattered droplets of blood onto the wheat, and sent

15

oscillations throughout the rat's body. Elyse had given it life.

It began to scream.

"No!" Elyse shouted.

The rat bit her finger and jumped out of her hands. It hit the floor nastily and began to crawl away. Its broken limbs jittered and kicked. Its red eyes bulged. It struggled across stone and dirt, like a black ophidian glistening in red.

"No," Elyse repeated, horrified.

She moved to capture it when Sindel came up beside her. Sindel looked from her sister to the rat, equally horrified.

"I—"

"It's done," Sindel remarked. "Look away."

Elyse shut her eyes as her sister grabbed the rat. She would not open them for a long while, not for hours after the snap.

⚜⚜⚜

Brilliant light.

The men lined the inside of the tent with strings of fluorescent bulbs. It was nearly sunset, hours before the sisters would take the stage, but the earth was already dotted with figures in mourning. Some leaned against rusted pickups, others were perched on hoods of cars, and more sat on shriveled winter grass. They waited beside coffins, pallbearers who were tired by the burden. Snow had not fallen, but the air was cold, and night was coming.

The sisters entered the tent, all clothed in midnight. Sindel was the oldest. Her blonde hair had just begun to turn grey, and the scythe she carried reflected in her brown eyes. Juliet walked behind her. Younger, with black dreadlocks tied into a high bun and a human skull in her hands. Elyse was the last. She was the youngest, nearly nineteen. She had brown hair with eyes like her sisters' and carried a single lily.

They made their way onto the stage, and laid their trinkets on the floor.

"This blade will never dull," Sindel said.

"This skull will never crumble," Juliet added.

"This lily will never die," Elyse declared.

"Behold!" the man on their right, Herbert, told the crowd. "The Sisters of Midnight."

There was no clapping, no sighs of wonder, only silence. They did not trust the sisters yet.

"Proof," Herbert said, nodding with understanding.

Elyse stepped off the stage and walked around the room. Her hand was grasped by many grieving partners. They pleaded with her. Bent on their knees and begged. She stopped beside a widower, a pauper of a man.

"Bring the coffin to the stage."

The widower removed the wooden veil and revealed his wife. Her body was cold, ashen, and the smell of rot was strong in the air. Herbert covered his mouth and nose with a handkerchief, but the sisters were unmoved.

Sindel, Juliet, and Elyse lifted the woman out of her coffin and laid her on the table.

Sindel bent over her. "I remove your sickness."

She kissed the dead woman's lips.

Juliet bent over her. "I undo the decay."

Another kiss.

Elyse bent over her. "I give you life."

A third.

For a time, nothing happened. The mutters of the crowd heightened and morphed into shouts. Cries of anger and wails of anguish were thrown about. Then the woman sat up. She screamed, bile and spit sprung from her mouth, and her nails scraped the table. Sindel grabbed her chin and turned the woman's face toward her husband. Only then did she quieten.

Her husband appraised her. There was color in her cheeks, life in her eyes, and she smelt of rain when it hits dry earth. New. He lifted her off the table and into his arms.

"Life!" Herbert shouted.

"It will be given," Sindel added. "All we ask is an offering of your greatest worth."

⁂

Elyse sat on the stage and rubbed a handkerchief across her lips. She did it with compulsion, until her lips bled. Sindel and Herbert were having a heated conversation, one she was too tired to involve herself in, and Juliet was attending to the offerings. Elyse was alone, isolated from the fluttering of the tent as it was pulled down and the scraping of chairs as they were carried out. She was floating, high above the disorder, yet unable to tear her eyes away from it.

A caterer dropped a platter. Elyse looked at the woman and smiled. She smiled back. The woman was young and attractive, but there was a shyness in her eyes that Elyse found mesmerizing. She got off the stage and moved toward her when Herbert grabbed her arm.

"Elyse," he intruded, "may I speak with you?"

She looked at the woman longingly then turned toward her uncle. "What is it?"

He followed her gaze. "Pretty, but not enough to endure the

17

consequences of attachment. There is another matter I would like you to consider."

"What is it?" she asked again.

"Come with me." He took her hand and pulled her out of the tent.

They hurried across the open field toward the dark of the forest's edge, but there was enough light bouncing off the treetops to see a man waiting for them. He was of a strong build and not grey enough to be considered old, but there was a look of sickness about him that his purple coat and fashionable spectacles could not suppress. A wheelbarrow lay in front of him, and a younger man within it. The sleeping man was covered in so many scars and bruises that he looked like a human scab. Elyse looked closer and saw that his neck had been broken.

"What is going on?" she asked her uncle.

He gestured to the older man. "This is Mr. Griffin, and his son Gabriel. Gabriel was involved in a car accident. Unfortunately, he did not survive. Mr. Griffin begs us to resurrect his son. He offers a large payment in exchange."

"Sindel did not agree?"

"No," Herbert answered. "She was quite tired."

"She was more than tired," Elyse remarked. "She was adamant. Gabriel's wounds differ in color; it was not one accident that caused them. I'll ask again, what is going on?"

Mr. Griffin grabbed Herbert and placed a dagger against his chest. The tip touched her uncle's flesh and sent a snail's footprint down his shirt.

"Bring back my son," Mr. Griffin ordered.

"I cannot do that," Elyse replied. "Not on my own. I need my sisters."

"Do it," Herbert said. "Sindel will not agree. She will not negotiate. Please, Elyse. Don't let me die."

"I cannot," Elyse said again.

Her voice trembled. Mr. Griffin pressed the dagger deeper into Herbert's chest, until his shirt was dyed like a blooming red flower. She looked into her uncle's wide, horrified eyes, then turned toward the cradled figure. He had a kind face, deep lines around his mouth from smiling, but he had clearly known pain. She wondered how he would react. Much better than the rat, she supposed.

"Do it!" Mr. Griffin shouted.

"Elyse!"

"Fine," she said.

Placing her hands on the wheelbarrow, she bent over Gabriel.

"I give you life," Elyse said, "and I apologize for it."

She kissed Gabriel and tasted death again.

He was unravelling. The sound of his moving limbs was that of a crinkled paper being smoothed out. Suddenly, a purple hand sprung forward. Herbert grabbed Elyse around the waist and pulled her back. Slowly, very slowly, Gabriel got out of the wheelbarrow. His head rested on his shoulder, and he struggled to find his feet.

"Herbert," Mr. Griffin said, "this was not what you promised."

Elyse looked at her uncle. "You planned this?"

"Not this," Herbert said. "It was your sister. She should have agreed. She—"

"She knew there was something strange going on," Elyse said. "She knew not to trust you, Uncle."

She shoved him away and approached the dead man.

"Gabriel, my name is Elyse. I can tell you are in pain, and I can help. Come with me now."

He looked at her. This was not the look of a lifeform being born anew, born tabula rasa and reasonable. There was a light behind his eyes, and recognition when they fell on his father. He jumped out of the wheelbarrow and came toward them.

"Run!" Herbert shouted.

He took Elyse's hand, and they hurried toward the tent. She looked over her shoulder and caught a glimpse of the dead man colliding with his father.

※ ※ ※

Gabriel was laid out on a shore of white sand. Smiling, he closed his eyes and listened to the eloquent waves. The sun was bright but did not radiate with heat. There was warmth, but not the kind that warms flesh.

He could hear her breathing as she lay beside him, soft breaths like spring on winter snow. He took her hand. They were aged and rough, worked from cradling him as a child. He held his breath, waiting for her to inhale, and synchronized with her. A child's action.

For the first moment in a long while, maybe in his entire life, Gabriel Griffin was content. He was content until his eyes were flung open.

She was leaning over him. For just a second, her face transformed into a mask of death. Boils and sores and hollowed sockets greeted him. He reached out and grabbed her, but she was pulled free. Gabriel maneuvered himself upright and tried to put his head on straight. He relented when he heard a soft, cracking sound. There was a smell in the air, a putrefying smell, all about him. It was inside him. He could taste it on his tongue. Feel it curdle in his stomach. The woman stepped toward him.

She called out his name, but he did not respond. She continued to speak. His body was bruised, his tendons burned with pain, and his eyes were

19

covered in a thin film of white that blurred everything he saw. Yet as he looked at the man standing far behind the other two figures, he knew him at once. It was his father. His father had brought him back from the dead. The great Mr. Griffin had lost his favorite plaything and would not be denied his longing.

His father had brought him back from the dead. His father had robbed him. Again.

Gabriel ran forward.

☙❧❦

"Did you note down the stock correctly?"

Juliet looked at her sister with exasperation. "Does it matter? You're just going to check again anyway."

Sindel laughed and held up her hands. "Just a question. We have to be gone by morning."

"Of course we do," Juliet replied.

She walked toward the offerings and placed her hand on a wooden pelican statue. The offerings were usually money, but they did not have to be. It was the thing that you valued the most. The thing you loved the most.

"Maybe we stay," Juliet said. She looked at her sister. "Maybe we stay, for a little while."

"You were named a little too correctly," Sindel replied. "There's a man who follows us from town to town. Peter Hale. I've seen him; so has Elyse. You cannot be with him. To do so is dangerous."

"Sindel—"

"I remove the sickness," her sister continued. "You undo decay. We take them away from the dead, but they remain with us. What happens if you become pregnant? Will you chance giving birth to a new species, one born in suffering?"

"There is a chance," Juliet said. "We were born healthy."

"We were the only ones," Sindel replied. "Our cousins did not survive."

"Every second we continue with this business, you become more and more like dear Uncle Herbert."

"Our parents gave up their power when they had us," Sindel remarked. "There are people to help; for that we must offer that which we love. I am sorry."

"Sindel! Juliet!" Herbert hurried into the tent with Elyse beside him. "We need to go. We need to go, now."

"What's wrong?" Juliet asked. She placed her hands on Elyse's shoulders and saw that she was crying.

20

"What have you done?" Sindel asked.

"There is a man alive in the world who shouldn't be," Elyse answered. "Herbert tricked me into bringing him back."

"Without us," Juliet said. She looked at her older sister. "I'll send the staff away."

"There's no time for that!" Herbert cried.

"We'll make time," she remarked and set off.

Sindel moved toward the opening of the tent and looked out. The earth looked colored in graphite, but lonely.

"He's gone," she whispered.

Elyse came up beside her sister. "He's gone."

"That's what I said," Sindel remarked. "This is not going to end well, Elyse."

"It should," Herbert said. "It was my mistake, I—"

She rounded on him. "You needed her consent, and you knew she'd give it. She was blinded by her affection, as she always is, and allowed herself to be conned."

"That's enough, Sindel," Elyse replied. "I made a mistake. If you thought he was in danger, would you not do the same?"

"This is not another one of your mistakes," her sister remarked. "This isn't a dragonfly or a rat, Elyse. This is a human being, capable of thought and madness. Madness will take him; to live inside a decaying thing will certainly drive him to it. We need to stop him before he kills more people."

"I'm sorry, Sindel."

She sighed and took her sister's hand. "I know. I know you are. We just need to find him."

Elyse turned to her uncle. "What do you know about Gabriel?"

"I know where he would go," Herbert answered with a grin.

❧❧❧

Gabriel vomited.

He stared down at the things he had brought up and closed his eyes against the squirm of maggots. There was no bile, no sensation of nausea, just something moving rapidly toward his lips. He vomited again, then placed his hand on the rusted fence. It opened with a creak.

Mr. Griffin was not the sentimental type and would certainly not spend money to tend to graves. Dirt creeped up the sides of the giant stone slabs, and weeds dotted with white flowers grew over. The old tombstones were disfigured, angels lacked limbs, and crucifixes were turned into road signs. Only a single tombstone and its accompanying grave looked cared for. Gabriel moved toward it.

He knelt in the mud and ran his hands across the stone bed.

"Mother," he whispered to the night.

Closing his eyes, he tried to remember the bliss of the white shore. He grasped for the memory, knowing it should be there in his mind, but his fingers continued to reach. Gabriel tried to cry, but the tears would not come. Rising, he went into the mansion.

He was surrounded by darkness but moved methodically. This building had consumed him in life. Even now, in the purgatory state Gabriel found himself in, he thought it engulfing. It was a shadow place, lacking moonlight and covered in clouds. The smell of his own decay stuck to him and embedded in the wood, but he could still distinguish the old man's scent. An accompaniment of perfume, polish, whisky, and blood. His hand ran along the banister as he ascended the left staircase, and he stopped at the top. The apex. The place where his mother had died.

He remembered the scene. Vividly. His father dragging her by the hair. Slipping the rope around her neck. Tying one end to the banister. Throwing her over.

Suddenly, Gabriel knew what he must do.

The answer came through the door.

❀❀❀

"Can you smell that?" Juliet asked.

She took a step forward, a step into the darkness of the mansion, and shivered.

"He's here," Elyse said.

"I'll wait in the car."

Sindel grabbed Herbert by the collar and pulled him after her as she entered the building. Moving toward the windows, she drew the curtains so that the moon dressed everything in light. The house was impersonal, done by an interior decorator who had no knowledge of the family living within. The enormous television screen was covered in dust, the cabinets showed trinkets of an age before Mr. Griffin, and an ostentatious chandelier hung over a red sofa that sat in a gold frame. Impersonal. A display of wealth, uncomfortable even to those who lived here.

"Mud," Herbert remarked.

He pointed to the staircase.

"Herbert and I will go upstairs," Sindel said. She turned to her sisters. "Check the rest of the house."

"Maybe I should poke around here," Herbert told her. "I'm too old to climb stairs."

"Check the rest of the house," Sindel repeated. She shoved Herbert in front of her.

Juliet and Elyse made their way into the kitchen. Vintage gas lights were fastened onto the walls. When Elyse turned the switch, she found that they were operational. The room was lit in an impregnable glow, depriving the things that creeped in darkness.

"Fancy," she remarked, pulling open a walk-in pantry.

Picking an apple from the shelf, Elyse rubbed it against her coat and moved it to her mouth.

"How can you eat with that stench in the air?" Juliet asked.

"That's so disturbing?" she replied. "We kiss dead and decaying strangers every month."

Juliet pulled back the bolt on a purple door and entered a gym. It was a room of steel and iron, with a large window that looked out onto the cemetery. Elyse knew that Mr. Griffin had used this room often, it smelt of him, and she wondered if the view of the cemetery brought him motivation. She weaved her way through one side of the room, and Juliet weaved her way through the other. She noticed that her sister was being very careful not to bump into anything and shielded her stomach with her hands.

"Does Sindel know?" Elyse called.

"What?"

"Does Sindel know you're pregnant?"

Juliet looked at her sister. Elyse could see that she was afraid, not of Sindel, but afraid of the child who grew inside her. She crossed the room and took her sister's hand.

"It will be all right," she said. "The child will be human. And healthy."

"I hope so," Juliet replied. She kissed Elyse's cheek and continued to explore the room.

"Juliet."

"Yes?"

Elyse hurried to the window.

"Look," she said and pointed. "One of the graves has been dug up."

※ ※ ※ ※

Sindel opened the door.

She stepped carefully inside, with Herbert cowering behind her. He was annoyingly close, standing a little to her right, and directly behind the gun tucked into her pants. Elyse had begged her to reason with Gabriel. She would try that, but she was also prepared to kill him. Power was not the only thing her parents had transferred to her. She was tasked with watching over her sisters. She was tasked with monitoring Herbert. She was tasked with a multitude of anvils, and the weight was inescapable.

Reaching out, she picked a frame off the desk. In the photograph, Mr. Griffin stood in the middle of his wife and son. His hands were draped over both of them, clenching. She placed the frame back on the desk, face down.

Her eyes were drawn to one of the drawers. The lock was scraped and had been broken. Sindel pulled it open and turned it out onto the desk. A baby's rattle, a handkerchief stained with blood, and a long rope fell out. They were unintelligible to her, fragments and pieces of the family's life, and she could not make sense of it. Yet she felt nauseous when she looked at them. As though they were foul. Tainted.

"Sindel?"

She looked up and saw that Herbert was shivering. Gabriel stepped out from behind him and grasped her uncle by the throat.

"Leave him," she told Gabriel. "Leave him, and let us talk."

"I will talk," he replied, "but I shall not leave him. Not until you have listened."

"What do you want?" Sindel asked.

"There was a girl who woke me up again," Gabriel answered. His voice had changed, no more than a whisper now. The maggots were still inside of him, feasting on every part of him they could reach. His larynx was no exception. "I want her to do the same for my mother."

"No. It is unnatural, and it is pain. You must go back to sleep, Gabriel. You have suffered enough."

"I suffered more than you know. Bring the girl to me, or your uncle will die."

"That was his plan too," Sindel remarked. "Mr. Griffin, your father, bartered with the same goods."

Herbert gagged and waved his hands frantically.

"Bring her!" Gabriel shouted.

Sindel raised her gun. "No."

She fired. Gabriel shoved Herbert aside and ran into the hallway. Sindel followed. She fired three more times. Bursts of light illuminated the mansion, and she could hear running. Two pairs of feet beneath her. One behind. Only Gabriel moved silently. She would have lost him if not for the smell. She fired a fourth time and struck him. He fell to the floor at the top of the staircase.

Sindel slid to a stop and appraised the wound. The bullet was in his shoulder. Gabriel grabbed her ankle and tugged her to the floor. He shoved the gun out of her hand. It fell through the banister and hit the ground. A stray bullet erupted from the barrel, grazing Juliet. Elyse ran toward the gun. It was five meters away.

"Sindel!" Herbert shouted.

Gabriel grabbed the oldest sister around the waist and lifted her off her feet. Two meters. He bared his teeth at her uncle. The sight of him, not only dead but rabid, was enough to make Herbert stop. He looked at his niece. The heaviness in her eyes had disappeared, and fear stirred there. One meter. He took a step back.

Elyse grabbed the gun.

Gabriel threw Sindel off the staircase.

She whimpered. Something in Sindel's spine had broken, and she was paralyzed. Her eyes focused on Gabriel, as he lunged for her uncle. Herbert dodged him and threw himself down the staircase. Gabriel disappeared into the dark. Elyse and Juliet knelt beside their sister, and Sindel turned her head toward them.

"He cannot remain," she said.

"We need to call an ambulance," Juliet replied. She produced her cellphone from her coat.

"No," Sindel remarked. She looked at Elyse. "Place the gun against my chest and pull the trigger."

"What?" Elyse asked.

"Do it," she said. Tears escaped her eyes and ran down her crow's feet. "I remove the sickness."

Juliet put her hand on the gun. "Give it to me."

Elyse pushed her away. She placed the barrel against Sindel's heart and closed her eyes. Taking a deep breath, she opened them again. She would not look away, not this time. Sindel smiled, and Elyse pulled the trigger.

Juliet grabbed Elyse by the shoulders and pulled her away. Herbert ran before them, held open the door, and slammed it shut when they were outside. Linking hands, the three of them stared through the colored glass and watched the process. Sindel was gone. Every sickness she had taken away, every injury she had healed, erupted from her in a wave of death. The wood around her turned brittle and weak, mirrors became murky, and noxious fumes erupted from her mouth and nose. It engulfed everything.

Glass broke, and the house collapsed onto their sister's wilting body.

※ ※ ※

"All right," Elyse said.

Wedging the cellphone between her ear and shoulder, she got her card out of her purse and swiped herself into the building. When she was inside, she dusted snow off her coat and pressed the elevator button.

"All right," she repeated. "Well, Juliet, I can't leave Herbert alone in the apartment on Christmas. I know Hale doesn't like him, but the baby does. I know. I will. Ok. Bye."

Elyse laughed as she got out of the elevator. Juliet sounded more and more like Sindel and less like herself. She walked down the hall, took a right, and stopped outside her room. Snow had melted on the floor in the shape of a boot print. It was not hers and far too large to be Herbert's. She looked at it a second longer then took a deep breath.

Reaching into her purse, she withdrew what she needed. Another deep breath, then the plunge. Elyse opened the door and entered.

She stepped in blood. Following the trail with her eyes, she saw that Herbert lay dead on the sofa. A woman was sprawled on the floor. She was lifeless, terribly decayed, and covered in a woolen blanket. Gabriel stood beside her, a gargoyle protector.

"Hello," Elyse said.

"Hello," Gabriel replied.

He advanced, but she did not retreat. He held out a photo, and she took it. It was a photo of the Family Hale. Juliet, Peter, and baby Sindel. Tucking the photo into her pocket, Elyse crossed the room. She moved toward the sofa and closed Herbert's eyes. When she was done, she knelt beside the dead woman.

"Do it," Gabriel commanded. "Bring her back."

Elyse took a deep breath and placed her hands on the woman's cheeks. It had been two months since she kissed the dead. Without one of the sisters, the process was disastrous. They would not risk it again.

"Do it," he repeated.

She looked up at him.

Shocked, Gabriel grabbed her coat and pulled her upright. A nail file hit the floor. Blood dripped from Elyse's mouth. She smiled. On her last breath, death left her lips and destroyed everything in her apartment.

WISTERIA

by Donna A. Leahey

Charles leaned out the back door and pointed an accusatory finger. "Dammit, Gia, look at this!"

It was obviously my fault. I had no idea what he was talking about, but still, it was clearly my fault. "What is it, Charlie?"

My husband's scowl twisted his handsome face into an ugly mask. He hated being called Charlie. I liked to pretend it just slipped out, but really, I did it just to annoy him.

"It's going to take the siding right off the house!" He pointed again, and sure enough, there it was, right under the eaves, a cluster of green leaves growing up behind the siding.

"Is that the wisteria?" I asked, turning to look behind me at the spot we planted the skinny twigs five years ago.

The thick, twisted stalk of the wisteria climbed the posts of the deck and created a dense, leafy canopy of shade in our backyard. Every spring, it erupted into an amazing display of pale, purple flowers hanging down and transforming the simple wooden deck into a spectacular floral show. Charles had argued so hard for the deck then spent so much time and so much of my money building it. Now I could barely convince him to set foot on it. I rarely tried anymore.

"I told you that damn plant was going to wreck the house! Do you have any idea how much it will cost to replace the siding?" He stood there, hands on hips, tall and manly and handsome, his tailored suit flattering the lines of his body. I was no longer impressed with his looks; beauty is only skin deep, but handsome is even more shallow.

I paused to take a breath. I supposed I could remind Charles—again—that it was he who brought the little wisteria cuttings home. It wouldn't help. I liked the pretty, purple flowers; therefore, it was my fault.

I studied the dark green leaves and pictured the vine crawling the eight feet under the deck before it reached the house, burrowed up under the siding, and then climbed up the wall before finding its way out again. Looking up at the slender seeking vines, stretching out, up and down, I saw how thick those vines could become. He was right; it would utterly destroy the siding. I hated it when he was right.

"There's no way to get to the vines with the deck here."

"Cut the damn thing down!" he demanded. "Just kill it. I'm tired of this!"

"With all the vines and roots, even if you did cut the main stalk, that wouldn't kill it. We'll have to pry up some of the boards."

He jabbed his finger towards me to punctuate his words. "Leave the goddamned deck alone!"

"Leave the goddamned wisteria alone, then!"

He cursed under his breath and slammed the door shut. Yep, that's pretty much how our conversations went.

I left him alone in the house and settled down on a comfy lounge chair under the shady canopy of vines and leaves. The wisteria had really taken off this spring. It had grown steadily since we planted it, but this year it grew faster and thicker than it ever had. On a rare pleasant evening with Charles, I'd joked that its roots must have found a bag of Miracle-Gro down deep in the earth. He'd glared at me as if I'd said something stupid then stalked away, but then, most of the time I talked he looked at me like that.

Gazing up into the lush, green tangle overhead, I smiled at how beautiful and wild it was. I loved it and would not let Charles kill it. Determined and ready to carry on with the fight, I started towards the house. I noticed another vine coming up from under the deck. This one hadn't made it behind the siding, but it was crawling up the wall. I frowned at it and looked again at the green tendrils reaching through the air. There were at least ten stretching towards the roof of the house. If they started growing up there they could take off shingles, maybe penetrate into the attic. It was as if the plant were trying to get into the house. Chuckling at the thought, I reached for the sliding glass door, and my laughter died in my throat when I noticed the tip of a vine pressed right into the door frame, as if poised to enter the house as soon as the door opened.

I pulled the door handle, but it was locked. I banged on the glass, and my darling little RooRoo came running, flinging his head back and braying out an alarmed bark. Roo bounced around on his dainty feet, his white-and-brown, fluffy tail curled up over his back, anxious and excited at the prospect that I'd open that door and he could jump on me.

"Charlie!" I banged on the door. "Charlie! Open up!"

He didn't answer for a long time, but Roo never got tired of barking, spinning in circles, and bouncing.

"Shut that goddamn dog up!" Charles yelled.

"I'm locked out!" I called back, pounding on the door and provoking more barks.

Muttering loudly enough that I could hear every word, Charles finally made his way to the door and let me in. He shoved Roo aside with the outside of his foot, provoking a growl and a snap. "If that dog bites me, I'll wring its neck."

My patience with him was done for the day. "Anything you do to my dog, I do to you!" I whirled about to point at the door. "Why did you lock me out again?"

"It was an accident, dammit! If I did it on purpose, your stuff would be in a pile on the front lawn!" He glared down at Roo. "And your dog, too!"

"God, you're hateful," I said. I picked up Roo, who proceeded to lick my face enthusiastically.

Before I could smile at my dog, Charles spoke up again. "Only since I met you. And for God's sake, don't let that dog lick your face. Disgusting!"

I slammed the door behind me, nipping off the end of the wisteria vine.

🕱🕱🕱

Our evening wore on as it usually did. We argued over what to watch on TV, his horrible smacking noises when he ate, his criticism of how I cooked the burgers—they were too well done, so I was deliberately robbing the burgers of all flavor and juiciness. Last time they were too rare because I was obviously hoping to kill him with an E. coli infection. His cat, Snowbelle, pissed in my shoes, but somehow that was my fault, too. Those were $700 shoes. I told him he was buying me a new pair; he laughed in my face. Snowbelle stared at me as if she understood every word and was laughing along with Charles. Little white-furred bitch.

By the time we went to bed, we were barely speaking. I'd won the argument over leaving the window open, and the room was too cold, but there was no way I'd close it. Instead I pulled on a sweatshirt and huddled under the covers. The calls of mockingbirds and chirps of cicadas carried through the open window. A dog barked nearby, and a car with a wheezing engine drove by.

In the silence that followed, I heard an odd scratching sound. I opened my eyes, more curious than alarmed, and saw a wisteria vine waving in the breeze, scratching back and forth against the window screen.

⁂

I woke early, fixed my coffee, and stepped outside to enjoy the cool morning air on the deck. Roo bounced around my slippered feet, his long coat dancing about his legs like the hem of a gauzy skirt. I smiled down at him; Roo was what kept me going some days. I let Snowbelle out into the backyard even though Charles preferred she stay indoors. I guess I was still mad. She immediately disappeared under the deck. It would be my fault when her white fur got dirty.

The breeze had a chill bite to it, but the sun was warm. I lifted my face to it before settling in my chair under the canopy of wisteria. I loved the morning, resting there under the lush green leaves, watching the world wake up. The irises were blooming, and I smiled at the beautiful blue flowers.

The wind picked up and the vines began to stir. I saw the one that had been scratching at my screen during the night. It arched up towards the sky then angled back towards my window, and I could see why it had eventually stopped scratching: it was pressing so hard against the screen that it had caused a deep dimple. I wondered if it would be able to break through.

I stood and walked out into the yard to get a better look. The wisteria had meant so much to me just a few years ago. The vibrant, green foliage; the pretty, purple flowers had seemed symbolic of my resurrected marriage. Once upon a time, Charles and I had been very happy together. He, a charming and handsome young academician just starting as an assistant professor, and I, the new graduate, pretty, young, and possessed of a trust fund just large enough to guarantee we'd never have to worry about paying our bills.

In our small town, social life revolved around the college. So Charles got to share my trust fund, and I got into the social events at the college. As he became more successful, I gained access to better events.

Twelve years later I couldn't pass for a co-ed anymore, and I realized that my husband and I were no longer happily married. Charles had nearly vanished from my life, always working late and going off to conferences. I began to wonder if he was having an affair.

God knew he had the opportunity with all those pretty graduate assistants. There was Angie, a chubby redhead who clearly adored Charles but went on to get her PhD. Then Shelly, the pale blonde, who ended up marrying her boyfriend and at least once a year called Charles to talk about maybe finishing her dissertation. They were followed by Monique, a fabulously beautiful and willowy young black woman; Nessa, blonde and plump; and Fae, a serious Native American girl, tall and slender. Every one

30

of them with a passionate schoolgirl crush on my handsome and charming husband. It was entertaining at the fall faculty dinners, spring cotillions, holiday parties, and summer barbecues watching his latest grad student try to pretend she wasn't in love with him. It wasn't like I didn't understand. I remembered being in love with him.

Then there was Melissa. Sweet, pretty Melissa with all the brunette curls and the big, pale-purple eyes. She made only the most token of efforts to hide that she was in love with my husband. Charles was gone even more than usual and my suspicion that he was cheating became certainty. I wanted to confront him, but I was unwilling to risk my social status over his dalliances. Before my resolve firmed, he came home and told me Melissa had left. She'd just packed up and left to be with her boyfriend back West without so much as a goodbye. Well, so he said, but I suspected she'd left because of Charles. I was just grateful that there was no scandal.

He was home that entire summer. He built the deck, an elaborate thing with three levels. When it was done we planted the tiny, frail shoots of wisteria next to one of the posts. For a while, it seemed my marriage had come back to life. It was a sham, though. Our marriage hadn't been resurrected; it had returned as a zombie shambling along in a disintegrating parody of life. It had just taken a while for me to recognize the rot.

I shook my head to clear the thoughts and returned to studying the growth of the wisteria. The canopy over the deck was a three-foot thick mat of dense, intertwined vines and leaves. The vines were always reaching and exploring, extending both from the high mat and from the ground, every one of them reaching towards the house. It gave me a chill. It looked as if the plant were attacking the house.

I heard a muffled meow, then a louder, angrier howl. "Snowbelle?" I called, but there was no answer. Roo, however, darted to my feet, his eyes wide, his whole body shaking. He was frightened of something, but I couldn't imagine what.

"Gia! Gia, dammit! Where's Belle-Belle?" Charles yelled out the kitchen window.

"How should I know?"

"Did you let her out?"

I huffed indignantly. "She may have darted out when I opened the door."

"Don't you leave her outside all day, dammit." He slammed the window shut, then immediately opened it again. "I'll be late tonight. Don't wait up. I have to review Allie's dissertation with her."

Right, I thought, her dissertation. I wanted to complain, but really, I liked it when he was out. It was the only time we weren't fighting. Was he sleeping with her? I didn't know, but I figured someone in the family should be having some sex. Before I could say a word, the wind rustled the wisteria. The vines swayed and reached for the house.

I work from home as a consultant and had a busy morning of calls, email, and video conferencing. It was afternoon before I remembered Snowbelle. I was tempted to leave her furry ass outside all day, but it wasn't her fault Charles was an asshole, and I would feel bad if something happened to her. I stepped away from my desk, snagged a can of diet soda from the fridge, and headed outside to find the cat. Roo flatly refused to come out with me.

Usually Snowbelle would be napping in a sunny patch on the deck, but there was no sign of her. I called her, but there was no answer. Worry began to gnaw at my gut as I called and called again. Snowbelle never strayed far. I finally decided that I would tell Charles she'd been asleep on the bed last time I saw her. My mind made up, I started into the house when I heard a low, quiet meow. "Belle?"

I looked up into the trees and under the furnishings, but was no sign. I peered into the thick canopy of leaves and vines over the deck, but she wasn't there either. Finally, I crouched to peer into the darkness under the deck—the last place I'd seen her. I thought I saw something white, but it was too dark for me to be sure.

I cursed and pushed myself to my feet before going back inside to find a flashlight. It was in the drawer where Charles always kept it—woe betide anyone who failed to return it to its proper spot! I flicked the light on while dropping back to my knees by the deck.

For a moment, I could only stare in complete shock. The few inches of space under the deck were completely filled with wisteria vines: a thick, tangled mass of life. I had the crazy idea that a mere heartbeat before the light hit the vines they had been churning over each other like a ball of earthworms. Then I gasped—I saw Snowbelle, trapped in the vines. Her white fur was dirty and matted and there was blood on her neck.

I raced back into the house and, for once, blessed meticulous Charles since I knew exactly where the gardening clippers were. I reached under the deck with the clippers, ruthlessly yanking at the vines, trying to get to Snowbelle. She was too far away for me to reach, so I grabbed at the vines and pulled, hoping to drag the cat closer.

She was well and truly trapped, with loops of vine around her neck and body, her legs and paws. I could almost reach her, so I started clipping. As soon as I cut the first vine, Snowbelle shrieked to life, hissing, spitting, and fighting. She was like a wild thing, but every move she made tangled her even further. Her blues eyes found mine and she stilled, panting in open-mouthed terror.

"I'll get you, kitty," I promised and cut another vine, but Snowbelle shrieked again, as if I'd cut her and not an inanimate plant. I frowned at the dark liquid dripping from the cut vines and brought the flashlight closer to see. It was red as blood, and thick, too.

Shuddering, I reached in and grabbed a handful of the tangle, and it felt like it wriggled in my hand. I fought the urge to flinch away; I was determined to save Snowbelle. I pulled, trying to get her closer, but the tangle didn't move. She screamed, a hopeless wail of pain and defeat, and exploded into struggles again. They didn't last nearly as long this time. Snowbelle was exhausted.

Gritting my teeth, I cut another vine, ignoring the blood-like sap. I strained as far as I could and just managed to get my fingers on her scruff. She cried out again, quietly, and I felt sure she was nearly gone. When I pulled, the resistance was strong enough that it felt as if the vines were pulling back. Snowbelle let out a final, horrible scream and then went silent and still. The vines abruptly let go, and I fell back, banging my head on the wall behind me, but I had the cat out from under the deck.

I tumbled back into the house, nearly tripping over a frantic Roo, and slammed the door, telling myself I didn't see a vine reaching for me from under the deck. Once inside, I looked down at the bundle of dirty, bloody fur in my arms. She was still; her chest didn't move.

"Oh, no, Snowbelle!"

I felt blood trickling from her body, and cocked my head to see the source. There were at least three puncture wounds in her soft, little belly. I frowned then suddenly turned away, barely making it to the sink before losing my breakfast. There were leaves coming out of the wounds. Out of the wounds. Had those vines been inside her body? I gagged again.

"Oh...Charles," I whispered. I could not let Charles see what had happened to his cat. With tears running down my face and my skin tingling, I wrapped Snowbelle in an old towel and curled her up into her favorite nap position before slipping her into a plastic trash bag. I stashed that inside a box, taped it securely shut, and then ran outside and stuck it into the neighbor's trash. God, how I hoped he wouldn't find it!

I looked back at the house and felt another chill. Wisteria vines with their deep, green leaves crawled over the roof. I stepped back, frowning. How was it possible the plant was growing so fast? Then I heard Roo's frightened bark. With a last sorrowful glance towards Snowbelle's makeshift coffin, I hurried back into the house.

"Roo! Where are you, RooRoo?" I called. Usually my little dog rushed right to me, but I didn't see him, and I didn't hear his claws clicking on the floor. "Roo?"

I paused, listening for him. A frightened yelp came from above. I turned and dashed up the stairs, two at a time, with images of those leaves protruding from Snowbelle's soft, little belly. Not my Roo!

The bedroom door was closed. Roo's barks were high-pitched and frantic as his little claws tapped against the door. I turned the knob and slammed into the closed door. It wouldn't open. I twisted the knob back and forth and pushed, and all the while Roo cried for me.

I hit the door one more time, and it opened with a crunch. Roo made his escape, darting between my feet and racing down the stairs. I stared into my room; no less than three vines had punched through the screen. One of them had wedged itself into the hinges of the door but the other two waved leisurely about my bedroom.

"This...this is insane," I murmured. I had to do something about the wisteria before it wrecked my home. I slammed the door shut behind me and ran back down the stairs. Grabbing my cell phone, I called Charles. It rang twice and went to voicemail. Of course he rejected my call. "Charles!" I said to his voicemail, "I'm doing something about the vines right now, and I'm going through the deck to do it. Call me, dammit!"

I tossed the phone onto the counter and found the clippers where I'd dropped them on the kitchen floor, but Roo was nowhere to be seen. I found him cowering behind the couch, his eyes wide and round, his little body quivering. "Stay here, little Roo," I said and reached to scratch his soft, floppy ears. He was still frightened and inched further behind the couch. "Stay here," I repeated.

I hurried into the garage and collected a crowbar. A trio of vines hung down from the trap door into the attic. I shuddered to think of the damage the vines had done up there as I hurried back to the door. I looked out onto the deck and my skin crawled. Just this morning the vines had been reaching for the house. Now they were all over it. The thick canopy over the deck appeared to be crawling off towards the roof, and more green leaves were sticking out of the siding and poking up through the boards of the deck. I kept hearing Snowbelle's last agonized scream. I didn't want to touch the vines at all, but to get to the part of the deck nearest the root, I would have to.

I gritted my teeth and reached up with the clippers. As the cut vine fell, thick red liquid dripped down around me. Where a couple of drops landed on my skin, they were as warm as blood. I almost bolted then, but I was sure if I could just get through the deck and cut the vines, this would all be over. Hot tears dripped down my face, but I stepped forward to cut another vine, and another. By the time I reached the edge of the deck, there was so much red splattered around it looked like a murder scene.

I started working with the crowbar, prying up boards, but it was hard work. They were secured by long nails to the structural beams that ran underneath. It would not be as easy as I'd hoped, but I was determined. As I worked, I imagined I could see the vines moving from the corner of my eye, but when I looked right at them, they only swayed in the breeze. My phone rang, but I'd left it inside, and I wasn't walking across the blood red spatters all over the deck. Besides, it was probably Charles, and he deserved it for ignoring my call earlier.

The sun was hot and sweat rolled down my body. My hands began to blister, and my muscles ached, and I still hadn't gotten the first board up. The phone rang again and again, but I ignored it. If Charles wanted to talk to me, he should have answered when I called the first time. Besides, I knew what he would say—he'd just yell at me to leave the deck alone.

I set the crowbar aside and grabbed the saw, offered up a quick prayer to the do-it-yourself gods that I wouldn't cut off a finger, and began to slice through the boards. I made my second slice, and as the boards began to fall through, sunlight struck tangled vines and earth it hadn't touched in five years.

The hard work took the edge off my nerves, and I began to concentrate more on the saw blade, the wood, and my aching back than on the vines moving in the wind. Roo had bravely come out from behind the couch and was watching me, sitting in the sun, his white fur shining. I was lost in my own head, imagining the cold earth soaking up the warm sun, when Roo began to bark. I glanced at him, surprised, and he became frantic, flinging his head back in a howl and bouncing on his toes. Turning around to see what had him so upset, I dropped the saw, the sudden silence as my finger came off the power button revealing the rustling of leaves and vines. I put my hands to my face and screamed.

A skeletal hand pushed out of the earth, the bony fingers reaching towards the sun. As the hand moved, the bones of the wrist and arm followed. At the same time, vines and leaves wrapped themselves around the bones, weaving themselves about, forming the shape of a human arm. Where the last joint of the ring finger was missing, a thin vine moved into place and completed the hand.

The seeking fingers found and gripped a sturdy beam. The wood creaked as the arm pulled, then a second hand of vine-covered bone pushed its way out of the sun-warmed earth. The hands pulled and twisted, straining to be free. I screamed again and slammed into the wall behind me hard enough to stun myself. A skull with shreds of hair still clinging with determination rose out of the ground. One pale white eye glared balefully at me before it fell out of the socket, and I realized it was only a snail. More vines began to wrap themselves around the gray and dirty skull.

Roo, safely on the other side of the door, let out a sound like a scream and vanished back into the house. I was glad. I didn't want him hurt. I wished I could run away as well, but I was held frozen in fear and wonder, like a mouse staring into the eyes of an approaching cobra.

Inch by inch the skeleton dragged itself out of the dirt like a flower blooming in the sun. Shoulders appeared and then ribs, filled in several places by helpful vines. As it moved, one of the ribs fell out and tumbled down into the dirt below. A skeletal hand released the beam, reached down to pick it back up, and held it in place until the thin, green tendrils secured it. It pushed on the beam like a swimmer climbing out of the pool. After the hips cleared, one dirt-covered knee lifted up out of the soil and onto the deck, and it was free, straightening up to stand on its two, bony feet atop my back deck.

Wisteria vines from above and below swirled around the skeleton, filling out a woman's shape, covering her skull to give her a face with a skin of smooth leaves and eyes of purple flowers. More flowers flowed over her shoulders to mimic the fall of long hair. I screamed again because I knew her.

"Mel-Melissa..." I stammered. "Oh my God, Melissa?"

A thin voice rustled like wind through dry leaves. "Where...is...Charles?"

In a bright flash, I understood. He lied, oh, how he'd lied when he said she'd left. She'd been right here all along.

Those purple flower eyes turned to me. How could a face made of vines and leaves have so much expression? Rage, pain, betrayal, and grief ravaged her features, made a face that had been lovely in life into a twisted mask.

"Charles," she said again, her voice low and slow. She walked closer to me, slowly, leaves fluttering around her. "Where is Charles?"

I turned to run for the safety of my house. I had just gripped the door handle when she snagged my hair and pulled me back. "Please! Let me go!"

I couldn't speak more because her horrible skeletal fingers closed around my neck. I grabbed at her, pulling away leaves. A finger bone snapped off in my hand, and I dropped it in disgust, but a vine merely lifted it back into place. I pushed and pulled and kicked and grew steadily weaker. My entire existence narrowed down to the crushing pain encircling my neck. The world narrowed and dimmed.

A distant sound—the front door slamming—brought me back. I opened my eyes as Roo began to bark. The skeletal figure looked away from me towards the front of the house, and my little Roo bolted through the narrow gap in the door. He charged at the viney figure and bit, stealing a bone from her ankle and racing away with it. Melissa's figure cried out and her grip on me loosened. I escaped the one way I could—I dropped flat to the ground and then scrambled for the door. Vines wrapped around my ankle and pulled me back towards the figure. Roo screamed in terror as a vine dragged him with a grip on one back leg, as yet another vine carefully tucked the bone back where it belonged.

Charles' voice carried through the house. "Gia! Gia, goddammit! Where are you! You stay the hell away from that deck! Gia! Leave it the hell alone!"

Abruptly, the grip on my ankle loosened and fell away. Roo let out one surprised yelp and raced to me, his body quivering, making little whimpering noises with each frantic breath. Melissa faded back into the shadows, pressing herself into the wisteria so that if I hadn't known she was there, I probably wouldn't have seen her. She lifted a bony finger to her face and shushed me.

"Charles! Help me! Help!" I cried, pushing myself up with an armful of terrified dog.

I ran for the door, but Charles appeared in the doorway. "What the hell is going on?" He looked out onto the deck, the weathered wood striped by the long shadows of early evening, and now marred by the hole I'd cut. His face first paled and then reddened. "What did you do, Gia?" he asked.

"Melissa...Melissa!" was all I could say.

His eyes turned towards me and went cold. "You found her then?"

"She's dead, Charles, but..."

His expression flickered like the frames of a movie as he considered his options. I was terrified at the thought that my fate might be one of the options he was considering.

"Gia, are you all right?" His voice was flat and emotionless. "Come here, darling."

I'd felt a lot of things towards my husband over the years: love, of course; anger; betrayal; resentment; hurt...but I'd never been afraid of him until that moment. "Charles, what...what happened to Melissa?"

He stepped out onto the deck. His eyes cut towards the hole in the boards then back to me. He sighed and shook his head. "She was going to ruin everything, Gia. She got pregnant. She wanted me to leave you so we could be together." As he spoke he stalked to where I stood against the wall and put one hand on each side of my head. "But I took care of it. She was out of the way and not causing any more problems in my life." He leaned closer, and the look in his blue eyes was cold. "Tonight would have been the night with Allison, but you screwed that up. She already thinks you're a cold bitch who doesn't deserve me. That I'm a 'warm and special man who deserves a woman who appreciates him.'"

I should have been listening to Charles, but the vines—the vines were reaching for him, and Melissa was coming. As frightened as I was of my murderous husband, I was even more frightened of her.

Charles reached to grab Roo from my arms. I screamed "No!" and

Roo chomped his hand. Blood began to pour down Charles' arm, and he flung Roo away. I screamed again as a vine snatched my darling little dog out of the air and yanked him into the canopy. "No! Roo! Roo!" I tried to shove past Charles, but he held me there.

Melissa erupted from the shadows, lumbering across the deck towards us. She grabbed Charles by the shoulder and dragged him around to face her. He froze, his head traveling up and down, struggling to understand. "Melissa?" he gasped.

"You killed me. You killed our baby," she said, her voice like wind though the leaves.

"Wait, Melissa!" He lifted his hands as if torn between his want to push her away and his reluctance to touch her.

She stepped into him, trapping him against the wall the same way he'd trapped me, and embraced him like a lover. He let out a horrified scream and thrashed, then his scream cut off as her skeletal mouth and vine lips closed onto his. His screams were muffled, his eyes so wide I thought they might pop out of his head. She began to drag him back, and though he fought her, she pulled him inexorably towards her hidden grave.

As soon as my way was clear, I ran to the last place I'd seen Roo. She could have Charles, but she couldn't have my dog. I plunged my hands into the vines and found his warm, furry body. I grabbed the clippers from my pocket and began cutting everything between me and Roo. I cleared enough to see him. There was a vine around his throat, and his tongue was purple, but he still struggled weakly. I clipped the vine around his neck and dragged him out of the canopy before turning back to see what had become of my husband.

Melissa held Charles tight, his body pressed intimately against hers. The vines that made up her face twitched into a smile, and Charles let out a gurgling cry as vines erupted out of his body. He jerked and twitched, but he was caught like a worm on a hook. The vines wrapped back around him, holding him in place. His eyes cut to me, pleading for help, but I shook my head. He buried a dead girl in my backyard, he'd get no help from me.

Melissa backed step-by-step towards the hole in the deck, the place where she'd dragged herself from the ground. Charles, fighting every step of the way, was pulled in after her. He called out to me one last time, "Gia, for God's sake, help me!" His voice was strangled and weak, and he reached back with his left hand, the fading light glinting off his wedding band. I shook my head again, holding a quivering and terrified Roo tight.

With Melissa so focused on Charles, I raced for the door. I nearly made it before a vine wrapped around my ankle and flung me to the ground. Roo was knocked loose, and he bounced through the open door into the house. He sprang back to his feet and barked madly as Melissa dragged me across the deck. My scream was cut off when my head banged against the wood, stunning me for a moment. It was nearly a moment too long, but when I came back, I remembered something.

Twisting my body and ignoring the splinters invading my skin, I dug the clippers out of my back pocket. Quivering with terror, I glanced up and saw a half-dozen vines reaching for me. Flinging my body to the side, I reached out with my left arm and hooked my elbow onto a sturdy wooden post. I stretched towards the vine wrapped around my ankle. I twisted and pulled until I held that vine between the blades of the clippers. I looked up at Melissa, but her flower-eyes were fixed on Charles. She didn't look at me until I cut the vine, then she flinched and her head whipped towards me.

Scrambling on my hands and feet, I raced for the door. A vine tangled in my hair and I chopped it, hair and vine both. Another found its way to my ankle just as I crossed the threshold into the house. I slammed the door on it then cut it as well, leaving a wiggling, cut vine-tip just inside.

Melissa glared at me; even the flowers narrowed in anger. She hissed at me, then Charles—his body full of vines—jerked once, twice, and went still. I pressed my hands to the glass, staring, as Melissa sank back down into the ground with my husband's body pressed to hers. Those purple eyes never left mine. She vanished from sight first, and I felt as if I'd been freed from some evil spell when her furious purple gaze finally broke. Charles's hand was the last part of him to disappear under the dirt. The wedding band he wore caught on a broken vine and slipped from his finger. The ring lay there alone in the dirt, its golden sheen fading in the last rays of the setting sun.

SHE COMES CALLING

by Lisa Finch

This old house whispers and shakes. It tries to fool me, but I know what I hear: just the wind as it tunnels through the eavestroughs. Or maybe the scraggly reach of branch against window pane.

But it won't be my granddaughter, Lynette. Not until later, when the sky is black and the trick-or-treaters are out.

I don't give out Halloween candy, so tomorrow I'll find my front door egged, my trees streamed with toilet paper. It's the one night of the year I can't function. You'd think they'd forgive an old woman who would answer the door if she could.

Have they forgotten? At Christmastime I make fudge for the neighbourhood. I hire students who want to earn extra cash shovelling snow. I hire them to mow my lawn in the summer, too.

But their memory is short, obviously.

When the doorbell rings, I nearly jump three feet. Can't they see my lights are out?

It's dark now. I picture Lynette slouching, making herself small against the brick, near the crowd, but not *with* them. She'll wait for her chance to get inside. After all, this was once her home, too.

Little Lynette, my little pet. I used to call her that.

More footsteps on the porch. Is Little Lynette among them? She'd go unnoticed, a lone Disney princess hidden by her hood, in the shadows.

I got close to her once, on a Halloween night five years ago. She'd been dead three months. I chased after her, down the stone walkway at the side of the house that led to our garden.

I could almost touch the blue cape she'd begged me to make. I called her name; she stopped in her tracks, we nearly collided. The smell of dirt and decay invaded my nose.

I gagged and ran inside before she could turn around.

Every year since, she's tried to come home on this, the night of strange possibilities. But I lock the door.

Now as I watch shadows leap through the slit in my curtains I wonder how I'll get through this. How will she?

A gloom settles in on me.

I pace back and forth until I settle it. But I must wait. The last trick-or-treater finally gives up the ghost, so to speak. I chuckle nervously at my joke.

I go to the door. She'll be there.

I open it a crack. Ripples of anticipation mixed with bone-chilling terror dance along my spine. She has her back to me. Her hunched figure patiently waits on my porch although she's never had the slightest encouragement.

Poor kid. She needs me.

How bad can she be? She's still my Little Lynette, no matter what. And it's only this one night of the year she comes calling.

She turns and I see she has no eyes, no face, just a rotting hole.

"My pet." I smooth her hair as she falters into my arms. "I'm sorry I kept you waiting. Forgive me?"

THE STRAY BONES TRAP
by Chris Kuriata

In all the lonely years I lay in the dirt—winnowing, turning yellow, itching from the bugs—it never occurred to me I might one day rise out of the ground.

On the last day of my life I crouched in the bushes spying on my parents as they unloaded groceries from the trunk, leaving their car engine running, which they never would have done had they known their daughter lurked nearby. Seizing the opportunity, I ran across the slushy road, being very nearly smashed into by a skidding Beetle filled with Bing Crosby's muffled voice. With a quick rip of the parking break, the stolen car rolled down the driveway, and I cheered. The roar of the engine promised me the freedom of a fresh start. I planned to drive to fabled California where the sun never stopped shining and orange juice ran like running water. I would leave the battered remains of my shitty life behind.

I should have known better than to be hopeful.

The roads conspired against me. Too poorly ploughed, I skidded and crashed into the leg of a billboard advertising Winston cigarettes. The steering wheel crushed my ribs and took a tooth. I regained consciousness to the sound of emergency sirens. After scrambling out of the wreckage, I begged the snow to cover my footprints so neither the police nor my shamed parents could track me down. They never did—I survived to make my fated rendezvous with the man who put me under the ground.

My memories have leaked into the dirt so I can no longer remember the manner in which the man finished me off. Did he drive into the privacy of the woods, allowing himself the leisure of savouring his activity, or did he do me all in a rush in the backseat, panicked the whole time someone would catch him in the midst of his bloodlust? My hollow skull retains only the tune which played on the radio when he opened his car door and invited me to hop in. I often hum this song, clenching my broken teeth together, making them vibrate and rustle the grass growing above me.

I am not buried in isolation—in a quarry somewhere or clogging up a marshy drainage pipe. Sometimes I hear voices. Men tinkering with cars in their garages. Barbeque grills being scraped. Children dancing through a sprinkler. My killer has placed me in his backyard, not a stone's throw away from his house.

Imagine being so confident no one would come looking for me that he buried my remains on his own property.

I am the only woman under the ground in his yard, which is strange. Men—the type of men who enjoy causing suffering—don't kill once and call the habit quits. It's laughable to believe I satisfied his savagery, cleaning out the dark cobwebs, transforming him into a docile gentleman who now tips his cap to passing ladies. He claimed more women after me, of that there is no doubt, but he buried none of them so close to home.

He must have known someone would come looking for them.

I think he dreaded the idea of a backyard full of mutilated women— under the ground together we'd bond; comparing observations, laughing at his pot belly and rotted buck teeth. Our laughter would bubble up through the soil, taunting him at night. He'd lean out the window, screaming at us to keep quiet, until the neighbours noticed his paranoia and hauled him off to Merritville Sanatorium.

Eventually, the house went quiet and the man disappeared. I wonder if he considered digging me up and hiding me somewhere else, afraid I'd be discovered by the new home owners. Maybe it wasn't his choice to leave the house. Maybe the bank took it. Maybe he was finally captured and locked up. I have no way of knowing; no one came by to whisper the news into the grass.

The yard has a new owner now. I hear the rumble of his car when the engine starts each morning. When he first arrived, I wondered what kind of a man he was. Did he work in an office wearing a sharp suit or in a factory wearing overalls? Did he like to sing? In the spring, would he plant a garden?

Soon, I understood the new owner wasn't much different from the old.

Not long after his arrival, I heard a sound that had been absent from the yard for a long time; the stabbing of a shovel spade into the thick, rich soil. This wasn't shallow garden digging—a loosening of dirt to sow seeds. No. The new owner grunted and dripped sweat as his heel pushed the blade deeper and deeper into the ground, lifting top soil, digging until he hit clay.

The bastard was digging a grave.

The new owner placed a tiny body into the hole; an animal curled up in a pillow case. He did not place the animal in its grave gently like one would a beloved pet but dropped the bundle from a good height, wanting to hear its dead weight smack against the cold ground.

With this act, the peace I had long enjoyed under the ground came to an abrupt end.

My surrounding dirt became loud; congested with the sound of transformation inside that little cloth casket. The animal swelled and gases gurgled inside, unable to escape under the pressure of the earth. The sound went on until a tunneling insect reached the body, making the first puncture and being washed away in a jet of fluid and gas. Alerted to the new burial, millions of tiny bugs sifted their way through the soil, hungry for fresh nutrients. Insects crawled all over me, using the insides of my bones as a short cut, their feet tracking dirt inside the places I had managed to keep clean all these years. I felt humiliated, filled with bugs like a rotting piece of fruit.

Before the bugs finished stripping the animal down to its bones, the new owner returned and split the yard open again. He buried a second animal. This time, he didn't dig so deep—repetition made him confident.

As the season went on, he returned to the yard with great regularity, shovel in one hand, a bloodied sack in the other.

For a time, I considered the animals were merely victims of the road, scooped broken out of gutters and given a decent burial so as not to upset children, but their numbers were too great to be natural. The first few had been buried in pillow cases, but the new owner soon abandoned this courtesy, and the new animals arrived in crinkly paper, like purchases from the butcher, wrapped in twine to keep the limbs pulled tight.

Collars jingled, and I understood the animals weren't feral or strays. They came fresh from homes of people who loved them. People who cried and made posters and searched, driving through the rain, keeping the car door open in the vain hope their beloved dog or kitten would jump in, grateful to be brought back home.

One night, the new owner's ghastly hobby changed.

A plastic bag dropped into the hole, and the new owner shoveled dirt overtop as quick as he could. Under the ground, I felt desperate vibrations, a dimming life struggling to free itself, pressing so hard against the dirt its bones cracked.

The new owner had buried the animal alive, and I decided this nonsense had gone on long enough.

For the first time in decades, I moved my arm. It passed through the dirt much easier than I imagined. Perhaps the fact it no longer fitted into a joint eased its mobility. I was spread through the dirt like fragments of broken china. Gathering as much of my incomplete self as possible, I rose out of the ground. Thankfully, it was still night time. I feared the glare of the sun, afraid the reflection off my stripped bones would blind any poor soul who happened to look in my direction.

The neighborhood slept gently under the soft blue light of the moon. No one would see me. I struggled to stay balanced on my busted stumps, standing less than half my original height. I must have looked terrible with so many of my teeth missing.

I got low and used my jaw to push the dirt aside, sifting through the soil until I heard the sound of bone hitting bone. One by one, I lifted the animals from their graves, pinching the back of their necks in my jaw like a mother cat. They were all so light. Dried husks. More fur than meat.

Mostly I pulled up dogs. Some cats. All were little. Young and defenceless—trusting of people. When the new owner opened his hands to them, I'm sure they rushed forward, thinking they had found a new friend, not smelling his previous victims until it was too late. They'd all made the same mistake I had.

At last, I came to the freshest grave. When I bit into the earth I felt a pulse. Astonished, I dug faster, tearing open the plastic bag wrapped around the animal. The small, curled dog was still alive.

The poor thing was too exhausted to be thankful. His tail did not wag. He could only lie on his side, breathing rapidly—foamy white drool leaking from his mouth. His tongue rolled out and his eyes clenched shut, caked with dirt. Likely, he wouldn't survive. If I still had my flesh I may have tried breast feeding him, something I remember a woman doing for a tiger kitten in a storybook my mother had read me over and over when I was a child.

I made my way towards the new owner's home, bringing the animal bones with me. I had no arms to carry them, but their joints and sockets were compatible with mine. A little patience went a long way, and I soon snapped every one of the hundreds of rib and leg bones onto my form.

Click click click.

I delighted in my new shape. The bones fanned in all directions, making me spherical rather than vertical. A belt of lower jaws circled my waist. A cluster of skulls perched over my head, their fangs pointing north. With each step, the bones rattled, tinkling like broken ice bobbing on the lake.

The house surprised me. All this time I envisioned a slanted, dilapidated shack—where else would men who put women and animals underground live? Yet the house held its head high, proud to be gazed upon.

The paint was bright, a welcoming red, complemented by white trim like frosting holding together the seams of a gingerbread house.

Fitting myself through the front door was impossible without reconfiguring the bones. *Click click click.* I pulled the skulls from atop my head and bundled them around my chest. The other bones shifted on their own, folding and snapping into new joints, giving me a shape that could pass through the doorway. Once inside, the bones migrated again, forming sturdy legs I used to climb the stairs.

My bones clanked every step of the way. Did the new owner hear me coming? I pictured him cowering behind a locked door, cradling his rifle, begging me to leave. I had no voice to call him out. My only sound was air whistling through my hollow bones. I moved faster and faster.

The inside of the house matched the outside—decorated with an exquisite sense of order and comfort. The wallpaper had been hung so expertly the seams were invisible. Soft white carpet covered the stairs, muffling my gigantic new legs. Picture frames lined the wall, guiding the way to the second floor. I rubbed my jaw over the glass, trying to feel the faces underneath. The frames held a family. They seemed happy, but who knows for sure; who could see into their hearts? Perhaps their happy expressions were only for the benefit of the photographer urging them to "smile for the birdie," and were replaced with creases and frowns the moment the flash faded from their eyes.

On the second floor, the bones rearranged themselves again. They clattered together, excited. A part of me now, the bones knew the gruesome use I intended for them.

I pushed the bedroom door open. The room smelled of apples—two brown cores lay on the bedside. They'd been gnawed by different sets of jaws. "His 'n Her" teeth marks. Two people slept in the bed. The new owner, and his wife.

I wouldn't look at the wife. She had no idea what kind of man she slept beside. She never imagined him cruising down the street, opening his car door at every corner waiting for some beloved pet to trot out of their yard, foolishly trusting him enough to jump in. Maybe he held a handful of treats to entice them, or maybe they were just curious, wanting to see a world beyond their yard.

I grabbed the new owner under the chin. The bones reassembled again, standing tall over my back, reaching as high as the ceiling.

The bones jittered, eager to snap into their revenge, but doubt flickered in my hollows. Something wasn't right. The bones stood down, aware they had never been in the hands of the new owner. I lifted the sheets and ran my teeth over his fingers, nibbling the soft flesh under his nails. I tasted no dirt. His skin was smooth. There were no scars—no white ghosts from the nips and scratches of frightened, cornered animals.

I returned his hand to its place by his wife's side and retreated from the room. Could I possibly have wandered into the wrong house? Perhaps someone else had been jumping the fence and making the backyard their hiding place. Maybe it was even the original man who put me in the ground, elderly now, with only the strength for killing animals, his days of luring women into his car long behind him.

Halfway down the stairs, I remembered the framed pictures. I ran my jaw over them again, feeling the shape of the new owner and his wife and, finally, the person standing between them.

Of course.

The boy's bedroom reeked of fresh dirt. His sneakers, lying beside the bed, were frosted with a good inch of the backyard. He'd tracked mud full of animal blood across the carpet. His mother often scolded him, saying for the one hundredth time to take off his shoes in the hall. Not anymore. In the new morning, when his mother found him, her mind would be far away from such banalities.

The bones jittered in the boy's presence, some of the smaller ones raising goose bumps. They had been in his grasp before, cracked and crushed between his hands. Without a doubt, the killer of animals lay before us, tucked beneath freshly laundered sheets.

I thought of the young boys I'd known. The vicious ones who raced through the school halls, safety pins tucked between their fingers, jabbing girls. Always girls they jabbed, these young cowards with wicked cackles. I used to believe the taste for suffering eroded as they grew up; once men with daughters, they looked back on their wild days with shame and revulsion. But I knew that wasn't always true. I remembered the man who pulled his car door open, how eager he was for me to jump in, wanting to jab me and make me shriek.

Would the boy's fascination with capturing animals abate, or would his hobby continue into manhood, until he used his grown-up hands to reach for bigger, two-legged prey? The man who put me under the ground was once like this boy. I wonder how many animals he buried before me.

The bones rattled, impatient for me to begin constructing my revenge. I started with two hip bones, snapping them off me and arching them across the boy's neck. They became support beams on which I built the frame. The construction was steady. The bones cried to surround him. Box him in like a sarcophagus. Let him see the enormity of what he had done. I complied, building a prison from their bones.

I worked diligently, fitting pieces together. When the boy awoke and found himself trapped, he'd pound against the wall of his victims, trying with all his might to break through. But the bones would hold firm. I wove each vertebra and rib tight. They'd refuse to part, keeping him as immobile as an animal frozen in the soil.

I attached the skulls last. They demanded to hang over the boy's face, their fangs pointed at his eyes. When he awoke, he'd stare into the vacant socket of every animal he'd smothered in his pip-squeak hands. Would their faces be familiar? Would he know who they were? How could he not?

Once I'd completed building his monument of shame, I prepared to return under the ground, the only place I felt comfortable. The boy had no chance at escape. In the morning, I would hear the crack and crash of the heavy bone trap collapsing. The skull's fangs would pierce his eyes. He'd choke on a thousand, tiny macaroni bones. A few worms who hitched a ride into the house by hiding in the hollows would drain the boy into a husk, no heavier than one of the animals he put into the yard. Maybe the worms would be hungry enough to strip the boy to his bones, and he'd be lost in the jumble of all the others.

The animal bones cheered me farewell as I floated gracefully down the stairs. I hadn't felt so light since my final days haunting the street corners. I remember my father's shame. He used to drive through those seedy neighbourhoods, finding me perched in a row with the other hopeless girls. He never slowed down, never opened the door for me, not even on the nights rain fell. After awhile, whenever my father's headlights washed over me I turned away, hiding my face, but I wish just once my father had stopped and opened the door. I might have jumped in. I might have surprised us both.

Outside, a gust of wind lifted me high into the air. As light and flexible as a leaf, I swirled around the chimney and through the tree branches before gliding over the backyard. I couldn't wait to be back under the ground. I'd pretend I was a little girl again and the soil was the stack of quilts mom used to pack over me on long winter nights.

I looked for the boy's last victim, intending to cradle the little dog's body in my arms, let him turn to bone against my breast, but the spot he had lain in was empty. All that remained were paw prints in the loose dirt, heading far away from here. I hope he found his way home.

Comfortably in my grave, I reached above to pull the soil over me, but my hands felt nothing. Mystified, I clawed the earth over and over before realizing I no longer had arms to grasp with. Every surviving bone of mine went into the construction of the boy's trap. My hollows were no longer a part of me; they stayed behind, holding hands with the animal bones, waiting to spring the moment the boy opened his eyes.

I experienced a moment of panic before relaxing. What use had I for my tired, yellow bones anyway? Covered in cracks and crumbled at the edges. Good riddance.

At last, I rested in the open soil, bathing in the blue light of the moon.

I'd been released from the burden of my body. Any moment now, another gust of wind would come along and blow me away completely, like dust blasted off the edge of a table. Once the body is gone you can be everywhere. At last, I'm free to stop remembering forever.

THE GLORIOUS DEAD

by Dawn Vogel

Frank woke to the sound of soft groaning. The horizon did not yet show the first glimmers of dawn, and the campfires had burned low enough that the only light came from their glowing embers. Frank peered through the darkness to locate the source of the sound. A sharp motion to his left drew his attention. The retching sound that followed explained the nocturnal movement. The men of the 19th Regiment Kentucky Volunteer Infantry had suffered from a variety of maladies since the beginning of the campaign. Hardly a day or night passed that some poor soul was not running off to follow the dictates of his illness-ridden body.

Frank considered going back to sleep, but he was wide awake. He rose and walked across the campsite, scanning the other bedrolls. He found the sleeping form of his cousin, Alexander. Frank had promised his aunt he would look after her son, barely eighteen to Frank's twenty-four. Alexander's soft snores put Frank at ease, but he continued moving through the encampment to see who was sick tonight. His eyes landed on an empty spot, where a book and pencil lay in place of one of the men.

The book was open to the most recent entry. "May 25 – 9 o'clock, not much firing this morning." Scribbled beneath the entry was a signature, "J. J. Ray." Frank frowned and closed the diary. If James Ray had signed his last entry, he must have been feeling even more poorly than he had been in the past months. One of the older men in the company, James had not taken to the change in climate as they had moved south. Regardless of age, Frank still felt a bit of paternal concern for all of the men entrusted to his command.

Another moan of pain drew Frank's attention, just a few dozen feet from the camp. He called out, barely louder than a whisper, "James?" The only response was the sound of dry heaves. Frank moved nearer to the source of the noise.

A long moment passed before James spoke, his voice feeble. "Sorry, Cap'n. Didn't want to wake no one. Been real sick tonight."

Pine lingered in Frank's nostrils, masking the scent of James' vomit. The feeble light of the embers did not penetrate the treeline. "It's all right, James. Do you need some water or something to eat?"

"I can't keep nothin' in my belly. Not even water."

Before Frank could admonish James to go back to the surgeons in the morning, another, louder groan pierced the stillness. The fine hairs on the back of Frank's neck leapt to attention. The noise sounded like a strange combination of an animal growling and a human cry.

"What was that?" James asked.

"Sounds like a hurt animal." Frank slipped straight into command mode, his mind whirling. "Wake Davey Parsons and send him out here with a light and our rifles. Be quick and stay quiet. And if you feel sick again, go to the other side of the camp next time."

❧ ❧ ❧

Frank waited in a tree, about ten feet above the ground. Although the sound could have been a hurt animal, he was not taking any chances. Something about the too-human cry tickled at Frank's memory.

When Frank saw James returning instead of Davey, he dropped down from the tree and landed in front of the older soldier. James jumped and clapped a hand over his mouth, dropping the two rifles cradled in his right arm. The weapons clanked off of one another as they crashed to the ground and slammed the hood of the lantern shut, breaking the silence. James' left hand remained firmly on the handle of the lantern. Frank was thankful for that. James was a good man, but he was a farmer, not a soldier. Keeping the flame of the lantern out of the underbrush was as much as could be hoped for right now.

"Where's Davey?"

"I couldn't find him, Cap'n. His bed was still warm, but he weren't in it."

A long, low whistle came from a short distance away. Frank froze for a moment, then took the lantern from James. He cracked open the hood and looked around. Davey walked out from between two of the spindly trees, a grin a mile wide on his face.

"You hear something out here?" Davey asked.

"I thought it might be a hurt animal you could help me track," Frank

52

replied.

Davey shook his head. "Not if it's the same thing that woke me. I've heard a lot of injured animals out in the woods. Even foxes don't cry like that. It sounded more like a wounded man."

"Big Sam weren't in his bed either," James said. "Do you think he went and got hurt?"

"May have," Frank said. Big Sam was a former slave who had escaped to the 19th Kentucky's lines earlier that year. While the leadership of the unit had debated whether or not the President's Emancipation Proclamation had set Big Sam free, the African seemed more than happy to help out around camp. "We ought to look, at the very least. I wouldn't want him to be left out alone all night."

⁂

Clouds raced across the May sky, obscuring the moon for minutes at a time. Frank had hooded the lantern again so barely any light escaped it, lest anyone in the city of Vicksburg was watching. When the sky grew completely dark, he and the two other men stopped moving. The ground around the battlefield was littered with holes and mounds of earth, where countless bodies had been buried earlier that day. Trying to traverse the area in the dark was a fool's errand. Davey might be able to manage such a feat if he was alone, but Frank knew better than to try, especially with the way James stumbled every few steps.

Frank began to feel as if this entire excursion might be a fool's errand. Even if Big Sam had wandered out this far, the odds of finding him were slim at best. The fact that they had not heard any more groaning suggested one of two things: either they were going the wrong way, or whoever had been groaning was no longer capable of making a sound. But he knew he would not sleep a wink if they returned to camp without investigating.

The three soldiers rounded a bend in the road, and Frank and Davey immediately ducked low to the ground. James remained standing for a few moments longer, his instincts not as ingrained as those of the other two men. Ahead, they saw a low campfire, with two men standing opposite one another.

One of the men was tall, straight, and broad across the shoulders. He held a shovel in one hand, tensed as though he was ready to strike out with the makeshift weapon at any moment. The faint moonlight glistened on his ebony-colored skin. Though the darkness reduced most colors to shades of black and white, the campfire gave off just enough light to reveal Big Sam's wide red sash around his waist.

The man opposite him was hunched and twisted, with one arm

53

hanging limp. He stood a few paces back from the fire, just far enough that details of his appearance were harder to see. His skin looked ashy gray, and darker patches on his clothing looked like they might be dried blood.

The air smelled faintly of smoke, underlain by an aroma earthier than wood. A shift in the wind brought a whiff of sage, along with Big Sam's clear voice, toward the three soldiers. The words he spoke were not English. Frank's skin crawled as he finally remembered the last time he had heard such speech. He sunk even lower to the ground, and gestured for his compatriots to do the same.

"What's he doing?" James asked.

Frank paused for a long moment before answering. Despite having seen such a ritual with his own eyes, he had a hard time admitting he believed in such superstitious nonsense. "Voodoo." His voice was flat and barely crept above a whisper.

Davey arched one eyebrow at Frank. "Voodoo? That's nothing but a heap of mumbo-jumbo."

"I wish that were true," Frank said. "Do you recognize the man across from Big Sam?"

Davey turned back toward the fire. "Henry Franklin?"

Frank nodded. "I saw him take a bullet to the chest three days ago. I didn't bury him myself, but I'm pretty certain he was dead."

"Are you trying to tell me that Big Sam raised that man from the dead?" Davey asked.

"I didn't want to believe it. But the noise I heard earlier, the cry of pain, is the sort of noise that sticks with you. I heard it once before, after one of my father's slaves had died."

James blanched in the pale lantern light, but kept silent. Davey shook his head. "I thought all that was just stories."

"So did I, till I saw it." Frank chewed at his lower lip. "I wasn't much more than nine years old. Alex was only three. I don't suppose he even remembers it. I can't forget it. I don't know the words Big Sam is saying, but I do know that's what I heard that night."

Without another word, Davey stood up and strode toward Big Sam. Frank leapt up after him, and James scrambled to join the other two soldiers.

"What are you doing, Sam?" Davey asked as he neared the fire.

Big Sam's chanting faltered as he half-turned toward the three men. Perspiration stood out on his brow, despite the cool night air. "Not...now," he stammered. As he turned his attention back to the mangled person in front of him, he was barely able to raise the shovel up in time to ward off the attack that came from the creature. Thwarted, it let out a piteous moan, then shambled away from Big Sam.

"Damn!" Big Sam shouted. "I almost had it."

"Had what?" Davey demanded. "What in all of God's creation do you think you're doing, Sam?"

"I'm sorry, Mister Davey. I gave Mister Henry one of my auntie's *gris gris*, for luck. Only it turned out it wasn't no luck *gris gris*. When he got buried today, it made him rise up out of the grave. I was trying to put him back in it." He gestured limply with the shovel.

Frank let out a long, shuddering breath and asked the question he dreaded the answer to. "What is he then?"

Big Sam grimaced. "My auntie would've called him a zombie. It's bad, bad mojo. I got to get him back in the ground before he starts making more."

"Making more?" Davey exclaimed, running his hands through his hair. "More like him?"

"Yessir, he's going to run around and bite anyone he can find, and they're going to fall down, and then get back up. One makes a second. Two make more. It just keeps going."

"He ran in the direction of camp," James said feebly. "I think I need to sit down now." His knees bent, and he fell to the ground.

"Get up," Frank snapped, feeling his temper rise. He tried to calm himself before speaking again. "We don't have time to sit. Sam, you better tell us everything you know, and do it while we're running back to camp."

James began to stand, but collapsed again. "There's somethin' wrong with my leg." He lifted his pant leg and winced. Frank turned the lantern light toward James and cursed under his breath when he saw the wide scrape that ran along James' calf.

Davey moved to James' side and looked at the wound. He probed James' leg gently, eliciting a scream of pain from James. "How long have you had that scratch, James?"

"It was mostly healed," James moaned. "I took the bandage off it before I went to bed. I guess all this walkin' around tonight made it sore again."

"Has the surgeon seen that?" Davey asked.

"Not for a couple of weeks. I'm scared to go back. I seen too many men gettin' their legs sawed off for less than this. I don't wanna lose my leg. I got a wife and six kids back home. Who's gonna take care of them if I lose a leg?"

Davey looked up at Frank and mouthed a single word. "Gangrene."

Frank nodded and turned to Big Sam. "How fast can that thing move?"

"Fast as a man. Maybe faster, on account of it not needing to rest anymore."

"Can you carry James?"

"Yessir, Cap'n Frank. You and Mister Davey just watch your step, as

I don't think I can carry all y'all too."

"No use in sneaking anymore," Frank agreed. "Even if the Rebs see us now, I'm more worried about what's back at camp." His thoughts flashed to his young cousin for a fraction of a second. He focused again by reminding himself that the quicker they stopped the zombie, the more likely it was that Alex and the other men of the 19th would make it home safely. He threw the lantern hood wide open as they moved toward the camp.

⚜⚜⚜

Frank had thought that they were not too far behind the zombie. When they arrived, he realized that single creature had made fast work of the sleeping soldiers in the 19th Kentucky's camp. The campfires had been built back up, casting their light across the scene, but Frank saw only a few clusters of men in the area. Most of the soldiers looked terrified, clutching their weapons to their chests rather than trying to fire on the approaching attackers.

He saw several men who had been bitten by the zombies. Huge bloody gashes in their throats or arms pumped forth streams of crimson, as they collapsed to the ground. It was like the battle all over again. Although the Confederates had not used their teeth and hands to rend apart the Union troops, the bloodshed looked all too familiar.

Also unlike the results of the siege on Vicksburg, the fallen soldiers did not remain strewn across the battlefield. After the men collapsed from blood loss, they remained still for less than a minute before they rose and began their own personal assault on the remaining survivors. Their movements were slow and jerky at first, but soon became like those of any normal man, sometimes even more fluid than in life.

Frank's levelheaded leadership kicked in as soon as he had observed the situation. "Big Sam, take James and find the Colonel. Tell him to get as many of the men who are still living as he can, and retreat to Brigade Headquarters. Davey and I will find the ones who can help us most, and we'll take care of this. Can you think of anything at all we can use to find the first one?"

"He ought to still have the *gris gris* tied on a string around his neck. It'll be a little bag, the same color as my sash. If you can get it away from him, he'll go back to being dead."

"What about all the ones he's bit? What'll happen to them?" Davey asked.

"I don't rightly know, Mister Davey." Big Sam's voice faltered. "I wasn't expecting none of this."

Frank clapped Big Sam on the shoulder. "We'll do what we can for them, too. Godspeed, Sam."

Big Sam, with James riding piggyback, skirted the edge of the campsite. The former slave scanned the chaos for an officer, while James kept an eye out for any approaching zombies.

Davey spared a sidelong glance at Frank. "So, you really think we're up for this?"

Frank half-smiled. "I am if you are." His grin faltered for an instant, but the look in Davey's eyes told him that his friend had seen it. "Davey, if you see Alex, and he's one of those things, just pretend he's not my cousin for long enough to put him out of his misery."

Davey nodded solemnly and turned his attention to the carnage around them. Frank let out a long breath, mentally steeling himself for what had to be done.

Without pausing to breathe in again, Frank drew his sidearm and took aim at the nearest zombie. Reciting a brief prayer under his breath, he fired. The shot struck the zombie directly between the eyes. The zombie staggered a few steps, nothing but momentum propelling his husk forward.

"Nice shot, Frankie boy," Davey said. "Save one of those for the *gris gris*." Davey's face split into a wide grin, and he let out a terrifying war whoop. He strode toward the fracas, pausing only to scoop up a saber from the grasp of a dead man. The corpse twitched, and Davey drove the sword through the newly awakened zombie's throat.

"Like shooting fish in a barrel," Frank called out. Davey raised the dripping sword in a quick salute and dove into a group of zombies. Frank watched patiently, aiming before each shot to ensure he would not hit his friend or any other living person.

All the while, he watched for any sign of Big Sam's *gris gris* around the neck of one of the zombies. He saw occasional flashes of red, but inevitably they proved to be blood staining the clothing of soldiers and zombies alike. Frank and Davey were not the only soldiers fighting back against the zombies. A few others, near the fringes of the campsite, shot rifles and pistols at the zombies that approached them. Davey, however, was the only one brave—or stupid—enough to wade into the midst of the zombies. He was also singing "The Battle Hymn of the Republic" at the top of his lungs, punctuated with grunts as he ran his sword through the necks of nearby zombies.

"Fraaaaaank." A deep, drawling voice to his left drew his attention away from Davey. The man was about thirty feet away, missing a large chunk of hair and skin that had covered his skull. Though the zombie looked dimwitted, faint recognition registered in its eyes.

The same recognition flashed across Frank's face. "Alexander." Frank looked at his cousin more carefully in the firelight. He hoped he had imagined the injuries, but they were even more apparent the closer he looked. A long, dark stream had worked its way down Alexander's shirt from the collar. The gaping wound above it still pumped forth blood. The air smelled of copper, and Frank winced as he comprehended the source.

Frank's arm was as heavy as lead as he raised his pistol. Though he had given Davey orders to pretend the boy was not Frank's kin if it came to that, Frank found himself unable to do the same. He did not look forward to having to tell his mother's sister that it was he, not a Confederate soldier, who had killed her only son.

Alexander extended his hands, covered in gore, toward Frank. Frank took a shot out of instinct, forgetting his gun was still aimed low. The bullet hit Alexander's right knee, who only lurched slightly. Backing away, Frank reloaded his pistol. He took a second shot, aiming for his cousin's left knee this time. If he disabled Alexander long enough to find the first zombie, he might be able to spare his cousin.

"Frank, aim for their heads!" Davey shouted. "Nothing else will do anything to them!"

Frank waved in Davey's general direction to acknowledge the advice, and turned back to Alexander. His cousin had stopped approaching but was now gnawing at the neck of another soldier. The victim's name escaped Frank for the moment. He knew the other soldier was only a boy of eighteen, just like Alex.

Frank's military instincts clicked, and he made his decision. Alexander would never be able to live with the thought of having killed one of his comrades. Frank did not relish the thought either. At least he would do so in control of his faculties. He raised his pistol. "I'm sorry, Alex. I'll give your mother your best." He pulled the trigger and watched as the light in his cousin's eyes faded.

Frank crouched down to close the eyes of the dead boy. As he straightened back up, he noticed that a hush had fallen over the camp. Davey's singing had stopped. He whirled around, trying to locate his friend. "Davey?"

Davey's sword arm flailed as one of the zombies gripped him by both shoulders. The zombie bit a large chunk out of Davey's neck, and Davey let out a gurgle. Frank rushed to his friend's side and seized the sabre that had cut down so many of the zombies already. He plunged it through the neck of the zombie that had just attacked Davey, pulling to one side until the sword came free. The zombie's head lolled to the right, and it crumpled at Frank's feet.

Davey had also fallen to the ground, and lay twitching in a pool of gore. "Gimme...pistol," he gasped.

Frank turned his head away from Davey, preparing to shake his head "no." As he turned, a flash of red caught his eye. The color was richer than that of the blood that coated the entire area, and it glowed with malevolent power. "Hold your horses," he muttered, and charged toward the first zombie.

Behind him, he heard Davey's voice growing gravelly and strained. "Frank. Pistol. Kill me."

The zombie with the *gris gris* around his neck moved in Frank's direction. Then it stopped, eyes narrowing, and darted into the midst of a large group of zombies. Frank stopped, trying to calm his racing heart. He picked up a discarded rifle and checked the barrel. Methodically, he raised the gun to his shoulder and sighted along the top. His breathing slowed. He watched the mass of zombies writhe and shift in front of him. Finally, he saw the *gris gris* again, and took his shot.

Just as the zombie fell, the report of a pistol echoed the rifle shot. Frank wheeled and looked for the other gunman.

Davey's right hand flopped to the ground, an officer's pistol in hand. Fresh blood blossomed from a wound in his temple. Frank was barely aware that the zombies had stopped. The men of the 19th Kentucky muttered in confused tones around him. All he saw was the blood flowing out of his friend's skull.

"Davey, you idiot!" Frank shouted. The light had begun to fade from Davey's eyes. What little expression remained in them was a mix of fear and regret.

"I'm sorry, Frank," Davey whispered. "I couldn't let myself become one of those things."

Frank knelt and grasped his friend's hand. "You never were one of them, Davey. You always knew which side you were fighting for, even to the end." Davey's body shuddered, and Frank leaned forward to close the dead man's eyes.

TEMPORARY

by S.D. Hintz

"Look at him, Pete. He's a frigging zombie."

"Of course he is, Lynn. What do you expect?"

"I expect him to leave his cubicle once in awhile."

"He's a copywriter. His ass is stapled to that chair."

"It doesn't mean he has to be an anti-social Nazi."

"Give him a break already. He's a new hire. He doesn't know anybody. Maybe he wouldn't be an anti-social Nazi if you talked to him."

Lynn rolled her eyes. "Yes. Anyways…I have a lovely slush pile screaming to be read."

Pete nodded, sipping his Starbucks. "Hear, hear. I've got more SASEs than the mail room."

Pete disappeared into his office while Lynn lingered by the break room, staring at the new hire. There was something she loathed about him. Maybe it was the fact that he lacked a bio, or she had yet to tap into the rumor mill. She knew his name was George Carpenter. His hair was oily and the texture of black wool. He had Elvis sideburns and beetle brows with a five o'clock shadow to match. His beady, bloodshot eyes were unblinking, locked on the computer screen.

Lynn glanced at her slacks. She picked off lint and let it float to the Berber. She looked back to George. He had worn the same outfit two weeks straight: an off-white button-down, navy blue Dockers, and a frayed gray clip-on. That bothered her. It was obvious the man didn't dress to impress. He was in a professional environment, for Christ's sake.

She nibbled her lip, dwelling on George like a fruit fly. Why had her boss hired this loser? Or was he a temp? That was it. He had to be a temp. One of those jobless bums from Hattan Staff. She had yet to meet a temp that was worth half of minimum wage.

"Lynn?"

She jumped, relieved that there was a lid on her sloshing latte.

Her boss Gaines Artiss knitted his penciled brows and wrinkled his nose. "If you plan on asking George to a power lunch, I suggest you do so. The slush is only getting deeper."

Lynn shook her head and smiled weakly. "Yes, because I so admire a man who never changes clothes."

"I recall you wearing those same sequined pumps yesterday and the day before."

"Shoes are one thing." Lynn bit her tongue, remembering that she was speaking to the guy responsible for hiring and firing. "Never mind. I have a medieval romance to read."

"I need your feedback on that Connor sub by noon."

"And you'll have it."

Lynn strode past George's work area, sniffing the air.

God, he smells trashy.

She wondered if he had washed his armpits in the last month. She smothered the smell by sipping her coffee, and then plopped down at her desk four cubicles from George.

She shook her mouse. Outlook blinked through the England screensaver. She had one email from "Pesky" Pete. The subject line read: SO…

She double-clicked on it and enlarged the pane.

DORRIAN JUST TOLD ME GEORGE NEVER REPLIES TO HIS EMAILS. THOUGHT YOU'D FIND THAT INTERESTING.
PETER JENKINS
ACQUISITIONS EDITOR
GALLOWAY PRESS

Lynn replied.

REALLY? LET'S FIND OUT.

LYNN HARGROVE
ASSISTANT EDITOR
GALLOWAY PRESS

Lynn searched George's name in Outlook and then typed him a

playful message. She figured he would be more apt to reply as opposed to receiving a business request.

She simply typed: WAKE UP! ☺

A simultaneous reply *dinged*, startling her. At first she thought she had misspelled his email address. Then she saw *his* name rather than the Postmaster. She clicked on it.

> I CAN'T.
> GEORGE CARPENTER
> COPYWRITER
> GALLOWAY PRESS

I can't? What the hell does that mean? He's been out on the town all night with the hobos?

Lynn half-stood, peering over her cubicle wall. She spotted George, stiff, perfect posture, dazed on his screen. She sat down and shook her head. God, he was pale. And his eye sockets were dark ovals. Maybe he had the flu. He looked as if he might spew chunks on his keyboard at any second.

The slush pile of bubble mailers teetered in Lynn's periphery. She minimized Outlook and grabbed the top submission. She blinked hard. She had to stop thinking about George. She had way too much work to do. She blamed her intrigue on her mother, the gossip columnist. The busybody trait was programmed in her DNA. She wouldn't be appeased until she knew the copywriter's story.

She tugged the stapled sample chapters from the envelope and scanned the title page.

MILADY'S LUST
BY CAROLYN CONNOR

"George?"

Lynn's head snapped in the direction of her boss's voice. She craned her neck. Gaines approached George's cubicle with a manila folder in hand, waving it like a Chinese fan. George failed to acknowledge that he had heard his name. He gaped at his monitor, shoulders square.

"George! Wake up, man! There's something missing here. Reed Michaels doesn't end his epics in mid-sentence. Where's the rest of it?"

George was unresponsive, save for the drivel that dangled from his chin. He remained stone-faced and statuesque.

Gaines waved the folder before the monitor. "George! *Hello?*"

George turned his head, his joints cracking. His stare was blank. His throat gurgled as if he was on the verge of belching out a reply.

"Mr. Carpenter! Where is the rest of the Mr. Michaels manuscript?"

George lifted his arm, shoulder creaking, and pointed at the folder blocking the monitor. His voice was deep and grating when he spoke. "There."

"*There? In there?* Are you implying that he ended the next *War and Peace* with a hyphen?"

George tapped the folder. A spit bubble popped on his parted lips. "There."

"I swear to God, George, if Mr. Michaels has a more complete ending lying around your sty of a cubicle, you'll be cleaning out your desk!"

Gaines yanked back the folder. He then whirled and stormed to his office.

George dragged his callous hand down the monitor screen until it slapped onto the keyboard. "There."

Lynn noticed that the entire office was distracted, their gazes locked along her own line of sight. She knew George was screwed. When Gaines returned with word that the manuscript was indeed incomplete, their new hire would live up to the title "temporary."

Lynn's Outlook rang.

Speak of the devil.

The subject line read: WHERE ARE THE PR QUERIES??

Lynn opened the email.

> I NEED THOSE COPIES FOR MY 9AM ROUNDTABLE.
> GAINES ARTISS
> EDITOR-IN-CHIEF
> GALLOWAY PRESS

Damn.

Lynn had forgotten to retrieve the paranormal romance queries last night. She left the Xerox to its vigorous printing of thirty color copies but neglected to gather them up. She chided herself for being in such a hurry to clock out and catch happy hour at Applebee's. She prayed the stack of papers sat untouched in the copy room.

She looked at her PC clock. 8:54 a.m.

She cursed under her breath, stood, and hurried across the office, eavesdropping on murmurs and tapping keys. She glanced at George's cubicle as she passed by. It was deserted.

Where the hell did he go?

She wondered if he was digging in the recycle bin for the missing pages of the Michaels manuscript. Either that or he was searching for a new trashy wardrobe: maybe one of those biodegradable Glad bags.

Lynn rounded the last cubicle. She paused at the break room doorway and poked her head in. "Scrawny" Tawny Dane dunked a tea bag in a hot pink mug. She wore a dirt-colored sundress and matching high heels; a twig costume, her frizzy blond hair canopy. If someone opened the refrigerator door, Lynn was certain Tawny would blow over into the bulletin board.

Tawny half-turned and regarded Lynn with a raised brow. "Good morning, Lynn."

"Have you seen, George?"

Tawny raised the other brow. "You're really wet for this guy, aren't you? You haven't stopped talking about him since Monday."

"Oh, go purge!"

Lynn huffed and headed to the copy room, straight down the hall, concentrating on the two cubicles on her right. "Scary" Harry Pendleton and his thinning combover gabbed about some *Ellery Queen* drama. That man needed a life…and a man. Her ear trained on the adjacent carpeted cell, like a bee buzzing to the next blossom for nectar. "Overweight" Kate Winslow's jowls jiggled as she exchanged recipes. Lynn was surprised she hadn't eaten "Scrawny" Tawny.

The machine gun whir of the Xerox snatched Lynn's focus. She veered into the copy room with her game face on. If anyone had moved her queries or was in the midst of doing so, they were going to be swallowing her slush pile.

Lynn stubbed her toe, stopped and donned a squirrel-in-headlights stare. George stood at the copy machine, drooling on the console. He stared straight ahead, as if using x-ray vision on the wall.

Then Lynn noticed what he held in his wrinkled hands. It was her query pile. The author's underlined name had caught her eye. She opened her mouth to snap and then clamped it shut as George's stench hit her like a Hollywood wind machine. It was olfactory hell. Odors from every orifice, air conditioning from his putrid pores. Lynn gagged and held her breath, refusing to inhale his rotting compost aroma. Why hadn't she whiffed it before? It should have permeated throughout the office.

Lynn plugged her nose and pointed frantically. "Mine!"

George remained in his conscious coma. His greenish-yellow drivel splashed on the copies he held.

Lynn flipped her lid. Her boss needed those queries in five minutes. "Goddamn it! Give me them! They're mine!"

She snatched the slobbery pile. George's grip was viselike, and the papers tore in half. His neck twisted—a snap, crackle, pop—while his vacant gaze searched for the disruption. It followed the drool. He dropped the copies, and they scattered on his tattered loafers.

Lynn was beside herself. The nerve of a temp tearing up her paperwork and spitting on it. Her blush deepened to crimson, and she trembled. "You son of a bitch! What the hell is the matter with you? Those were my copies!"

George looked down, still drooling, watering the Berber and papers. "There."

"*There?* What, are you satisfied or something?"

George opened the Xerox, crouched, and gathered up the soggy shreds. When he stood, knees cracking, he grabbed Lynn's half of the queries.

"Yes, George! Throw them away! You've ruined them! Now what?"

George slapped the whole mess of papers on the Xerox glass. He gaped. His tongue fell out, as if his mouth had defecated, staining the queries. He then slammed the copy machine shut. Lynn's grimace was splattered with blood and chunks of muscle. Her mouth dropped to scream, but the latte had dried her throat. She choked and hacked while George left the copy room.

What had just happened? Had he really smashed his severed tongue in the Xerox? Who would do something like that? Lynn struggled to compose herself, bridled her anger. Her leer landed on the copy machine. It was dripping with blood, probably conducting a MRI on the twitching muscle.

A prolonged squeak snatched her gaze. The fax machine beside the Xerox was spitting out a document. The bold headline glared at Lynn.

CRYOSTAFF
Affordable Temps – Indefinite Hours

Lynn approached the fax machine, nosiness overcoming her present shock and disgust. The word "Temps" confirmed her suspicions about George. She removed the document from the tray and read it.

> Dear Employer,
> We are delighted to inform you that two additional CryoTemps have attained eligibility status. We hope you have been satisfied with George Carpenter's performance and dependability. Please contact us at your earliest opportunity to reserve further replacements.
> Thank you.
> CryoStaff
> "Temporaries of the Future!"

Temporaries of the future?

Lynn's hand shook as she mulled over the fax. George was some kind of cryogenic freak! Did that mean he was…dead? No. No, that was just stupid. This wasn't one of her paranormal submissions.

Lynn took a deep breath. She looked at the wall clock. 8:59 a.m.

Shit. Gaines is going to want his queries. What am I going to do? She shut her eyes, seeking her inner yoga. *That's it. He wants a copy. I have his copy. I'll throw it in his face and get George out the goddamn door. I'll show him the copy room and the blood. That'll convince him.*

Lynn marched into the hall and barged into Gaines's office.

He peered over his wire-rimmed reading glasses and straightened behind his mahogany desk, startled by the intrusion. "Ahh, my queries."

Lynn waved the fax. "What the hell is this?"

"I thought they were my copies, but I now see there's only one. Where are the rest of them? Christ, you're not giving me incompletes, too, are you?"

"You're hiring…" Lynn stammered over her word usage, paranoid of sounding loony. "Some kind of dead freaks! George just slammed his damn tongue in the Xerox! Look at me! His frigging blood's on my face!"

Gaines eyed Lynn incredulously. "George just went home because he bit his tongue pretty badly on a Bruegger's. I…I don't even know what to say to that, Lynn. Is this some kind of 'dog ate my homework' excuse?"

"You know damn well what this is!"

Lynn slapped the document on the desk.

Gaines glanced at the headline and met his editor's infernal gaze. "I believe it's what they call junk fax. It's not nearly as enticing as the Hawaiian trips for a hundred dollars."

"You're lying! You're using them! You're using that trashy temp agency of freaks!"

"Lynn, if this is about George…"

"I'm gone! I'm done! I'm taking the day off! Have some other goddamn lackey get your copies!"

Lynn stormed out of Gaines's office. She knew he would never admit to employing some illegal temp service, some basement lab of mad morticians. Who would? Besides, he was probably saving on overtime or evading taxes.

Jesus Christ, I must've sounded like a lunatic. I don't care. I don't care if it wasn't my business. George made it my business. Gaines is involved in illegal activity. It's illegal. There's no way… There's just no way!

Lynn pulled a Flash Gordon, snippets of gossip falling on deaf ears. If she hurried, she could catch George before he vacated the premises. And then what would she do? Ask him if he wanted to come clean? What if he conceded that he had leprosy? After all, his tongue fell out. No. No, he was a nasty temp from a chest freezer, nuked to life in a microwave, probably on the damn "popcorn" setting.

Lynn jabbed the down arrow and paced before the elevator. She poked it five more times for good measure. After a New York minute, a *ding* sounded and the doors clunked open. She nearly charged in and then staggered back as traffic emerged.

Lynn's eyes widened and her face reddened. Two men in gray jumpsuits with CS embroidered on their lapels wheeled hand trucks. Strapped to the carts were six-foot tall crates. A frigidity bit her skin as they passed by into the office. She stared after them, knowing damn well that Gaines had hired more diseased temps.

The elevator doors began to shut, breaking Lynn's trance. She snuck inside and punched the "L" button. Her head swam, overloaded with more information than a busybody could handle.

Gaines lied to my face. That bastard! One of those temps was probably coming to replace me. There's no way in hell they can edit Carolyn Connor's crappy manuscripts. I'm the one that makes her look good. They're deadbeats! What are they going to do?

The doors rattled open. Lynn spotted George at the entrance, making his exit. She dashed through the lobby, determined to have a last word with him. He stepped outside, head held high, limbs looking robotic.

"George!"

Lynn barged through the glass doors, head snapping in every direction.

George stood near the curb on a wheelchair lift that elevated him toward the floor of a gray van.

"George! Wait, damn you!"

Lynn lunged, attempting to clutch his Dockers and snag his attention. Instead, she lost her balance off the curb and stumbled headfirst into the street. An ambulance barreled into her, destroying the left half of her torso and thrusting her back. Her body collided with the van door, which slammed on George, bashing in his skull.

The ambulance screeched to a halt. Two EMTs rushed to the scene. A trio of men in gray jumpsuits beat them to the punch and surrounded Lynn.

"We've got this one. She's as good as dead. We'll save you the paperwork."

The EMTs considered the request reasonable, waved their hands, and climbed back into the ambulance. Traffic whizzed by, disinterested.

The men in jumpsuits lugged Lynn into the van, where she landed beside George, bleeding temporarily in unison. The lift folded and the doors shut, snuffing the dark cloud of manufactured microbes.

Mercy Brown and Me

by Christine Lajewski

This is a very short memoir. I'm only fourteen—not that much to tell—and I'm only covering the past fifteen months. I don't have a lot of time, either, just a few hours until darkness falls.

Mercy Brown is my best friend. Let's start there. I'm writing this on the last day of October, 2016, and she died in 1892. No matter. We are good friends. She is lonely like me and, no, she is not a vampire.

If you live in Rhode Island—and even beyond—you probably know the story. Her mother and older sister had already died of TB and her brother Edwin was sick as well. When Mercy got sick, she didn't linger like the other members of the Brown family. She went quickly. She was stored in the charnel house at the Chestnut Hill Cemetery because the ground was frozen. Edwin got sicker and it looked like he was doomed. Out of desperation, George Brown, her father, and some friends opened the hut to inspect his daughter's body. It looked to them like Mercy had been moving around. They thought it could only mean she was a vampire, insatiably sucking blood from her own brother. They cut out her heart, burned it on a rock and fed the ashes to Edwin. With medicine like that, I guess it's not surprising that he died, too.

I met Mercy Brown one year ago. I never really liked kids my own age—too immature. The friends I did have turned on me. I would have preferred to hang out with my eighteen-year-old sister, Gina, but she usually didn't want me around. Probably she was worried I would tell Mom what she did with her friends. But every once-in-awhile I got lucky. One of those times was when she had to pick me up from the art fair at the junior high school.

It was November first, the Day of the Dead, and she had a carload of people. She didn't want to drive all the way home with me so she pulled over on a side street and we all walked to the Chestnut Hill Cemetery with cans of beer stuffed in the front pockets of our hoodies. We hiked right to a big pine tree leaning over the headstones and there it was: Mercy Brown's grave.

I knew the story but like an idiot I asked, "Why are we here?" Everyone laughed and I felt stupid.

"Tonight's the night for wandering souls," Gina said, as if that explained everything.

We drank beer and spilled it on Mercy's grave. Gina's friends left nips of vodka and peppermint schnapps and Jaeger Meister. They scattered pennies around the tombstone. (I didn't understand that, either, but I wasn't going to ask.) They all began to drift in different directions, hoping to run into Mercy, I guess, but I stayed to examine the grave goods. There were crystals and the devil card from a tarot deck. I saw a passkey from a local motel and a torn photograph of a guy—someone's ex-boyfriend, I suppose. (Was Mercy supposed to haunt him?) There were two headbands with springy alien bobble heads attached. I was only thirteen but I could see that this poor dead girl was whatever people needed her to be, starting with her dad and continuing to the present day. It struck me for the first time that my big sister was kind of silly and immature. (Sorry, Gina.)

I looked up to find I was completely alone. I panicked—who wouldn't? I followed the sounds of voices to the charnel house on the far right of the cemetery. My sister was there with her friend, Laurinda. "This is where they kept her body and cut out her heart," Gina said. "This is the most haunted part of the cemetery." Like she knew.

"We've never seen her, though," said Laurinda. "I don't think they keep bodies in there anymore." They joined the others wandering among the graves, searching for anything even remotely ghostly so they'd have something to post on Facebook. I leaned against the door of the charnel house. It was a stone building backed by a stone wall. The roof was covered with dirt and overgrown with shrubs and weeds. I heard Gina call, "I got to get you home, Julia. It's a school night." But, nervous as I was in the darkness, leaning against a house of the dead, I didn't want to leave. When I finally pushed myself away from the door, I heard a girl's voice: "I would give anything to leave this place, too."

I almost pissed myself as I ran to my sister. But then I started thinking.

You see, Mercy Brown is a girl with a hole in her chest. Mercy Brown is a girl with her heart ripped out. If you ever had your heart ripped out, if you know what that feels like, you can understand why she feels stuck. I do know so, of course, I went back.

I took the late bus home from school a few days after my first visit to the graveyard but got off at a stop close to the church. It was November in New England so the sun was already setting. I ducked into the shadows behind the stone wall bordering the cemetery. And as I approached the stone crypt, there she was, sitting on the roof in the tall weeds that grew there. She wore a white dress trimmed with wilted lace, all of it yellowed and stained brown and green with some kind of terrible death fluids. In the center of her chest was a hole. The material around the hole was torn and fluttered in the cold wind like trembling moth wings. The edges were black, from either old blood or mold. I don't know which.

Our eyes connected and I thought she was going to cry. She reached out one hand to help me up to the roof. "Everyone else looks through me," she said. "How is it you can see me?"

I sat down next to her and said, "I'm Julia and I know how it feels to have your heart ripped out." Before I knew it, the whole story poured out of me. Of course, I had to explain it in a way a girl from the 19th century would understand. I told her how just last summer I was in love with a high school sophomore who asked me for some naked pictures. I sent them to him and the next thing I knew my picture was everywhere. Mercy looked confused. I said something like, "It's easy to take pictures now. You don't have to sit a long time. It's like one second and then it's done. And then it's too late. You can't do anything to stop where it goes next." I told her he had done this before with other girls and they were too embarrassed to say anything. I didn't bother sharing how the police talked to all of us or how it hurt even worse when they said we all could face felony charges for distributing child porn. All this, thanks to an asshole who I thought loved and respected me.

I couldn't really explain, either, how people were trashing me on Facebook. The nastiest posts came from people who were supposed to be my best friends. It was so humiliating. There was only one junior high school in town, so I was stuck dealing with everything and hoping I could just ride it out. First term was ending and I'd already stayed home sick for twelve days.

But Mercy understood betrayal. She stroked my hair and whispered, "Poor Julia, poor girl. How could a respectable young man treat his sweetheart that way? I would have died of mortification." Not even Mom had said something like that to me. She just kept asking me why I had been so dumb and didn't I know that some boys out there just wanted to use me.

The ghost girl comforted me but I felt ashamed all over again, partly because I was looking at it from her perspective and partly because I was afraid she was a little disappointed in me, her new and only friend. She was nineteen but she seemed much younger. I was embarrassed to think of all the things I knew—even the nasty words I'd heard—that she would have been clueless about. Then she squeezed my hand. It felt like slipping on a soft but freezing cold glove. It was wonderful and exciting, like a toboggan racing down an icy slope. My heart overflowed with happiness. I knew she understood my broken heart and would never turn her back on me.

She sighed, "You loved and were betrayed. I was never in love. There was a young man who could have been a suitor but once the sickness came to me, he went away. Consumption frightens people so."

"You were betrayed after death," I said. "A father should never treat a daughter that way, dead or not."

"Yes, I don't understand why he thought I could ever harm my own family." She put her hand over the hole in her chest and moaned as if it hurt. It was my turn to squeeze her hand.

We sat in silence for a while, just feeling each other's pain. Before I knew it, the sky went crystal black and the stars came out. I lay back on the roof and watched as they shimmered in their slow overhead procession. Mercy placed a cool hand on my forehead, like I was a little girl, sick in bed, and strangely, I felt like I was home. I don't know how long I lay there, stargazing, almost in a trance. My phone vibrated in my pocket and I realized I had missed dinner. I started the lonely mile-and-a-half walk to my house. I don't know why but my legs trembled like they were going to collapse when I climbed off the crypt. But I felt stronger as I got closer to home.

I phoned Mom to tell her I was with Kayla, one of my used-to-be friends. She didn't like my new friends, the ones who also got caught sexting, so I lied to keep her from getting too angry. It was too late. I could tell she was pissed.

I got grounded for two weeks. No surprise there. After the sexting incident, my parents didn't trust me to do anything. And if I wanted them to trust me again, the only thing left for me to do was sneak out my window in the middle of the night, walk to the cemetery whenever I wanted to talk to Mercy and make sure I was back in my bed before dawn.

It was the best friendship I ever had. I could talk about my problems, my hopes, my dreams and she would listen. Then it would be her turn. Of course, Mercy's problems were always the same: "I'm so lonely. I want to be with my family but I can't move on. I sit here day after day with no one to talk to. People visit my grave to leave useless things and make fun of me." It was amazing how she could stretch this handful of complaints out for hours.

I remember a conversation we had shortly after Christmas. Mercy was sadder and lonelier than usual, and most of the night was spent obsessing about her feelings. Finally, I asked her why she didn't just walk away. Mercy replied, "You know why. My heart was ripped out of my chest. I'm not really me. No one can find heaven if they're not whole." Gazing into her misty eyes, I realized she had nailed exactly what I'd been feeling all these months. We both burst into tears and wrapped our arms around each other. It felt the way falling backwards into a big snow drift should feel: soft, kind of floaty, and dryly cold. Cold everywhere, seeping into my lungs and bones but without numbness or wet, achy pain. Without any pain of any kind.

After that, I was sneaking out of my room a couple nights every week throughout the winter. The following morning, I would get ready for school, even though those midnight visits left me so tired I could barely stand. As soon as my parents left for work and my sister was off to school, I collapsed. The school had my cell phone number instead of my parents' so they left messages with me or on the house phone, which I erased before Mom and Dad came home.

Of course, they found out when report cards were sent out. Mom thought I was depressed. My guidance counselor said I needed therapy. Dad said, "Don't they have some pills she can take?" Mom said, "She's not sleeping. Look at the dark circles under her eyes." Gina yelled at me, "They love you and you're scaring them." Even the only two living friends I had, the girls I called the sexting twins, said I looked like crap. We drank and smoked together but it didn't help. I yes-yessed everybody and went through the motions of whatever they suggested (except I wouldn't take any pills) and continued to visit Mercy whenever I could. How could I abandon someone who needed me so?

Then, one day last spring—I think it was April--I stopped by the cemetery after school. I didn't see Mercy so I visited her grave, making a mental list of all the foolish stuff people left at the tombstone. There were sealed envelopes—maybe fan letters or death day cards from last January, all dirty and tattered after months in the rain and snow. There were also little plastic alien figures. Someone seems to think she never died; she was just taken away in a space ship. There was a sketch of a sad looking boy sealed in a plastic bag. Maybe a self-portrait? On the other side, he wrote, "I need you, Mercy." It was all about what they wanted Mercy to do for them. None of these people understood what she was really about.

Organ music drifted from the church, sad and slow and kind of creepy, like someone was practicing for a funeral. I was so focused on the pile of graveside silliness, I didn't notice when the music stopped. I jumped and nearly screamed when a woman's voice said, "There really are vampires, you know."

When I turned, I saw the organist, a woman with glasses on her nose. It was kind of hard to place her age. She could have been forty. She could have been sixty. There were hollows under her eyes like she hadn't slept for a long time. "I've seen you here before, over by the wall and the crypt," she continued. "You've got a thing about Mercy Brown, haven't you?" I tried to tell her I didn't but she ignored me and said, "It's okay. I was fascinated by her when I was your age. But she's not your friend. She's not safe. Do you know what a psychic vampire is?"

I'd heard the phrase before but I shook my head. The woman continued, "It's that one person everyone knows who always sucks the energy out of a room. They're the needy ones, the ones who are all about emotion but no one's feelings matter but their own. They're always looking for support and they leave their family and friends drained and worn out. Does any of this sound familiar?"

I wanted to tell the woman that I wasn't drained, not one bit, even if I was losing sleep. But there was a haunted look on her face that said she knew something about Mercy that I did not. I remember I felt kind of jealous about that. But I could also hear Mercy's voice in my head, "She envies you. She's always wanted to be my friend but I never let her." I felt proud when I told the woman, "She's not like that at all. She's *my* friend. No one else listens to me the way she does."

"Does she?" The woman sounded sarcastic. "Listen, dear. Go home and search for my name: Margaret Chopin. You'll find a story from forty-two years ago. It's what happened to me when I started telling Mercy Brown my troubles. She listened at first, then somehow the conversation was always about her. I remember crying for her every night until I fell asleep. And then . . ." Margaret went silent, as if the story was too painful to continue. Finally, she just said, "Look it up. And while you're at it, read the story of Mercy Brown again. I mean, read it carefully. She lies. And please, don't come back here." As she turned and walked down the drive, she said, "Call me if you need to talk."

She gave me no contact information so I didn't know how I was supposed to call her. But I wasn't about to ask. She scared me with her shadowy face and creepy organ music. I didn't want to give her my name or a thank-you or even a screw-you.

I looked across the cemetery and spotted Mercy peeking around the corner of the stone vault. She did not look happy. She obviously did not like this Margaret Chopin but the way she stared at me made it clear she was angry with me. Her face was all purple and green, her eyes glassy black. I felt scared. Really scared. I turned my back on her and ran to the road as fast as I could.

After dinner, I researched Margaret Chopin. There were several stories but the one at the top of the list was about a fifteen-year-old girl who disappeared one January night—January 17th, to be exact, Mercy Brown's death day. She was missing for two days before one of the church maintenance men opened the vault to get a snow shovel and found her barely alive, curled up in the dirt, wearing nothing but a sweater over her clothes. The story she told was that she wasn't trying to kill herself. She drank a few beers and fell asleep. But she couldn't tell anyone how she ended up inside the locked crypt.

Obviously, Margaret meant the story to be a warning. But all I could think was: She got to see the inside of the crypt.

That night, I saw Mercy in a dream. The door to the vault was open and she sat inside, her head buried in her green and white arms as she wept. Slimy, olive colored tears plopped and puddled like jelly in the dust. I stood outside, calling her name over and over but she ignored me. I wanted to comfort her but every time I tried to go through the door, something pushed me back. "Look at me, Mercy. Look at me," I begged but she just kept on sobbing. In desperation, I threw my body against the entrance only to be hurled back into the dirt. I stared up at a foggy, yellow sky and right into the face of Margaret Chopin.

Her face was all warped and distorted with rage. She grabbed my wrist and dragged me to my feet. "I told you to read," she screamed. "You didn't read!"

"I did! I did!" I cried.

She just kept screaming at me, "You didn't read! You didn't read!" And Mercy wailed in the background. But there was still no way I could get inside the vault.

My alarm went off and I dragged myself out of bed and off to school. I couldn't concentrate on anything. I didn't want to be there. I wanted to sit inside the charnel house with my friend. Even worse, I was being haunted, right there in the junior high school. The hall monitor looked like Margaret. The lunch lady—the skinny one with hair the color of brass—looked like Margaret. Then, somewhere between third lunch and last period, I felt dizzy and hugged the wall on my way to the nurse's office. Waiting inside was Mercy, in her dirty white dress with the blackened hole. Her face was beautiful again, all frosty blue and white. She blew a kiss to me. When her breath reached my face, it was so cold it hurt. I realized then I had a raging fever. It felt like my sweat was freezing into droplets of ice. Mercy sighed lovingly, "How wonderful. Now you're sick, too." Everything went black and I woke up in an ambulance taking me to the hospital.

The doctor said I had been incubating a case of mono. They said I was raving deliriously before I collapsed outside the nurse's office, talking to people who weren't there.

"Who's Mercy?" Gina asked when my family gathered around my hospital bed. "You been talking to the vampire girl?"

"I thought she was talking to someone named Margaret," said Mom.

"They're my friends," I lied. "They're new at school." I didn't want to say anymore so I pretended to fall asleep.

A day later, I went home. It turns out getting sick was one of the best things to happen to me. I had a tutor visit me three times each week. Schoolwork was easy for me, so I convinced my parents and teachers to let me finish the school year convalescing at home. My grades improved enough for me to pass eighth grade with respectable Cs. Mom and Dad were happy.

Once or twice a week, Amanda and Mariel, the sexting twins, skipped school to hang out at my house. Sometimes they brought that legal synthetic pot anyone could buy at this gas station near the school. "It's totally harmless," they said but it made me see Mercy's dark, angry face in my head, those pond scum tears sliding down her green face.

Sleeping and dreaming, sleeping and dreaming, sleeping and dreaming. Except for my school work, that's all I did. My dreams were filled with voices and images from the cemetery but I couldn't make out what the spirits were saying. There were new graves and empty graves. Maybe one of them was mine. Sometimes, Margaret bitched at me while Mercy sat inside the open crypt, like a dead princess in her throne room. Finally, after weeks of trying and failing to enter the stone house, I found myself inside. I was seated next to my dear friend, feeling that lovely chill seep into my bones until I came apart, piece by piece, turning into white diamond chips that floated all around Mercy, settling on her shoulders like a snow queen's mantle. I was emptied of all other needs but one: to shroud and to protect her. When I woke, I thought I'd never been happier in my entire life.

The dream was an invitation. I knew it in my heart. I didn't feel up to a long walk but I returned to the cemetery that morning as soon as the house was empty. Mercy was nowhere to be seen. So devastating. Walking all the way home without speaking to her? The thought was unbearable.

Other people came and went, leaving flowers for loved ones. I pretended I was doing the same, standing before random graves with my head bowed. I didn't bother reading the information on the markers until I stopped at the fifth headstone in one of the back rows. What I saw made my knees shake. My legs gave out and I collapsed on the grave of Margaret Chopin.

She had died fourteen years ago, in the same month and year I was born.

I wanted Mercy as I never had before. I needed her to stretch out her hand and raise me up from Margaret's grave; needed her to stroke cold fingers across my forehead, the same fingers that brought that icy no-feeling to my body, my heart and my soul. But she left me there, lost, completely abandoned and alone. I sat until I felt strong enough to go home. By the time I walked through the door, I was exhausted. I tried doing some research but couldn't concentrate. I was too jumpy and anxious to sleep so I took a warm bath. No lights, some scented candles and lavender bath oil. As I toweled off, I caught an image in the bathroom mirror. It was the face of Margaret Chopin. I shrieked but as the fog on the mirror cleared, I saw that the darkly shadowed eyes, sharp cheekbones and unhealthy yellow skin was mine.

Somehow, I ended up hiding under the blankets on my bed. I don't know how I fell asleep after seeing something like that but I did. I was completely out of it. Gina woke me for dinner hours later. After supper, I did my internet search and found those stories about Margaret I hadn't bothered to read. The first was her obituary. It said she passed "suddenly at home." Everyone knows that means she either OD'd or committed suicide. The story underneath that was a profile of her son, who had grown up to become a psychologist. He spoke at the high school a few years back about suicide prevention among teens. He shared his feelings about his mother's death.

Gina appeared over my shoulder. "Oh, is Doctor Chopin speaking at your school?"

She could see I was confused by the question, so she continued, "He spoke at an assembly when I was a freshman. We all talked about it at dinner that night. Remember?"

I couldn't recall ever hearing anything about Dr. Chopin or his mother before. But I didn't want to give away what was happening to me, so I lied, "He might be speaking to my friend's youth group. Don't know if I want to go." Then I pretended to be busy with a history report.

It bothered me that I forgot learning about Margaret long before I met her but, in the end, decided it didn't matter. What was important was why Margaret wanted to keep me away from Mercy. Clearly, the woman had a lot of problems but blamed all her bad feelings on a poor, bedraggled ghost. I wasn't like that. If I was lonely, if Mercy no longer wanted to talk to me, I could only blame myself. Still, I didn't need that crazy old bitch haunting me, so I reviewed the history of the Brown family again. There was lots of stuff, from historical societies to personal blogs. The stories contradicted each other. Some claimed her father helped cut out her heart. Some said he wasn't at the cemetery at all. Some even said she was a real vampire.

Margaret called Mercy a liar. But if Mercy was dead, would she even know who had mutilated her? If her father gave permission, that was still a betrayal. Margaret was the one who couldn't see the truth. She was no different from the people who left tokens on the grave: Mercy Brown was what this depressed, suicidal person needed her to be.

Stupid girl. Stupid, crazy girl, all passive and freezing to death, waiting for someone else to make things happen instead of taking charge of her situation. I wouldn't make that mistake.

I didn't need Mercy to be anything but my best and truest friend. I understood what she really wanted. She had to have me all to herself, supporting her, listening to her. No talking to other dead people. I had to admit I kind of liked that. I felt loved. I felt special. No, I used to feel loved and special. Now I had to think of a way to make up for being disloyal.

First, I researched how to keep ghosts in their graves. That would keep whiny Margaret out of my dreams and show Mercy I was unfriending the old lady. Then I turned my summer into a scavenger hunt for the things I needed. I made trips to the beach with the sexting twins and searched old barns throughout the area.

I had all my supplies by mid-July and made a midnight visit to the cemetery to decorate Margaret's grave. First, I made sure she wasn't out roaming around. I stood in the middle of the cemetery and announced, "I think I'll just go over and visit Mercy for a while." When Margaret didn't respond, I felt sure she had to be resting in her coffin that night. I placed iron horseshoes at the four corners or her grave. I followed this with a solid line of shells outlining the plot and extending behind her marker. When I finished, I crept along the stone wall to the charnel house and hoped against hope that Mercy would show. She didn't. I placed a rose quartz heart on her grave. It was cold as stone but it was better than no heart at all.

Then, on a truly unbearable summer night, I sat alone on our deck, sweating and watching the stars come out. My mind drifted. I went into that star-trance again. Suddenly, all my sweat evaporated and my warm breath formed clouds in the wintry cold air. My heart danced with joy. There was no mistaking the sign. Mercy hovered nearby and she was letting me know I was forgiven.

Later that night, I waited for everyone to go to sleep and hurried to the cemetery. Mercy was floating around the back rows. When I caught up to her, she was laughing about what I had done to Margaret's grave. "It serves that busybody right," she said.

"I'm sorry. I'm so sorry. She tried to make me think I couldn't trust you," I cried. The next think I knew, we had thrown our arms around each other, sobbing. I felt myself sinking into that wonderful, gigantic, painless glacier.

We sat with our backs resting against a neighboring tombstone. The events of the past weeks, the sickness, the dreams, the fear, poured out of me. Mercy planted a cold kiss on my forehead, then sobbed out her story, although I could have recited the whole, weary rant, word for word: "My heart was ripped out of my chest, I can't leave this place until my heart is restored but it can never be restored, I'm so lonely, so lonely, so lonely." I tried to comfort her, but she just kept repeating it, like a chant. I didn't know how to stop her.

Then I did something desperate, something I'd never done before. I placed my hand right inside the hole in her chest. I don't know why but I thought it might comfort her--like putting an arm around her. An ice dagger stabbed me right in the heart and I felt everything Mercy felt—the sorrow, the betrayal, and the devastating loneliness. I had no doubt which Mercy Brown story was the truth. She had not lied about her father's betrayal or about her own innocence. At that very moment, I knew she would never, ever lie to me.

And I threw out an idea. "I could come here more often if I could hide out with you in the vault. No one would know I was there. I could spend hours and hours with you without anyone noticing," I told her.

She pulled my hand from her heart and turned away. "The vault is locked and I don't have a key," she replied.

I wanted to cry. But I didn't dare ask her about Margaret or question anything Mercy said. She would get angry again.

"There's nothing to see in there. I've walked every inch of this graveyard for over a hundred years. It's just dirt, stones and loneliness," she continued. "If it's so important for you to see the charnel house, you'll have to think of some way to stay here always." She just stared at me, waiting for my reaction. But I didn't know what to say.

I went home. I could not get this conversation out of my head. It occurred to me that Mercy had not magically pulled Margaret into the crypt. Maybe she sat and waited outside, probably hidden in the tall weeds on the roof and when she reached those last moments just before death, she did this out-of-body thing to go inside. The maintenance guy looking for a shovel found her just before she took her final breath.

That was my inspiration for a wonderful surprise. I knew I would have to wait for a night when movement between the real world and spirit world was easy, so I continued to visit my friend throughout the summer and fall but kept my plans to myself.

That brings me to this moment. I wrote most of this memoir throughout Halloween day. Now I am hiding behind the stone wall, waiting for all the idiots who bring meaningless crap to Mercy Brown's grave to finish wandering around and calling out to the spirits to show themselves.

☠☠☠

Hours have passed. There's not a single living soul left in the cemetery but me. I went to the grave to look over the new gifts. My pink crystal heart was gone. I'll have to remember to hunt down the defiler as soon as I get the chance. Someone modeled a Slender Man out of clay and leaned it against the tombstone. Each hand grips the arm of a clay boy and a clay girl, leading them to their mysterious doom. What a stupid gift. Everyone knows Slender Man isn't real, except for some middle school kids who tried to make a human sacrifice to him. And what's his connection to the Exeter vampire anyway?

"What, no Bloody Mary? No Ouija board?" I called out.

Midnight has come and gone. It is now officially the Day of the Dead.

I am sitting on the ground, my back against the wooden crypt door, writing the end to my story. I hope when my family reads this, they will know that I do love them. Mom, Dad, Gina: You were good to me. You didn't do anything to make me unhappy. I will miss you but I found someone who understands me like no one else does. I hope you appreciate and understand the devotion I have for my dearest friend, Mercy Brown.

Before me stand two spirits: Margaret and Mercy. Someone must have broken the boundary of shells around the woman's grave. She's escaped to warn me not to do what I have planned. But her voice is weak. She might as well be talking from a mile away. Mercy is saying nothing at all. She is still as an ice sculpture and twice as beautiful, her stained and faded dress fluttering in the cold autumn wind. She smiles at me and nods as I take the big kitchen knife out of my backpack. And now she is twirling and dancing, laughing and clapping her hands. She is so delighted with my surprise.

I will only be able to start the process. I will plunge the knife close to my heart but not through it. It must not be damaged. The blood on these pages will tell all of you that I followed through on my loving pledge. Mercy will finish the job. She has promised to take me into the charnel house once I am out of my body. Then she will remove my heart from my chest and divide it in two. We will be joined forever by the heart shared between our two bodies. Hand in hand, we will walk together into our beautiful hereafter.

THE RED LADY

by Joni Chng

You have probably seen her somewhere. Perhaps you walked by her on a crowded street or saw her sitting alone in a dimly lit corner of a café you frequent. You could have seen her walking out of a theatre after a show or standing at a newsstand across the street. Maybe it is just your imagination, but you could have sworn you caught a glimpse of her from a train window once and may be convinced you are being stalked.

It is impossible to not to take notice of her. She wears a form-fitting, bright red dress, with a hem that stops above her knees, and matching heels, with a black trench coat over the outfit. The top-half of her face is always concealed under the brim of a black fedora hat that matches her coat, leaving only her blood red lips visible and wavy crimson hair cascading down her shoulders. If she is in close enough proximity, her perfectly manicured, red fingernails may have also caught your eye.

She is a stunning vision in red and black, but there is something uncanny about her that would turn heads. She seems out of place, like she belongs to a different era of time or a different world. For those who have heard about her, there is no shortage of tales to explain her origins. Some say she is a time traveler, lost in the wrong decade and searching for a return portal. Others even theorize she could be a top-secret government agent without a civilian identity. Bring up the subject around Chinatown or some ethnic communities, and you may hear talk that murder victims dressed in red will return from the dead to exact vengeance.

Who is this lady in red? you wonder. Why does she keep showing up around you? More importantly, what does she want with you? The earliest accounts of her sightings started circulating around the 1960s, but how she came to be harks back to a simpler time.

The year was 1948. In a dingy little diner, in one of the shadiest parts of a city that supposedly never sleeps, a lone waitress was working the graveyard shift. No one knew her name nor cared, and what little was known about her came from vague and inconsistent hearsay. Word had it that she was a small-town girl with big dreams of headlining at the most prestigious theatre in the nation. She came to the big city in pursuit of stardom, but life was tougher than the aspiring actress imagined. So to make ends meet in between auditions and acting gigs, she took up a waitressing job.

This diner she worked at was one of the few establishments that opened late into the wee hours. It was close to 3 a.m. on a Monday, and there was not a single customer in sight, so our anonymous waitress decided to call it a night. She hung up the apron that protected her red dress—she had come to work after a rehearsal, —then donned her black trench coat and fedora – two article of clothing she was never seen without during these chilly months. She stepped out into the windy autumn night and took to the quiet alley off the main road, which was a shortcut towards her apartment. She walked at a brisk pace, not because she was afraid of potential dangers that could be lurking in the shadows, but because her mind was running through the script of her next role. In two weeks, she would be starring in the leading role of a tragedy. This could be the breakthrough role she had been holding out, for that would make a year of hard work and perseverance worthwhile.

As she made it back onto the main road, the budding actress felt the chill in the air biting into her skin. Hands securely tucked in the pockets of her trench coat, she quickened her pace. By the time she was walking past a park close to where she lived, a distant shuffling could be heard, along with the clicking of her favorite red heels. She stopped in her tracks to ensure it was not a product of her imagination. Besides the wind howling and tree branches rustling, there was complete silence. She resumed walking, and there it was again. This time it had become distinct footsteps. She was being followed!

Without looking over her shoulder, she quickened her pace. The footsteps had stopped by the time her apartment building was in sight. She breathed a sigh of relief and got into the elevator, pressing the button to the eighth floor, where her unit was. Entering her apartment, she bolted the door and turned on the lights. Before she had the chance to hang up her hat and coat, she was startled by the presence of a tall and imposing man in her living area but was overcome by relief when she saw who he was.

He was a fellow actor. The one time they played a couple on stage a few months ago, their chemistry was so intense that a romance blossomed after the last curtain call. However, the spark between them had fizzled out a bit since he had been down on his luck. She remained his source of moral and financial support, and was just as disappointed when he failed to land the role for the male lead in the upcoming play she would be in. They could have recreated the magic of their first collaboration.

Her relief at seeing him was short-lived when she could smell alcohol in his breath and saw rage in his eyes. Since she was cast as a leading lady, he had made it clear he was not keen on her working alongside the actor portraying her love interest. She had even witnessed one of his fits of jealousy, when he saw her in the arms of her on-stage lover during a rehearsal. True to her suspicion, he had come to serve her with an ultimatum—give up the role or give up on them. In no way would the rising star give up on an opportunity of a lifetime, so she opened the door and politely asked him to leave.

Instead of walking out, her angry suitor slammed the door shut and bolted the both of them inside the apartment. He intended to make her pay for her roving eye. She tried to reason with him, but the alcohol had already muddled his rational senses. He grabbed her by the collar of her coat and swung a heavy hand at her. She fell to the floor, but before she could get to her feet, he pulled her up by the neck and continued the vicious assault. He was determined to leave her face battered and unfit for the stage. Mustering all the strength and willpower that was left in her, the actress managed to push her attacker away and hurled herself at the glass window, shattering it and falling to her death.

The tragic end of a starlet caused quite the media frenzy, but due to lack of evidence in the case, her assailant was never brought to justice. Fourteen days later, the play premiered with a reserve actress replacing the deceased leading lady, but another incident was stealing the spotlight. A struggling actor was found dead in the bathroom of his apartment in what appeared to be a freak accident. He had the faucet of the bathtub lodged in one of his eye sockets. From personal journals and letters, police were able to identify him as the man who had been romantically linked to the recently killed actress. He seemed to speak a lot about her in his writings, dated after her death, with long passages describing that she had returned to him.

The world gradually forgets a tragedy, but will the dead who have been done wrong ever rests? Stories of a female spectral figure sighting in the darkest nooks and crannies of the city has become a staple urban legend.

Some claim that she appears to warn someone of impending hurt and betrayal by a loved one. Other stories say that those who are jinxed enough to see her face underneath the fedora should take it as a sign that death may come upon them soon, and it would be wise to watch their step or chance a deadly mishap.

As time passes by, even ghost stories become nothing more than entertaining fables. Alas, neither the passage of time nor societal progress and technological advancement changes the lowly depths people are willing to go in pursuit of their ego gratification. The story of an average pencil-pusher in a tech firm is one such example. This corporate slave was a typical millennial who, by society's standards, had it all. He graduated from a reputable tertiary educational institute and worked at a well-paying job that afforded him a nice place to live, a functional car, and the latest gadgets and gizmos which had become the daily necessities of his generation. Yet, he it did not stop him from feeling victimized by unrequited love for a woman.

The object of his affections was a bright and beautiful colleague of the same age and equal social standing but of a higher professional rank. He had his eye on her even before her promotion to the managerial team, which placed her as his superior. It continued to both excite and frustrate him to win her over. Every time he made an attempt to get her attention, she never gave him the time of day, just like many of the women in his past. *Never mind,* he thought to himself; with patience and perseverance, she would one day realize that no one could love her the way he could.

To his disappointment, she chose to shower her affections on another man. Devastated that his object of desire would not reciprocate his devotion, the young executive spent many of his lonely evenings in the company of alcohol at a bar in a remote part of town. How could she be so blind to his love for her? What does he lack that the other fella had? *Women…they need to be put in their place!* Each night he tried to drink away the despair of rejection, the more those disdainful thoughts grew. His heartbreak and disappointment slowly morphed into anger and resentment towards the woman he once loved. *No…* He could not just let all the time and emotions he spent on her to go to waste! He would make her pay for it by taking her away from the other man and then returning her to him—used and a little damaged. That would teach her to be grateful for all he had done to please her.

One night, when this victim of unrequited love was at his favorite bar, he was distracted by the sight of a lone woman. She was sitting at the table in the far corner of the bar, but there was neither beverage nor food on the table. Had the wait staff not noticed her presence? The place wasn't that crowded tonight; it was a weekday.

From where he was sitting, he could see she was wearing a red dress that exposed her neck underneath the black trench coat. His eyes travelled down her long, shapely legs, crossed under the table, and ended at her pointy red heels. Her hands rested on the table, fingers interlocked. His eyes couldn't help moving up to her pristine crimson fingernails that matched the color of her expressionless lips. In the dimmed lighting, he could tell she was looking straight at him, although the brim of her fedora shielded her eyes. For a brief moment, he toyed with the idea of approaching her and struck up a conversation to see if he could get her number or perhaps get her home. He turned away to order another shot, and when he looked in the same direction, she was gone. *So much for the fantasy!* He went back to being immersed in his own thoughts of vengeance upon the one who had rejected him.

As days and weeks went by, he continued to observe his former object of desire at work. There was a spark in her eyes ever since word went around that she had her heart stolen by one lucky fellow. The more he watched her, the harder it became for him to contain his hatred for the woman who had deprived him of the love he so deserved.

His window of opportunity was presented one Friday evening when she accepted his invitation to go for a drink at his favorite bar because her boyfriend had an important work engagement. They talked about the latest news headlines and exchanged some office gossip. They were both deep in conversation when he noticed a familiar presence in his peripheral vision. There she was again, at the same table and looking straight at him with her eyes hidden under the hat. She may have tugged at his curiosity, but his attention tonight was on his objective.

After they had finished their drinks, he offered to treat his co-worker to another round, since the night was still young and it was a Friday. When she was distracted by a text message from her boyfriend, he slipped a ground-up pill into the cocktail. He knew everything was going his way when, 20 minutes later, she began to feel drowsy, and he led her to his car on the pretense of sending her home. She was barely conscious by the time she was in the backseat of her car. When he got into the driver's seat and started the ignition, he looked up and saw the red-clad woman in black trench coat and hat again. This time she was standing in the shadows, as if observing his every move. Her presence was starting to stir a sense of unease in him. He turned his attention to the road and drove off but took a quick glance at the rearview mirror. The mysterious woman was gone.

The road towards his apartment building was dark and winding. With his acquired target lying unconscious in the back seat, he was going a little above the area's speed limit. The sound of thunder crashing and lightning flashing across the horizon intensified his focus on the road. He needed to make it home before the storm; otherwise the rain would only slow him down. But it was too late when raindrops started to hit the windshield and became a downpour in a matter of seconds.

He was approaching a cross junction when he saw her again, the specter in black and red, standing in the middle of the road under a sole street light. He hit the brake pedal, but it was too late; he was going to run her over. He squeezed his eyes shut and braced himself. Instead of hearing the collision sound of metal against flesh, the sudden stop caused him to jerk forward and bump his forehead against the steering wheel. He steadied himself and slowly looked up to see what damage he had done. There was nothing.

He got out of the car under the pouring rain to have a look, expecting to find a pool of blood and a mangled body in front of his car. He found nothing, nor were there any traces of a person ever having been in front of the vehicle. *What's wrong with me?* He only had two drinks and was barely even tipsy. It couldn't possibly be the booze, but he was certainly seeing things.

He got back inside the car and stepped on the accelerator, this time going faster than before. Drenched in cold sweat mixed with rainwater, he looked over his shoulder to see his unconscious victim sprawled across the backseat. She was almost his! That thought itself was enough to send a rush of excitement coursing through his veins. He just had to get her home, and then he could have his way with her. She would not be the same woman again after tonight!

When he turned his attention back to the road ahead, he caught a sight that sent a chill down his spine. In the rearview mirror, the unmistakable silhouette of a person in a fedora sat in the backseat. Startled, he spun around to see nothing more than his drugged colleague. When he returned his focus to the road, the headlights were shinning on a familiar figure in black trench coat and red heels. Reacting on reflex, he swerved to avoid running straight into her, but the speed he had been driving and the heavy downpour worked against him.

The vehicle skidded out of control and slammed into a tree, with the driver's side taking the direct hit. The concussion snapped the driver's neck and shattered his ribcage, causing the broken bones to collapse in and crush his heart. His unwilling passenger in the backseat, who was still knocked out, remained unscathed. On his dying breath, he looked up to find the beautiful grim reaper standing before him. The edges of her lips curled into a smile as she looked up from underneath the brim of her fedora and met him in the eyes. Her face was the last thing he saw before a cold darkness took over.

GIRLS FROM JUMBO
by John Biggs

Animal tracks mark the freshly fallen snow around the cabin. Raccoon and possum prints by the trashcan, deer tracks everywhere else—as if a small herd had come around to make sure the hunters were gone.

Michael stands among the trees; he looks for signs of human life. No lights behind the cabin windows, no smoke, no thumps or bumps or human voices. He turns to see what Kenny has to say before he remembers. His only friend is in McAlester. One of those broken-home-visitation things Michael's dad is always going on about.

Pills make it easy to forget the loneliness. Michael swallowed two, on his walk to the cabin, or was it three? It's easy to lose count when no one is around to share. Kenny won't be back till summertime.

Dad told him, "Gone and good riddance," earlier this morning.

"Bad company ruins good morals," Dad said. "Right out of *First Corinthians 15:33*." He'd have said more but he had a meeting with the mayor.

"May his days be few; may another take his office. *Psalms 109:8*." That's how Michael's father summed up politics in Jumbo, Oklahoma.

"I hate you, Dad." Michael looks around to make sure no one is close enough to hear. Mom's pills make it hard to think quietly, but they help pass the time since Dad pulled him out of Moyers High.

Home school means reading Bible verses and looking after mom and roaming the woods behind the old Jumbo Cemetery after the bow hunters have gone home.

The snow around the cabin looks like sugar. Michael samples it—a little sweet, like the slush in Seven-Up cans that got shoved against the back wall of the fridge. Snow and Mom's pills turn the forest bright and fresh. Bird songs are full of hidden messages like when Dad speaks in tongues. Messages channeled from ghosts of men who died so long ago the only thing left of their language is Pentecostal gibberish.

The bird songs break through Michael's threshold of understanding. *The hunters are gone. Check it out.*

Michael funnels his hands around his mouth so his words will penetrate the cedar log walls. "Hello in the cabin." His voice bounces back to him. The words mix in the winter air and fall into a completely different message. *It's yours again.* Plain as day. It could be Mom's pills talking, or God, or one of the old Choctaw spirits from when this part of Oklahoma was Indian Territory. It doesn't matter.

Michael takes a zig-zag path to the front door—the way a cat crosses an open space—so nobody watching will know his destination until the very last minute. He turns around so he can see his footprints mixed with deer tracks in the snow. They look like primitive writing scrawled on the ground, too old and mixed up to understand. He stares at the footprints in the snow trying to sort things out. He presses his back against the door. When it pops open his decision is made.

He says, "I hate you Dad," again for no particular reason. He steps inside the cabin.

Colder than Michael expects. Darker too, but his eyes adjust in seconds. The windows are filmed over with frozen dust, so the sunlight fills the interior with polka dot shadows.

Michael reaches into his pocket and selects his third—or is it his fourth—pill of the morning. He places it on the tip of his tongue, rolls it backwards until it slides down his esophagus like a two-year-old on a sliding board.

"Slippery slide." Michael's voice sounds foreign and dangerous like the godless communists Dad told him had infiltrated the public schools and Catholic churches and even the Jumbo city government. Michael has to get his filters working again. Keep his thoughts from breaking through the silence barrier.

"Loose lips sink ships," he says through lips loose enough to destroy the U.S. Navy. It's too soon to feel the effects of the last pill, but the cabin seems to tip on its axis so the sunlight can get a better angle.

Yellow white light filled with dust motes and shadows of dust motes make it hard to see, but in the corner of the cabin, laid out on an old threadbare carpet fragment is a man's long coat covering something shaped like a human body.

It might be paranoia; that happens sometimes when Michael passes the three-pill frontier.

"Anybody here?"

He's seen coats like this one. Long and gray with imitation mother of pearl buttons. The kind of coat men wear to the Jack Fork Holiness Church where Michael's dad tells his congregation about heaven and hell. Every adult man in Jumbo has a coat like that—except bow hunters visiting from Tulsa.

No reason to suppose the collar of the coat will be significant, but Michael begins there. He folds the coat back carefully, as if a nest of rattlesnakes is sleeping underneath. He stops folding when he uncovers Janie Impson's face.

"Dead." The word slips out before Michael thinks about asking Janie, "Are you okay?" because she's way too still to be okay. Still pretty. Still very pretty. Pretty enough to be the homecoming queen in Moyers High where Michael went to school before it got overrun by communists.

"Janie..." nothing left to say. He brushes a stray lock of jet black hair away from her forehead; he presses it against her scalp.

Janie cut her hair short earlier this winter after her mother passed away. Put it into the coffin the way some Choctaw girls do. Michael's dad said it's a heathen practice.

"Margaret Impson's in hell with her daughter's hair," Dad said. "All heathens go there in the end."

A circle of dusty sunlight gathers over Janie's face. A pair of polka dot shadows settle on her eyelids and make it look like they are open.

Maybe Janie is real and dead or maybe she's an image from a fantasy in the back of Michael's mind. Something that floats to the surface like words he never meant to say out loud.

Her face is cold to the touch—too solid for a fantasy. His hand moves away from Janie's hair, works its way under the long coat as if an invisible chord is pulling it. The hand stops when it reaches Janie's breast.

"So this is what it's like." Does it count as second base if the girl is dead? Is Janie really dead? He leans an ear over her lips, listens for breathing sounds and hears them. Hers or his?

Then words: "Kiss me, Michael." Did she say that? Did he?

So close. A little kiss won't matter. Janie Impson is way too dead to mind. Michael lowers his lips over hers so they intersect at right angles, like a plus sign, like a cross. Cold and solid, they taste of lipstick mixed with buttermilk.

Michael pulls away as soon he thinks about what it means to kiss a dead girl. He's out of the cabin spinning excuses so fast it takes him two tries to close the door. He runs straight across the snow, stops when he reaches the trees, turns to make certain Janie isn't following.

The new string of footprints across the clearing looks like an exclamation point at the end of a message from God. *Get out of here and don't come back.*

Good advice, even if came from Michael's imagination.

❀❀❀

"You read those verses from the *Apokalypsis*?" That's what Dad calls the *Book of Revelation*, because it was written in Greek before King James got ahold of it. Dad knows a few Greek words, like Alpha and Omega and baklava. He peppers conversations with them to prove he's an educated man.

"Tell me what you learned." Dad sits at the head of the kitchen table getting ready to say grace over lunch but first he wants to know if there's any special spin he should put on the prayer for the sake of his son's education.

Michael says, "Whore of Babylon!" before his dad can ask any more specific questions.

Mom interrupts with, "Don't like such talk at the table," so Michael is off the hook. She sets three places with paper bowls and plastic spoons and Bounty paper towels instead of napkins.

"We're having Ramen noodles with soda crackers and cans of diet Coke," she says. "M&M's for dessert." She'd started with salami sandwiches but, "my pills made things too complicated for meat." Before she's finished setting out the drinks, Mom's mood turns south. She flops into her chair at opposite from Michael's dad and sobs.

"Ain't right," she says. "That sweet little Choctaw girl's gone missing."

Michael says, "Janie," out loud before he can stop himself. He's almost forgotten about the dead girl in the cabin. The way she looked under the grey long coat. Pretty as her picture in the Moyers High School Annual. Michael feels tears leaking from the corners of his eyes, because Janie Impson isn't a picture in his yearbook anymore, she's a dead girl in a deer hunter's cabin and he hasn't said anything about her to Mom or Dad or anyone.

"What's that on your face?" Dad draws a vertical line across his lips to show the location of the blemish.

Michael wipes his mouth with his paper towel napkin. It comes away with a red streak on it. Red as lipstick on a dead girl's lips.

"Must have cut myself," he says. Fast thinking for a boy on stolen pharmaceuticals who's just gotten to second base with a dead girl. What would Dad think about that? What would everybody think? Even Mom. Even Kenny.

Mom's pills shift her into a more cheerful gear. "Girls from Jumbo don't have their faces put on milk cartons." Giggles bubble up behind her words. "'Cause girls from Jumbo always come back." She breaks into a madhouse laugh that reminds Michael of a horror movie he saw last

90

Halloween.

Dad clears his throat. He has plenty of phlegm when he wants the room quiet.

He puts his hands together like the sculpture in front of Oral Roberts University and tries to figure out what kind of prayer to say over Ramen noodles and diet Coke.

"Put something in for the little Choctaw girl," Mom tells him. "Poor little Janie Impson."

Janie's kiss burns Michael's lips. They feel swollen. He wipes them with the paper towel again, but nothing comes away—not lipstick, not shame.

Dad is usually good with prayers but Janie Impson's name catches in his throat. He lapses into the Lord's Prayer and then something about casting the first stone and then goes on to the careless ways that get young people into trouble.

"The way Janie Impson probably got herself in trouble." Dad prays with his eyes closed. Michael keeps his open so he can keep watch for quick changes in emotion that sometimes fall on Dad along with the Holy Spirit.

Dad tells God how Janie Impson wore skirts that were too short and pants that were too tight, and how she brushed up against men sometimes even when there was plenty of room, and maybe one of them just wanted to teach her a lesson.

"God bless her anyway, I guess." Dad says a few words about Ramen noodles before his prayer finds its way to Jesus. He recites the first line of *The Sinner's Prayer*, and starts in quoting *Psalms*. By the time he's done Michael and his mother have fallen asleep. Mom's hands claw at the tablecloth the way a dog dreams of chasing rabbits. Michael rests his head on the table between his Ramen noodles and his diet Coke, dreams of Janie Impson.

"Your kiss brought me back," she tells him. "Like in fairy tales only not all at once." Janie Impson says Michael's mom was right about girls from Jumbo. "One way or another we come back."

※ ※ ※

The snow has melted in the clearing around the cabin. There are deer tracks in the mud and Michael's footprints and some footprints that don't look like Michael's. They don't look like Janie Impson's either.

He opens the cabin door slowly, because the footprints are too mixed up to tell whether somebody is still inside. He tries to call out, but the only word he can bring to the surface is, "Janie!"

Her face is covered by the coat again. A rectangle of sunlight frames her body. The shadow of the window grill forms a cross over her chest. A Bible rests at the shadow cross's center. Gold letters on the Bible's cover say,

91

Jack Fork Holiness Church.

Dad's church.

Time for another pill. Michael had been pretty high when he was here before. High enough to kiss a dead girl. High enough to touch her breast. Had any of that really happened? He pulls the coat away from her face (again?) and there she is, warmer now, but still room temperature. Her lipstick is smeared, so Michael licks his fingers and uses them to clean her face.

Softer than before. Almost like a real live girl. He kneels beside her. Maybe he'll think of something to say, an apology for kissing her, an apology for touching her breast.

"Sorry, Janie."

He folds the coat down further, so he can see how she is dressed. A white blouse, with buttons askew, as if they'd been fastened by someone in a hurry. Someone who didn't want to be around a naked dead girl any longer. Someone who'd come back and left a Bible on her chest to make up for what happened earlier. One more person who needed to apologize.

Michael pops another pill. He feels his hands move over Janie's buttons, just to re-fasten them. Just to get them right, because a pretty girl like Janie shouldn't have to sleep forever in a mis-buttoned blouse.

"A very pretty girl." When he's unfastened all the buttons there is really no point in missing the opportunity. Is there? All the harm that can be done has already happened. So he pops another pill, chews it so the bitter taste will take the edge off what is happening. As if it isn't Michael who's about to undress a dead girl without so much as a please or thank you. As if it was someone else doing this; someone not as good as Michael. Someone who stole his mother's pills and doesn't always believe in God.

"Best not to think that way. Right Janie?"

He places the Bible between her legs, which are still covered by the coat for the time being. That's when he notices the music.

It's hard for Michael to get his thoughts in a straight line but when he does he understands the music has been there all along.

"He Touched Me" by the Blackwood Brothers. Michael recognizes it from the gospel music on dad's car radio. FM 90.9 out of Idabel. He listens while he inspects Janie's breasts. No bra, but there are bite marks and bruises, not as pretty as he imagined. The marks tell a story, like the footprints in front of the hunter's cabin, like the birdsongs and his father's language of tongues. The story of how Janie got inside this cabin.

Michael doesn't want to think about that story. He doesn't want to touch Janie's breasts anymore. Doesn't want to look at them, so he looks around the cabin's interior until he finds the radio.

Station identification follows the song—90.9 all right. Dad's favorite channel. The announcer asks listeners to, "Pray for little Janie Impson, the missing girl from Jumbo. She's been gone two days now and her daddy wants her back real bad."

Michael turns the radio off, goes back to checking the damage done to Janie Impson. He pulls the coat completely off; sends the Bible bouncing across the cabin floor. It lands spine down on the floor, just like Janie Impson. Its pages fall open to *Galatians 5:19*. "Now the works of flesh are evident."

Michael almost hears his father's voice reciting the verse. He pops another pill. Time to see what other damage had been done to Janie Impson.

❧❧❧

Dinner is diagonally cut peanut butter sandwiches and Gator Aid. A bite is missing from Michael's in the exact center of the crust free base of the triangle. He doesn't remember doing that even though he quit taking pills before he left the cabin. It seems like days have passed since then but he knows it's been only a few hours.

Janie told him, "It's time to give up the pills, Michael." He hears the echoes of her voice bouncing around the kitchen. He sees her transparent image superimposed over Mom and Dad like a ghost image on a television set with bad reception. Janie sitting in an overstuffed chair back in the hunter's cabin. Naked and bruised, her hands placed in her lap in a gesture of modesty, one eye closed, the other half-open in a glazed wink. There are things Janie wants Michael to do. He's done some of them already.

Memories circle in his brain like a flock of vultures over a dead high school homecoming queen. They'll get down to business when the time is right. The radio Michael brought from the cabin plays a Dolly Parton song: "Daddy Was an Old Time Preacher Man" on 90.9 FM.

"Where the devil did that come from?" Dad doesn't look like he approves of FM 90.9 anymore, or peanut butter sandwiches and Gator Aid, or his wife or his son, or anything else in Jumbo, Oklahoma.

Mom holds up a copy of *Biskinik*, the Choctaw Nation Newspaper. Dad especially doesn't approve of that. Janie Impson's picture is on the front page. An old photograph, taken before she cut her hair. The headline over her picture reads, "Jumbo Girl Still Missing."

Mom says, "Chief Gregory Pyle asks everybody to say a prayer for Janie."

Dad swirls his Gator Aid and shoves his peanut butter sandwich triangles around his plate. His lower lip trembles like a televangelist on the evening news who got caught giving in to temptation.

"Heathen rag." He points his finger at Janie's picture while he tries to think of a suitable Bible verse. When none come to him he thumps his finger

93

against his Gator Aid glass and makes it ring.

Mom turns the volume on the radio up all the way when Dolly Parton finishes her song and the announcer asks anyone with information about Janie Impson to come forward.

Maybe this would be a good time to say something, but Michael remembers how Janie looked sitting naked in the overstuffed chair in the cabin staring at him with her one glazed eye, and he thinks maybe he should go back and dress her first.

"Looky here." Mom tips the *Biskinik* back and forth so the picture of Janie Impson dances to the brand new song on the radio.

Michael doesn't recognize the music. Something country. Something religious. Something sung by men with deep voices.

"I never noticed how much Janie Impson looks like you, Michael," Mom says. "Especially since she cut her hair." She walks around the kitchen table and places the newspaper in front of Michael's dad.

"Same eyes. Same mouth."

Michael's dad wads the newspaper into a ball and throws it on the floor. He stands up and glares at Michael and at Michael's mother. He's stuck in one position like the best freeze-tag player in the world.

"Say grace before the bread goes stale." Mom holds up a sandwich so dad will get the idea. "And add a little something for Janie, like Chief Pyle said."

Dad starts to speak, but stops when Dolly Parton comes on the radio with "Coat of Many Colors".

"That reminds me." One of Michael's vulture memories comes in for a landing. "I found your Sunday coat."

"Found it in the graveyard draped over a headstone." It is a lie but he doesn't think it counts as a sin. Not compared to kissing a dead girl or touching her breast, besides, Janie wants him to say it just that way.

"Margaret Impson's headstone," Michael says. "You know, Janie's mom."

Michael decides to eat his peanut butter sandwich without waiting for a blessing.

Mom remembers how, "Janie put her hair in Margaret Impson's coffin." She turns the radio off. Silence settles over the kitchen like a long coat falling over a dead girl's body in a hunter's cabin.

"Got to go." Michael's dad backs out of the kitchen like a middle-aged white man doing the moonwalk.

"Got a meeting. You know, with somebody..."

"I shook the cemetery dust off your coat," Michael says. "Hung it in the closet." He washes down a bite of peanut butter on white bread with a big gulp of Gator Aid. His appetite is coming back as the pills wear off. Funny how fast things change once you get on the right track. He smiles as he remembers the surprise in Dad's Sunday coat.

"You look exactly like her when you smile," Mom tells Michael.

"Doesn't he, Daddy?" Her husband is already looking in the hall closet for his coat.

Michael wonders how he'll react when he finds Janie's panties in the pocket.

⁂

Janie Impson is friendly now that she is dead. Now that she and Michael have so much in common. He builds a fire, using deadwood collected from the forest. Starts it burning with kitchen matches and pages from the Jack Fork Holiness Bible.

The *Book of Revelation* gets the kindling going. Michael doesn't like to leave Janie sitting naked in a cold cabin now that the temperature has dropped again. Once she's warmed up, once her muscles loosen and her joints thaw, Michael might try to dress her.

The fire catches hold, but he tosses a couple of *Psalms* into the flames just to be sure.

Janie's blouse is cold and crisp in Michael's fingers, as if it had been sent to a laundry in the arctic circle. Her skirt is short with pleats, like a cheerleader's uniform. It is black. The color that takes everything in and gives nothing back. Michael's breathing deepens when he thinks of the places that skirt covered when Janie was alive.

It might be made of linen, which reminds Michael of the old Russian dictator who still lay in state. Dead a hundred years, still looking like he fell asleep in his coffin.

Janie doesn't look like she's asleep sitting in her overstuffed chair. More like she's waking up. Both eyes are open now; her mouth is open too. Michael sees something move behind her teeth. He no longer wants to kiss her.

Not so pretty anymore. Michael can't tell whether that thought comes from Janie or from him. It doesn't matter.

"I hate you Dad." He says that so Janie will know that's one more thing they share.

Michael shakes the skirt in front of the fire. He looks at the label in the waistband. Not linen. A synthetic blend. The material feels delicate. Feminine. The kind of thing that danced around the legs of the prettiest girl in Moyers High School. A fabric that brushed against her legs in places Michael is not supposed to touch.

Janie's legs are swollen. The backs of them have turned grey.

95

"Lividity," Michael tells her. That's when blood is pools in the lowest vessels and leaks into the skin.

"No need to feel bad," he tells her. "It happens to everybody sooner or later." But he knows she does feel bad. He knows because he and Janie are so much alike that the only real difference between them is death.

He thinks about how pretty Janie Impson used to be before somebody put a stop to that.

A sound rattles in the back of Janie Impson's throat. Something between a laugh. and a memory of what it felt like to dress in her white blouse and her pleated black skirt and stand in front of the mirror and look at herself the way she knew the boys would look at her.

Another sound. This one from deeper inside Janie Impson as the heat from the fireplace warms the memories:

Of how desirable she was.

Of how sweet it was to feel that white blouse drape across her breasts.

Of how the hem of her pleated black skirt stroked her legs like a nervous lover's fingers.

Michael carries Janie's skirt and blouse into the cabin's bathroom. The odor of the chemical toilet seeps into the partially enclosed space as the kindling in the fireplace burns brighter. He looks so much like her in the bathroom mirror, especially in the ambient light through the open bathroom door. He holds the blouse over his chest and turns his head the way he remembers Janie turning her head when she was homecoming queen.

Exactly like her if he holds his mouth just so and closes his eyes halfway, and looks up as if he's too shy to make eye contact with someone taller.

More like her after he's removed his clothes and put hers on. The blouse and skirt fit perfectly, the feel of the fabric on his skin matches memories Michael knows were never his. The sensations intensify as he moves and before long he's parading around the cabin, showing off for Janie Impson who is smiling at him with a mouth that looks ecstatic and ghastly.

Michael executes a dancer's spin that makes the skirt stand out like an invitation to see what's underneath. He watches the spin through Janie's eyes and feels it with the parts of him that still are the sole the property of a teenage boy.

The spin slows down when the cabin door opens. Slow enough so he can see his father in the long gray coat with Janie's panties in the pocket. Dad has a shovel in one hand and a green trash bag in the other. He drops both when he sees Michael/Janie spinning like a music box ballerina in the hunter's cabin.

Dad screams in tongues and takes off running for the trees.

Michael tries to think of a good reason he is wearing a dead girl's clothes. He calls after his father in a voice sounds like Janie's shouting an accusation.

He and Janie are in this thing together. His father is in it too but in a much different way. Michael holds the naked body of Janie Impson in his arms—much lighter than he expected—and follows his father through the woods.

He catches up in the Jumbo Cemetery parking lot, where Dad is in his car, grinding the starter, pumping the accelerator pedal until the air smells like gasoline. The engine coughs and sputters like an old man laughing, but it will not take hold.

Dad screams when he sees what's moving toward him through the headstones. Not a woman's scream but very close. Michael wonders if every man in his family has a woman's soul inside him trying to come out.

Dad clutches his chest and slumps over the steering wheel. Prays at the speedometer until he runs out of things to say. Turns toward the sound of the passenger side door opening. Stuck in that position as if his curiosity has turned him to a pillar of salt.

Michael slides Janie across the seat until she's sitting next to him. Dad tries to turn away but his body isn't following orders anymore. He gives up after a short struggle. Closes one eye before he takes one final breath as if he's winking at a private joke between him and Janie Impson.

"So long, Dad." The winter wind teases its way under Janie's skirt—cold and persistent as a preacher's hands—as Michael walks back home.

Dad didn't seem too happy to see Janie again, but things will go better with Mom. She's always glad to see one of the girls from Jumbo.

THE NAKED WOMAN

by Theric Jepson

Usually only toothy, nether-dwelling monsters or horned, vase-breaking imps hide out of sight of the adult mind, but she didn't seem like a monster or an imp at all. When the boys of Miss Garner's third-grade class saw her pass the school yard during afternoon recess wearing nothing but a Polly Pocket backpack over one shoulder, they hid behind the evergreen bushes and watched, fearful the monitor would see them and call their parents. It didn't occur to them that a woman without clothes next to an elementary school might be the one who would get in trouble—or at least in more trouble than the naturally curious third-grade boys watching her. She was grown up, and grown-ups don't get in trouble. Boys get in trouble.

She walked by the next day during lunch, backpack-free, but carrying a Sesame Street umbrella crooked over her right elbow. She attracted a crowd. Already her lightly orange-blonde hair and smooth, milky curves were the stuff of playground legend. All but a few children lay on the ground near the fence to watch her walk by. Every movement was a lesson, every bounce a revelation, every jiggle an education.

The monitor saw the children tittering by the fence and walked over to see what they were up to. She barked at them, demanding intelligence. One boy, a dark-haired frecklefield named Ralph, pointed. The monitor turned to look but failed to see the naked woman, six inches taller and a hundred years younger than herself, walking by. That's when they knew.

The big item of conversation that afternoon however was not why grown-ups couldn't see the naked woman—that may have been strange, but it certainly was not outside the realm of possibility—but how she managed to walk so briskly on the sidewalk in her bare feet. That wasn't soft cement, they knew—that was unpleasant, poky stuff.

She didn't show up again until Friday. School was already over, and most of the kids had already left when Ralph, his sister, and a few of their friends saw her walking down the same sidewalk, wearing a baseball cap.

"There she is!"

They ran to the sidewalk and followed her, keeping about a half-block behind. They crossed Clay Street on the light (she had walked through traffic without looking) and followed her down to Boise, where she crossed again without looking.

"Maybe she's a ghost," said Sabrina, a frecklefield herself with dark brown, ear-length hair that made her look more like Ralph than his sister did.

No one answered. They had all thought this. They weren't happy with Sabbie for saying it aloud.

The naked lady kept walking up Sixth to the dead end then headed up the bike trail. The kids stopped to consult.

"Do you think this is where she always goes?"

"Do you think she lives in there?"

"I wish we had our bikes."

"Do you think she knows we followed her?"

"Doesn't she pay attention to *anything*?"

"I wish we knew who she was!"

"Why doesn't she wear clothes?"

"Do you think she will in winter?"

"Do you think she's dead?"

They all stopped and looked at Sabbie. Finally Ralph said, "Come on," and they headed up the bike trail.

If the sidewalks were bad on feet, the trails would be worse. Except for the most used paths, it was tough not to pop bike tires on goatheads or rusty nails and impossible not to get burrs in socks. It the kids hadn't been so far behind, they would have stopped to de-weed themselves every few feet. But she was getting away.

She left the path, and Ralph held down one barbed wire with his foot and pulled the other one up for the girls to get through. But Sabrina hesitated. "She didn't go through the fence."

"Knock it off," said Ralph. "She's right there!"

So Sabbie went through then held the wires for Ralph, and before the kids knew it, they had caught up with their prey. She was sitting on an old kitchen chair and reading a newspaper. A busted wagon and a paint can lay knocked over beside her. She closed and reopened the paper to turn a page and did not see them.

"She can't see us," they whispered.

Sabbie gnawed her sleeve.

They soon discovered that any day she walked by, and most days she didn't, the naked lady could be found in the fields on the other side of the fence from the bike trails, sitting on her chair. She did different things—filed her nails, did crosswords, ate chocolates—but she was always there. And she never saw them watching her.

Unspoken rules developed for who could watch her when. Only one group could see her at a time, and a sort of rotation developed. Groups of girls usually went right after school. They would watch her and talk about the shape of her breasts or the funny yellow hair between her legs and imagine what it would be like to be a woman. A woman with large round breasts and fur between her legs. Some of the older girls, in fifth and sixth grades, tried to pluck their eyebrows and style their hair to look like the naked lady. Some of the boys made fun of them, but everyone understood.

The boys would come later, after dinner. They came and told jokes and dared each other, desperate to find out if she would notice being touched. Even the younger boys felt there was something magical and important about the naked woman. Their little, fledgling bodies told them so. It felt like magic all the time, as she would sit there, painting her toenails. They didn't know why, but they tried to recreate the magic—drawing her in their notebooks and on the margins of their arithmetic tests. Which was what alerted the teachers.

They emptied the boys' desks and bookbags but only found more of their crude, little-boy drawings. They checked the girls' desks. More of the same. The girls focused on different features, but there they were—naked women.

The principal called a special faculty meeting. Halfway through, Ms. Prachett suddenly gasped. "Oh-oh-oh!" She stood up. "Look at their hair!"

They looked. They noticed. Every drawing. The same hair. Bold. Full. When in color, blonde and red.

"Either the children are sharing one magazine, or there is a real woman," they decided at the end. They told themselves that whatever had happened, it was over now, but they each feared that an exhibitionist was purposefully perverting the school.

The naked lady walked past the school again on Monday, and although she attracted a crowd as she fought to keep her scarf tied in a nonexistent wind, most of the children kept their place in line for the slide or on the swings or struggling to become king of the hill.

But the monitor still noticed. After the faculty meeting, she had decided to bring binoculars to school, and now she searched in the direction the children were looking; she checked each house window, but nothing. She checked the children, and now they were looking in another direction. She tried again. Nothing. She looked at the children. She noticed their gaze was not fixed, but it moved. Northward. She tried to follow their gaze. There was nothing there.

Winter came and what had been a near daily trek for most became weekly at best, and only for a few. Her occasional walks past the schoolyard still attracted attention, but interest waned as interest does, and the naked lady passed early into myth and fable for most of the children.

Ralph and his sister and their respective friends took it upon themselves to keep tabs on what they now freely referred to as their ghost—after all, what else could survive the snow so unconcernedly wearing nothing but a bow in her hair or a charm bracelet round her wrist or a single fuzzy glove? Nothing. So it was a ghost, and the ghost was theirs.

The first warm day didn't come till April, and that day Sabbie missed school. When Ralph and his friends went to see their ghost, they saw Sabbie leaving by the bike trail that led to Fourth Street but they thought nothing of it. So she was feeling better. Good. The other girls would be pleased.

They stayed only long enough to determine that the naked lady was there and what she was doing (toe touches) and wearing (some sort of hat) and then they left, writing their findings in a notebook dedicated to that purpose.

It wasn't for several weeks that they realized that the naked lady's hair was changing from its lemony-red blonde. There were strands of dark brown, and the overall color had deepened. The patch between her legs was following suit. The next week her hair was shorter, and after that it was pinned back with bright pink barrettes that reminded them a great deal of the type Mrs. Hogeson had given her best girl students at the end of second grade. The ones Sabbie had worn almost daily until recently. "I lost them," she shrugged.

The next day was the first of June. ("I can smell summer vacation," the principal had said during a mystery-meat lunch, which everyone agreed was hilarious.) The sun was bright and warm, bees were buzzing to the playground clover, and Ralph was blessed with a revelation inspired by the squirrel his dog had killed two days earlier.

"Did you know," he said during recess with the easy confidence born of invention, "that naked ghosts will talk to you if you bring them something dead wearing their favorite clothes?"

His friends buzzed. They tried to think of what her favorite clothes might be. What had she worn the most? Gloves? Her baseball cap? The Rainbow Brite t-shirt that wouldn't cover her breasts?

"No," Ralph said. And he tapped his head.

Of course. The barrettes. They pulled out the notebook. For the past forty-five days, whatever else she had worn, the bright pink barrettes had been a constant. Sabbie may have lost hers, but who else had some? They ran over to the chestnut trees where Ralph's sister was jumproping with friends. Sabbie sat against the tree, quiet.

Naked! Naked! Lady! Hey!
Where do you go when you want to play!
Over to the castle!
Over to the woods!
Just don't eat the baby child,
Cuz it's no good!
It's no good!
Say it one
Say it two
Say it three times!
It's no good!
Say it four
Say it five
Say it six times
It's no good!
Say it seven
Say it eight—

Ralph's sister botched it and said she should get to try again 'cause, "If you don't break ten / You should get to try again," but her friends wouldn't let her. Ralph interrupted them and explained his plan. The girls agreed it ought to work and brought up the obvious fact that they would have to bring the barretted squirrel at midnight. Several of them still had their barrettes, and they all agreed that whoever could sneak out would meet at the end of Sixth at 11:30 with all the barrettes they had and go see the naked lady together. No one was quite sure she would be there after dark, but Ralph knew more about ghosts than anyone, as he pointed out, and besides, it would be fun. By fun, they all knew, he meant scary. Spying on a ghost with the sun out was one thing. Going at midnight was another.

The bell rang, and they all ran in. A few minutes later, a lone girl was sent back out. She wandered over to the chestnut tree and told Sabbie the bell had rung. Sabbie opened her eyes and blinked. She stood up. They went in together.

At 11:30, Ralph was so tired he thought about not going. Besides, if he didn't go, no one else would bother showing up either—he was the leader after all—but just as he was just about to pull the blanket back up under his nose to keep the spiders out of his mouth, his sister came in. "Come on!" she said. Ralph jumped up and got slipped back into his lucky jeans and they snuck out of the house together, Ralph pausing in the backyard to sneak the dead squirrel from his dog.

They rode their bikes, which made the night colder than expected, but Ralph's winter coat had still been under his bed, and his sister said she was never cold in June. When they reached the end of Sixth, three girls were already there, each bearing barrettes, which they clipped onto the squirrel's tail amid squeals of "Gross!" and "Eww!"

"What do you think she'll say?" they asked.

Ralph considered. "Maybe she'll answer questions."

"Maybe she grants wishes!"

"No, that's genies, dummy."

"Well, maybe she's a genie."

"There's no girl genies."

"Maybe there are."

"Besides, genies don't have legs."

The girls folded their arms and turned away. They hated it when a stupid boy was right.

Ralph's sister had a watch that glowed when she pushed a button. It was 11:43. They wanted to go now, but...

"We need more boys," said Ralph. "For safety." The girls laughed and made fun of the idea but agreed to wait.

At 11:48, a boy came. "Finally!" said the girls. They agreed no one else was coming and hurried down the trail. Where the trail neared the fence, one of them tripped over a bike. "It's Sabbie's," said Ralph's sister. "Look. Those streamers from her birthday on the steering wheel."

"It's not a steering wheel," said Ralph.

"How long do you think she's been here?"

"I bet she found her barrettes and came to make her talk before we got here."

"Not fair."

Don't worry—it won't work. It can't! It's not midnight yet!"

They all looked at the glowing watch. Its green shine made them look like ghosts themselves. They giggled. They probably would have started laughing, but Ralph walked over to the fence and, holding down the bottom wire with his shoe, held it open. Once everyone else was through, the other boy held it for Ralph.

They had worn their own path during their little trips, and they went up it now, single-file, watching their feet in the darkness. Suddenly, they stopped; the ones in back peeked around those in front and, after they had seen, started taking steps back. The naked lady stood at the end of the trail, her naked backside reflecting a sun that was not there. She was staring at her chair. At who was sitting there.

"It's *Sabbie*," they gasped.

Sabbie must have heard them because she turned to look. Her eyes were wide and her mouth was opened, like she had been talking. But she didn't talk. And the invisible light bounced off her too. The clearing was bright, and the ruined wagon and paint can trembled. The chair seemed to move forward but stayed still. The naked lady was also still yet grew closer to Sabbie all the same. The children did not move. When Sabbie and the naked lady drew close enough, the ghost leaned forward and touched her face. Sabbie smiled. The lady took the barrettes out of her own dark brown, ear-length hair and clipped them into Sabbie's. Sabbie moved her lips again. The ghost stroked her cheek.

Then the chair was back in the center of the clearing, and the naked lady walked over to it. She turned around. She and Sabbie looked at the kids huddled just beyond their yellow-sun glow. And smiled at them.

"She sees us," said one of the girls.

"She's so beautiful," said another.

The naked lady reached her hands behind herself and onto Sabbie's lap. She sat. Sabbie's head fell back and faded. The wagon and the paint can were swallowed by the light as the ghost quivered, and Sabbie's body shrank and stretched and glowed and darkened and fell, fell, fell. Her chest grew into the naked lady's. Her legs lengthened and absorbed their jeans. Her face aged into a woman's.

The naked lady stood. And then she was gone. And her chair. And the clearing. And the light. The next afternoon, after school, all they found was the wagon and the paint can—nothing else.

The girls began wearing their pink barrettes again. Every day. They went to where the clearing once was and threw rocks into the brush. They gazed out the school windows at the once wonderful sidewalk. And they waited.

Sabbie! Sabbie! Sabbie! Hey!
The naked lady wants to play!
You get her body!
You get her soul!
Just leave us a roadmap,
So we can go!
We can go!
Say it one
Say it two
Say it three times!
Take me too!
Say it four

Say it five
Say it six times!
Take me too!
Say it seven
Say it eight—

The boys went back to drawing dinosaurs.

DEAD MEN DON'T COUNT
by Lynda Clark

"It don't count as stealing if they're dead!" Crom tells you for the millionth time. Like he's trying to convince himself he ain't a thief. He hangs back even though the dead man's penned in. You've already done your part—dragging an old oak cabinet, a heavy farmhouse table and a low cupboard filled with pots and pans to keep the dead man from interfering with Crom's work.

The man's a few years dead. Little more than a skeleton clad in strips of foul-smelling, discoloured flesh, he bumps disconsolately against the cabinet, rattling the blue and white china inside. Little of his eyes remain, and yet you feel he's looking at you with a deep sadness, judging you, your actions, your life choices. As if there was any choice about it.

Crom gives the makeshift holding pen a wide berth. It makes no difference to the dead man. He continues resolutely bumping against the cabinet, will do so until he rots away entirely or one of the Registry comes and finishes him off.

Once he's safely past, Crom pokes out his tongue and waggles it at the dead man, as if he's outwitted him somehow. You hate Crom sometimes. His easy acceptance of everything the Home and the Registry tells him. Sure he's young, but still old enough to have a mind of his own. He notices you giving him a look, and says, "Everyone knows if they bite you, you get it."

You roll your eyes. "They only bite when people are mean to them. Which is all the time."

You've never seen one attack unprovoked. Never ever. When the Registry shot Mama, she was just going to stroke your hair. You knew it, because it's what she always used to do, and that's what the dead do. They get stuck in loops and repeat the actions they did when they were alive, over and over. Like a bit of them remembers, somehow. Mama was going to stroke your hair, not claw your face like the Registry man said.

"You'd be the expert," Crom mutters under his breath and you want to knock the smart words out of his mouth, but he's got work to do.

In the far corner of the room, there's a safe. It's big and old, the kind that needs careful, precise movements, like mending a pocket watch. You can't just explode these with dynamite like the new ones. They're sturdy and fragile at the same time. Some kind of moron, Dada called it, but you can't remember the proper word.

You think of Dada's big strong hands, the hands that made your breakfast every morning and packed your satchel for school, even after the bad times, even after there was no school and his hands was just bones. Dangerous, the Registry men said. Mama and Dada weren't no danger to no-one, least of all men with guns.

Crom has set down his bag of tools and is carefully laying them out. You leave him to it. He's so keen to rob this old man, let him do it alone. You wander back to the man's pen and idly poke through the drawers in the bottom half of the cabinet.

Mostly it's been picked clean already. There's just a couple of books and a dusty old box of photos. You drag the photos out and thumb through them, trying to find one of the dead man when he was alive.

"What are you doing?" Crom calls to you. He's on his knees in front of the safe, turning the dial with his ear close to it, trying to determine the contact area. "Stop shuffling paper around. I need to hear this!"

You doubt it's the photos affecting his concentration. It's the dead man. Crom is terrified of them. He saw some film when he was a toddler, too young to understand it was make-believe, some made-up thing about dead men who just wanted to eat people's brains, so he has it in his head that's how they actually *are*. His parents were took away as soon as they got ill, so he never saw what they were actually like after. He just has all these pictures in his head of them being like the movie dead men. Zombers, he calls them. Silly name for a silly idea. Even the Home don't let you call them that. Though they don't like you calling them people neither.

Your flicking fingers land on a photo. The man's wearing the same coat he has on now. It ain't all rotted and dusty, but it's definitely the same, with wide silky lapels and brass buttons. His eyes were blue when he had them, and he looks friendly in a sad sort of way. Same as now, really. There are more pictures, him playing with a little girl, him holding a fluffy little dog on his knee, him playing with some machine back when there was lectricity.

You realise suddenly that the only sound is the *click-click-click* of Crom spinning the dial to park the wheels. The dead man has stopped bumping and he's watching you. Well, not watching, 'cause he don't have eyes, but regarding you in that way they have.

It makes you smile and you ache for Mama and Dada. They was good parents, even after. Even the Registry lady was surprised. Expected a feral child, she'd said, not to find you all washed and brushed and well fed. She said it like maybe, just maybe, the Registry man shouldn't have shot them. Even though just hinting that was treason. If the Registry man hadn't been shaking so bad, you think he might've turned her in after handing you over to the Home.

You've leaned over the pen and given the box to him without even thinking about it and he's taken it in his bony hands. He clacks his jaw like he's thanking you, but everyone says that's silly, like thinking dogs have personalities. There's a chair in there with him and he sits down on it and puts the box on his knee and rifles through the photos, holding each one at arms length for a moment like he's looking at them.

"He ain't looking at them, you know," says Crom.

You wonder how long you've been watching the dead man, because Crom's all done and he has the tools back in the bag and the bag on his shoulder and all he's got out the safe is a little black box.

"What is it?" You ask, nodding to the box.

"He ain't looking at them, cos he ain't got eyes or a heart or a mind."

You take the box from his unresisting hands and open it up. There's two rings inside, both silver, both engraved with the same date, a date just before you were born.

"They just pretends to be alive so they can trick ya," Crom tells you sagely. "That's when they goes for your brains."

The dead man has stopped on one photo. He's been holding it for the longest time. Eventually he lets it slip from his skeletal fingers and it drops to the dusty flagstone floor. He slumps forward in his seat like a man defeated. You crane your neck to see the photo, while Crom tugs on your sleeve.

"Leave him, leave him for the Registry," he complains. "We should get back to the Home."

"In a minute," you dismiss him with a wave of your hand. The photo is the dead man, younger, not much older'n you and with him there's another man with dark nappy curls and they're clutching hands and gazing into each other's eyes and they're both wearing dove grey suits and brooches of flowers and happy smiles.

You wipe your eyes quickly and you know Crom's seen, but for once he don't rag you about it. He just swallows and puts the rings in his pocket.

"They was happy as Mama and Dada," you say, your voice high and childish.

"I know," says Crom, patting your arm, "I know."

CLOVES AND ORCHIDS
by Leigh Harlen

My sister's death wasn't a surprise. She had been reckless and sinful. She probably brought it on herself. At least that's what people whispered when they thought I couldn't hear.

But fuck them. Most of the people at her funeral hadn't even known her. Not really. Dozens of my classmates sat in the back of the room exchanging whispers. They were only freshman when Taylor had dropped out. Aunt Patricia, perched in a chair in the front row, had made it very clear that she thought Taylor was strange, a trouble maker, a *bad girl*. They were here to prove that weren't like her. They were good people because they came to the funeral of a girl they barely knew and didn't like.

The most egregious were our parents. Thanks to them I didn't even recognize the woman in the casket. The soft blue dress more appropriate to a child, the delicate cross around her neck, the wig of long, curly, blond hair. The paint and spackle covering her face failed to hide the fact that it was broken, smashed, dented, and torn.

That dressed up lump of putty wasn't my sister. My sister was strong and defiant. She cut off her hair and dyed it blue, she said "fuck" and "goddamn", and she wore tight jeans and sleeveless, low cut shirts to show off her tattoos and cleavage. This broken nightmare doll was just the pasted together picture of who my parents had wanted her to be.

The pastor walked to the front of the room and the incessant whispering trailed off. He blathered on about how difficult and confusing it was to lose someone so young. "It's hard for us to understand, but God has His reasons. She's in a better place now. She's with Him."

Bullshit.

Taylor was dead. My best friend. My protector. The woman who bought me punk records and headphones so I could listen to them in my room without my parents hearing. The one who locked Melissa Thompson in a bathroom stall and threatened to shave her head if she didn't stop harassing me and calling me "dyke."

I didn't think there was a God. But if I was wrong, I hated Him.

The pastor stopped talking, finally. Those of us in the front row stood and formed a line to walk past the coffin and "pay our respects."

I followed my parents to the casket.

Looking down at my big sister's dead body, I couldn't cry. I wasn't sure why. It was as if my feelings had been scooped out, leaving nothing but rage to rattle around in the empty cavity. Maybe it was because she looked like a stranger. Maybe it was my mom's face, buried in my shoulder, soaking my blazer with her grief. Maybe I was just too angry.

My dad took my mom's arm. She released her grip on mine and latched on to his.

"Come on, Beth." He gestured at me.

On the way out, I spotted Taylor's friends. A small cluster of people with piercings, mohawks, and black leather jackets huddled together in the back of the room. My favorite of Taylor's friends, Mel, smiled at me. For a moment, I felt relief. Seeing other people who truly cared about the real Taylor and who weren't here out of obligation or curiosity was comforting. I gave her a hug in spite of my dad's chilling glare.

We went outside to the waiting hearse. I climbed inside and scooted to the far window. The seats were cold and the air smelled like pine-scented air fresheners and menthols. The hearse shook as they loaded Taylor's coffin into the back. The driver got in and we began the drive.

An arched gate welcomed us to the cemetery. It was tall, rusted, and overrun with vines. The hearse bumped along the gravel road. Stone angels wept atop elaborate headstones and huge mausoleums housed generations of families. But as we went deeper, the grave markers got smaller, less ornate. Unadorned rectangles jutting out of the earth or just a flat plaque pressed into the ground with a name, a date, and a note that they were someone's beloved something.

We stopped. There was a perfect, rectangular hole in the ground framed by some contraption that I guessed would lower Taylor's coffin. It was surrounded and lined with bright blue plastic tarps and protected from the drizzling rain with a green awning.

A skinny man with oversized glasses and an impressive overbite opened the door and guided me and my parents to our spot at the graveside. Car doors slammed and other people began to fill in around and behind us.

Cousin Bret, Uncle Daniel, and four men I didn't even recognize carried the simple coffin through the gathered crowd.

Before they reached the grave, Cousin Bret's toe caught the edge of the tarp. He stumbled forward and released his grip on the handle. The coffin tilted and there was thud from inside. My mom moaned and squeezed my forearm so hard I was sure it must be bruised. The man behind Bret grabbed the front handle and steadied the casket. Bret stood up, his face flushed, brushed off his knees, and took the handle again.

I felt a powerful urge to laugh. I pursed my lips, but it threatened to force its way out. I dug my nails into the palm of my hand until I regained control.

When the casket was placed, the six men disappeared into the throng of people.

Behind me I heard, "I don't think I've seen her cry."

"That's cold."

I turned around. Lots of faces seemed to stop mid-whisper under my gaze. They all looked ashamed and guilty so I couldn't tell who it was I had heard.

A woman with a pretty, but slightly off-key, voice led everyone in a hymn. I didn't open the hymnal or even pretend to mouth the words like I usually did. This was when Taylor should elbow me in the ribs and tell me to fake it so I didn't get grounded when we got home. Then she would make up obscene lyrics and sing them just loud enough for me to hear.

I'd blush and laugh and, even though Taylor always tried to take the rap, my dad would ground us both when we got home. It didn't matter to Taylor, she'd sneak out after he went to bed anyway.

"Would anyone like to come forward to talk about Mary?" Pastor James asked. It fanned my already impressive rage when he said "Mary." She had started going by Taylor when she was twelve.

Aunts, uncles, and cousins all made their way forward and told stories about "Mary" and what a smart, pretty, sweet child she had been.

My dad cleared his throat and stepped forward. My mom gripped my hand so tight that my fingers went numb.

His eyes were red but he was stone faced. "My daughter, Mary—" His voice cracked and he cleared his throat.

"I remember—" His hands began to shake and tears started to run down his cheeks. He brushed them away and coughed.

"She was about three," he started again. His entire body began to tremble.

"My little girl," he choked out. He tried to cover his mouth, but sobs ripped out of his throat. He screamed, a hoarse, pained sound. He dropped to his knees in the mud and wailed.

I'd never seen him cry before.

Chairs creaked as people shifted, uncomfortable at this open display of grief.

Pastor James took my dad by the arm and led him back to my mother's side. He pressed his face into her shoulder, muffling his sobs.

Pastor James returned to his place at the microphone. "Let us now bow our heads."

"I'd like to say something," I said.

"Oh, I'm sorry. Please, Beth, come up."

I stood. My legs shook and I almost turned my ankle trying to walk in the pumps my mom had insisted I wear.

I wanted my grief to be pretty and appropriate. I wanted my eyes to tear up without breaking into sobs. I wanted to say something heartfelt and poignant about the sister I loved. The protective, kind, free-spirited woman that Taylor had really been. But as I looked around at the ghoulish, expectant faces staring at me and down at the polished casket waiting to go into the ground, all I felt was angry.

I pulled the microphone towards my face, so close that it was touching my lips. "This is bullshit."

I didn't take the time to savor the shocked and scandalized looks, I turned and walked away into the cemetery. No one followed me.

My heels poked holes in the ground and stuck with every step, so I pulled them off and left them lying in the mud. The headstones got bigger, grander, on the edge of the cemetery. I dropped down at the foot of a tree facing a large gravestone with the Virgin Mary perched on top. With her worn down features and empty eyes, the Virgin was more frightening than comforting.

The wind picked up and I smelled something. Clove cigarettes and a cloying orchid perfume, the kind you got in a large bottle for $20 in the mall. It smelled like Taylor.

I closed my eyes and inhaled. When I opened them I saw her. Short electric blue hair, a silver ring on each side of her lower lip that was curled in a cocky smirk.

"Taylor?"

The vision disappeared and her scent with it. Seeing my sister, my real sister, not that pasted-together stranger in the casket, made her death suddenly real. She would never call me "nugget" or text me pictures of herself making ugly faces when I was sad. She'd never pick me up from school to take me to the record store again. My sister was gone. Her body would rot and I would go through the rest of my life without her. Tears pooled in my eyes and then trickled down my face. They turned into a flood of salty tears and snot. I pressed my jacket against my face to muffle the sound and I cried.

✞✞✞

I got up off the damp grass and wiped my dirty hands on my pants. I'm not sure what time it was, the sky was just dark enough that I could see a handful of stars. I passed my discarded shoes and left them in the mud puddle. I came to Taylor's grave, now a mound of loose dirt. I didn't stop. I didn't have anything left to say or feel right now.

On the walk home, I stayed on the side of the road so I didn't hurt my bare feet on the pavement but I still seemed to step on every rock hidden in the grass. By the time I walked up the driveway, my feet were muddy and bruised. The garage was packed tight and I had to hold my breath as I wiggled past my dad's rusting, scraped, and dented car.

When I stepped inside, my parents were at the kitchen table. They were silent and looked haggard and deflated. A greasy casserole lied on the table in front of them.

"Where have you been? We waited for you at the cemetery for an hour. Cousin Bret looked for you," my mother said. Her voice was slow and flat like a toy whose battery was almost run out.

"I just needed some time alone," I said, sitting down at the table.

Without a word, my dad scooped out a dripping square of casserole and passed the dish to me. I followed suit and dropped the congealed cheese, wet noodles, and ground beef down on my plate.

I stuck my fork into a noodle.

"Wait until we've said grace," my dad admonished.

I sighed and he glared at me.

My parents bowed their heads and closed their eyes. I kept mine open. I always did, there was something I liked about being the only one with open eyes, refusing to participate in this silly ritual. After Taylor dropped out of school and my dad kicked her out, she never came home for family dinners. But before that, we used to both keep our eyes open, making faces and trying to get the other to crack and laugh. I usually won.

But now my refusal felt necessary. I wasn't going to thank the god who killed my sister for anything, especially not a plate of shitty food.

"Heavenly Father, we thank You for the meal we are about to receive. We ask that you watch over Mary in Heaven and please take care of her family still here on earth."

The smell of orchids and cloves pushed away the odor of tomatoes and salty beef. My mom opened her eyes. I couldn't tell if she smelled Taylor, too. She looked around, her face hopeful, a small smile at the corners of her mouth.

My father's glass tipped over, spilling water and ice cubes into his lap. He jumped up and knocked his chair over.

"Well, that was clumsy of me," he said. He wiped futilely with a napkin at the spreading dark water stain and forced a chuckle. He disappeared down the hall and into the bedroom.

My mother looked at me. The expression on her face was intense, but I couldn't quite read it. I thought maybe we shared some kind of understanding. If we did, she didn't say.

My father returned wearing a dry pair of pants. When he sat down, he didn't finish his prayer. He scooped up a bite of casserole and began to eat. I lifted my fork but couldn't bring myself to put it in my mouth. I let it drop to my plate. My mom didn't move, didn't even try to eat, she just stared at the cooling lump of food before her.

No one spoke another word the entire meal. No one scolded me further for my disappearance, told me to eat, mentioned Taylor's name, or even complained about how terrible the casserole was. My father smacked his lips between bites and scraped his fork on his plate but otherwise the room was silent. All of the unspoken feelings seemed to fill the room until it felt like I was choking on grief, anger, and guilt that wasn't even mine. But no one would acknowledge those emotions. Better to pretend that they weren't there at all.

❧❧❧

I didn't go to school for a week. When I went back, it was quiet. No one talked to me about Taylor or anything else. Maybe they were too scared. For now I was just relieved to be left alone.

Between classes I wandered into the bathroom. It would make me late, but my teachers had been cutting me slack. I read the graffiti while I peed. It was the same drivel it always was—

"Jenny loves Mark."

"Jamie is a slut."

"Not all who wander are lost."

I took a pen out of my bag and added to it. "Doesn't anyone just come in here to piss?"

The door to the bathroom opened, for a moment letting in the hum of voices from the hallway.

"I don't know why everyone is making such a big deal about it. I mean, a weirdo skank got run over. Was anyone really surprised? I bet she was wasted and wandered in front of a car. Or maybe she got caught fucking the wrong person."

Another girl laughed. "That's mean, Melissa."

"Maybe, but you know it's true."

I buttoned my pants and opened the door. In my head, I had a plan. I was going to scream at Melissa. Tell her to shut the hell up. Push her into a stall and hold the door closed until she apologized or someone sent for a teacher. It's what Taylor would have done. But as soon as I stepped out, my mouth wouldn't open.

For a moment Melissa looked guilty. But then she straightened up and smirked. "Speaking of freaks."

I washed my shaking hands in silence.

"Come on, Melissa. Not today," said Amanda. She was Melissa's less attractive, less bitchy clone. She had even copied Melissa's blond-streaked bob.

I started to walk away.

"They shouldn't let your kind into the girl's bathroom," Melissa said.

The air filled with the smell of cigarettes and flowers. I looked around, hoping to see Taylor standing behind me.

The stall doors slammed open in unison. I jumped. Amanda shrieked.

"What the fuck?" Melissa crossed her arms and glared at the stalls as if they'd behave if she just channeled enough scorn at them.

There was a metallic screech. The tampon dispenser started to shake and pull out of the wall. A tampon wrapped in yellow and white paper flew out of the machine and hit Melissa between the eyes.

Another pastel missile shot out and struck her in the cheek. It was followed by a barrage. She squealed and tried to bat them away.

Melissa turned to run, but the tampons continued to pepper her, bouncing off her ass and the back her head, some lodging themselves in her thick hair. She slammed the door open and fled shrieking into the hallway. Amanda ran out after her.

I leaned against the sink. A warm, husky laugh echoed off the walls. *Taylor.*

I started to laugh with her. I was so filled with relief and happiness that I couldn't stop. Tears streamed down my face. When at last I regained control, my stomach muscles were sore.

"It's really you," I said, when I caught my breath. What I'd experienced in the cemetery and at home hadn't been a figment of my grief-stricken imagination. Taylor was here and she was watching out for me.

She didn't answer. I didn't know if she couldn't speak or maybe scaring off Melissa had used up all her energy. I wasn't sure how it worked. This was my first haunting.

☠☠☠

When I arrived home, I opened the mailbox. Inside was a large envelope. I couldn't breathe. I pulled it out and it said, "University of

Michigan" in blue letters in the top corner.

The big envelope was the good one.

When I was sending out applications Taylor told me, "You're the smart sister. You're gonna get the fuck out of here. Just go someplace cool. If I'm gonna spend the weekends crashing on your couch, I don't want it to be in some snow-covered shit hole like Houghton."

I stuffed the envelope in my bag and ran inside. I wanted to open it without my parents ruining the moment by immediately worrying about my safety living so far from home. It turned out to be unnecessary, the house was empty. I raced up the stairs to my bedroom and sat down on the edge of the bed. I pulled the envelope out, slid my finger under the seal, and ripped. I dropped papers and glossy books on the bed and grabbed the letter on top and read.

"Taylor, I got in. And Ann Arbor isn't a shithole," I said.

I waited for some sign that Taylor had heard me, to tell me that she was celebrating with me. But there was nothing. I sighed and leaned back on the bed.

The air filled with the thick, pungent odor of cigarettes.

The letter ripped from my grasp and an invisible hand crinkled it up and threw it in the garbage can.

I sat up. "Taylor, what the hell?"

A silver-framed picture of Taylor and me at my twelfth birthday hurled across the room and smashed against the wall, taking out a chunk of red paint.

My hands were slick with sweat and my heart pounded, but I didn't run. I didn't understand what was wrong, but I knew Taylor would never hurt me.

"Are you angry?" I whispered. Fingernails ripped through a band poster on my wall. "But I worked so hard for this. You said you wanted me to get out of here."

A paperweight slammed into my mirror, shattering it. I screamed, but my body was so rigid with fear that it came out as a squeak.

"Please, stop. I don't understand."

The room went silent.

"Taylor?"

But nothing moved to indicate that she was still there.

I forced myself to take slow breaths until my heart slowed. As soon as I had calmed down enough to move, I climbed down off the bed and left the room, closing the door behind me. I leaned against the wall. Was Taylor angry because she thought I was leaving her?

I wasn't prepared to face Taylor's unexplained anger yet, but my parents would be home soon and I had no idea what I would tell them about the mess. I went downstairs and grabbed a broom and took my time climbing back up.

Afraid of what might be waiting on the other side, I paused with my hand on the doorknob. I forced myself to go inside. The room was still a mess of shattered glass, but my wrinkled and torn acceptance letter was on my pillow.

I was relieved at what I took to be an apology, though I still wasn't sure why she had gotten so angry. I decided to let it go. Taylor was dead. It was understandable that she wasn't dealing with it well. No one else in this house was.

⚘⚘⚘

The cafeteria doubled as the gym, so it smelled like a sweaty sock stuffed with burnt fries. I sat down at the lunch table, alone. Usually a few other friendless misfits would fill in around me, but since Taylor died even they were keeping their distance. A conversation behind me caught my attention.

"Did you see her?"

"No. But Janelle said she was screaming and had tampons stuck in her hair."

"I don't much like being on the rag, but damn."

I smiled. Taylor's prank yesterday on the most feared person in school was juicier gossip than a loser weirdo's dead sister.

The bench shook and I turned to see Melissa had invaded my solitary corner of the cafeteria. Her thick black eyeliner was smeared, giving her a raccoon-like appearance.

"That was some trick in the bathroom yesterday," she said.

"I didn't do anything." I took a deep breath and smelled floral perfume.

"Like hell you didn't."

"Seriously, I was as surprised as you." The smell got stronger.

"Look, you ugly little dyke…" A clump of Melissa's hair floated up. She swatted behind her and turned around. "Stop fucking with my hair," she shouted at a group of freshman boys. Their eyes went wide and they looked terrified to have incurred the wrath of the school's self-appointed queen bitch.

She turned to me and opened her mouth to speak. Her head jerked back and there was a loud *rip*. Melissa screamed, it was piercing and echoed off the wood floors. Something yanked her backwards off the bench.

Conversation in the cafeteria stopped and people stood up to get a better view of the commotion.

119

Melissa thrashed and tried to grab at her invisible assailant. Handfuls of gold-streaked hair with bits of blood and skin clinging to the ends flew into the air and tumbled down around her, creating a macabre halo.

The smell of orchids and cloves got heavier until I was choking on the fragrance. A cold breath touched my ear, and Taylor laughed. But it sounded different, it was angry and cruel. I froze. The incident in the bathroom had been funny, but I didn't want this. It was too much. But I couldn't think of a single thing to stop her.

Melissa pulled herself up onto her hands and knees and tried to crawl away. There was one last patch of hair on the back of her mangled scalp. Taylor gripped that last handful and tore, pulling Melissa several inches off the ground and dropping her back down.

Mr. Pruitt, one of the English teachers, ran over to Melissa. He looked around, his eyes wide and frantic.

Drops of blood trailed down Melissa's face. She pointed at me and muttered something I couldn't understand. Her eyes were rolling back in her head and she was mostly incoherent.

Paramedics arrived, hovered over Melissa, and then spirited her out on a stretcher. When the door closed behind them, all eyes glanced at me and then darted away.

I sat back down while teachers and staff fluttered around. They couldn't figure out what happened so they didn't know if they should keep us here for interrogation or evacuate the cafeteria.

"Taylor, please stop," I whispered. But there was no response. I wanted her to move on or disappear or whatever people normally did that she had been too stubborn to do.

※※※※※

As I walked home I contemplated what I should say to Taylor. Fictional ghosts always had unfinished business or wanted their murders solved. I didn't know who had run over my sister. The police said she was hit from behind, so maybe she didn't either. But who was to say that's what actually created ghosts? I climbed the stairs and went into my bedroom.

I sat on the bed. "Taylor, are you there? We need to talk about what happened today. I'm really glad you're still here and that you want to look out for me. But, what you did to Melissa was really terrible. She's a bitch, but you can't hurt people like that."

I smelled clove cigarettes and perfume. There was a rustle from the garbage can and a sharp pain when something hit my forehead. I stared down at a bloody shard of broken mirror that landed on my thigh and touched my forehead. My fingers came away red.

120

Even after seeing what she had done to Melissa, I hadn't believed she would ever hurt me. Warm, wet blood trickled down the side of my face. It tickled my cheek a little. Drops of red fell onto my bare arm.

When the shock wore off and my legs stopped trembling enough to walk, I left the house. My head throbbed, but I kept going. I wasn't sure where I was headed until I found myself at the side of the road where Taylor had died. Her apartment had been just up the street. I wished I knew where she had been walking that night.

My dad kept throwing away the flowers left by Taylor's friends at her grave. So they had turned the site of her death into their own memorial. There were flowers and pictures and I found it more comforting than the cemetery. It felt more like the real Taylor.

※ ※ ※

Two weeks later, the funeral home called to let us know that Taylor's plaque had been placed on her grave. My parents called into school so we could all go see it. Since I'd lost my black pumps in the cemetery, my mom let me wear my combat boots, hidden under a long skirt.

We were silent on the drive. I wondered what my parents were thinking and if Taylor visited them, too. I hadn't seen, heard, or smelled her since she hit me with the piece of glass. I talked to my empty room every night. I asked her if she knew who ran her over and if she was angry with me. I thought maybe she wasn't coming to see me because she felt bad for injuring me, so I told her that I forgave her even though I was still hurt and scared.

My dad stopped the car. Neither of my parents moved. My mom let out a soft scream.

"No." My dad's voice was hoarse.

I couldn't see from the backseat so I stepped out of the car to see what was wrong. Taylor's grave was surrounded by scattered mounds of dirt and broken pieces of granite and polished wood. I walked towards it. Doors opened behind me.

A pale, bare foot was visible over the mounds of dirt.

I stopped at the edge of the hole. Taylor's grave looked like it had been blasted open. The lid of her coffin was gone. Her body hung half out of the hole and half in. The dress she had been buried in had been ripped off. Bits of fabric clung to her shoulders, but otherwise she was naked, her stitched-together and discolored skin on full display. The cross and the blond wig were nowhere to be seen. Her hair had been shaved to fit under the wig so there was fine blue fuzz over her mottled and dented skull.

"Who would do something like this?" my mom said, between sobs.

121

My dad stepped away and started shouting at someone on his cell phone.

Of course, I knew who had done it. Was Taylor angry to be buried dressed up like that? Or just angry to have to be buried at all?

I had always understood Taylor. Or at least I thought I had. But I didn't understand what she was doing now, or why. Her ghost seemed like a stranger. Staring at her corpse's frozen, patchwork face, it felt like my sister had died again.

҉ ҉ ҉

I leaned against the car and watched while my dad screamed at two police officers and the funeral director. I couldn't tell him that his anger was misdirected. I wondered if he knew that. To distract myself, I ran my fingers over the gouges and dents in the old car's paint. I thought that one on the fender might be new, but it was so hard to tell on the beat-up piece of shit.

The police and the funeral director drove off and my parents came back to the car.

We left the cemetery. My dad didn't turn to go home.

"Are we still going to the restaurant?" I was surprised. I didn't think anyone would be in the mood for a public family dinner after that.

"We still have to eat," my mom said, her voice trembling.

My stomach knotted. The restaurant would take us past Taylor's roadside marker. "Are you sure? I'm not very hungry, now."

"Your grandparents are expecting us," my dad said. His voice was firm and I knew there was no arguing with that tone.

The flowers, candles, and photos came into view and my mom made a strangled sound.

There was a women next to the memorial. She was limping and rubbing her arms as if to keep warm. Her back was to us, but I recognized her short electric blue hair and bare, tattooed arms.

"Taylor," I said. I regretted it for a second, afraid that I was the only one seeing her.

My dad slammed on the brakes and the tires screeched. Then the car sped back up.

"Stop the car," my mom said.

"I can't," my dad shouted.

The car swerved onto the shoulder and we plowed into Taylor's back. Bile burned my throat when I felt the bump of her body under the tires.

The car stopped. The motor died, the radio went silent, and the interior lights went out.

Taylor appeared in front of the car. Her mouth was open in a scream,

132

her teeth covered in blood.

She raced forward and reached through the window and grabbed my dad around the throat.

"Why? Just fucking tell me, why?" Taylor slammed his head into the steering wheel.

I didn't know what she wanted to know. Why was she dead? Why was she still here?

Another question crossed my mind but I was too afraid to think it.

My dad started to whimper. "I'm sorry."

Taylor let him go and stared at me. Her eyes were filled with rage and confusion, but seeing me seemed to make her pause.

I needed to say something, but I didn't know what. Before I could figure out what to say, she disappeared.

The engine started back up and soft music came from the radio. My dad sat gasping and sobbing for several minutes. When he calmed down he pulled back out onto the road.

"Was that...really Taylor?" my mom whispered.

My dad shook his head. "We're all just upset."

I wanted to argue. It was a ridiculous lie. We had all seen her. I could see the bruise forming on his forehead from where she'd smashed his head into the steering wheel.

"Why did she ask you why?" My mom's voice had an edge I'd never heard before. I thought it might be hatred.

My dad didn't answer. His face was pale and his hands shook as he reached over to turn the radio up.

My mom continued to stare at him.

"I don't know what you're talking about, Mary's soul is in Heaven, not here asking questions," he said at last.

It was obvious he was lying. But she didn't ask again.

❧❧❧

I opened my bedroom window and climbed out. Taylor started sneaking out when she was twelve, but I'd never had the guts before. I walked the thirty minutes to the cemetery and sat down in the damp grass by her grave.

Taylor hadn't appeared again since that night on the road. I wasn't prepared yet to ask any of the questions that night had raised, but I did want to say goodbye to my sister properly.

Kneeling in the wet grass, I reached into my bag and pulled out a fifth of whiskey that I had stolen from the cupboard that my dad thought none of us knew about. I opened the lid and poured some out onto the ground.

"Cheers, Taylor."

I took a drink. It was my first drink of anything stronger than communion wine. It burned my tongue but I liked the way it warmed my stomach and made my cheeks flush. I'd rehearsed over and over what I should have said to Taylor on the road. I hoped she could hear me now.

"Taylor, thank you for watching out for me, I'm going to be okay now. I don't know how or why you died, but I'm sorry, you didn't deserve it. I love you."

For a moment, I thought I smelled clove cigarettes and floral perfume. But if it was there, it drifted away on the wind.

I took a can of spray paint from my bag, shook it, and pulled off the cap. I wiped dirt and moisture off Taylor's grave marker with my sleeve.

In electric blue letters, I covered up "Mary" with "TAYLOR."

DEATH IS BUT A TEXT AWAY

by Kate Coe

They say you never stop learning. Well, let me pass on one of my favourite lessons: never believe anyone when they tell you something's a simple job—particularly if it deals with ghosts, spirits or the undead. It won't be simple. It'll be bloody hindering awkward.

How do I know that? I'll give you three guesses, and the first two don't count.

Oh, and another lesson for you? Always get payment in advance. You can work out how I discovered that one for yourself.

Anyway. My name is Ghost. I'm an assassin, thief and odd-job person...and, incidentally, I can talk to ghosts. And the reason I don't trust anyone when they tell me they've got a simple job for me started when I got a phone call as I was walking down The Strand in London on a wet, windy and plain yucky October morning.

"*Yo, sunshine.*" That's my boyfriend, Luk. "*I've got a simple case of an invisible thing that's throwing stuff around. Fancy dealing with it?*"

"Poltergeist?"

"*Yup.*"

"Do I get paid?"

"*£100.*"

"You bargained a hundred quid for a poltergeist?" I'm impressed.

"Sure. Who and where?"

Fifteen minutes and a short stroll later, I'm standing outside an office building near Lincoln's Inn Fields. Luk's waiting for me by the front door, lounging with his usual air of disreputable charm. He's dressed in ripped jeans and a leather jacket, and gives me a rakish grin as I stroll up. "So, ready to be target practise?"

"How come they only just realised they have a poltergeist?" I ask as Luk gestures me in.

"Basement got rebuilt into offices and things started moving. Then things got thrown. Friend of mine called me in as he knows I like freaky stuff." He winks at the receptionist, whose face turns pink as Luk adds, "And kinky stuff. This is Ghost. She's just visiting."

"I'll do you a pass." The receptionist seems happy to have a reason to stare intently at his computer instead of Luk, who leans an elbow on the counter and adds to me, "And then I called you, considering it looks like a simple haunting and I can't hear the damn things."

And that's where one of my problems lies. I'm one of very few people in this world who can hear ghosts...and believe me, most of the time I don't want to. It's not because the dead are scary or anything: most of the time, they're lonely, bored and really, really dull.

So I'll admit I'm a little bit excited to be doing something with an interesting ghost for a change, even if it does mean I get used as target practise. I really should learn to be more pessimistic. It'd stand me a lot better in the long run.

We get passes, and Luk heads towards the elevator. And the first thing that hits me as I step into the room at the bottom is a computer monitor.

Seriously.

I mean, I dodge, but...it's throwing monitors? This poltergeist is a bit more powerful than I'd thought.

"Uh, it wasn't this bad earlier," Luk says, shifting his hands and muttering a word that brings a sphere of energy up around us. It'll ward off the worst of whatever's thrown. "It was throwing paper, not screens..."

I glance around. It's a small-ish office, with five desks. The room's lit with two light-wells at the far side and banks of lights in the ceiling, and it's got the usual office stuff: a shelf of files and paper, computers on every desk, office chairs, bins...which are now scattered everywhere across the floor. Hmmm.

I look up and stare straight at the figure hovering in the middle of the devastation. "So? Got anything to say?"

It recoils. Most ghosts find out very quickly that normal humans can't hear them, and even most of the magical folk can only peripherally feel their presence. To have someone fold their arms, stare straight at them and give them sass is a bit of a shock.

This one recovers quite fast, and a keyboard comes flying towards me. It bounces off Luk's shield.

"Throwing things ain't going to work," I tell it. "Talk. T-a-l-k. I know you can."

"I want vengeance!" Spirits aren't usually too composed. Any that stay in this world have some sort of strong emotion, or unfinished business, but after a few years in the company of their own heads they're usually insane.

"Vengeance for what?"

"Vengeance!"

"Who has wronged you?" I sometimes think a degree in psychology would be a useful complement to my rarer skills.

"Vengeance!" Things start flying again.

"Oh, for..." I turn to Luk. "Anyone done any research on this building? Did they find any skeletons when they were digging the foundations?"

"Not that I know of." He shrugs.

I roll my eyes. Sometimes Luk is a serious chocolate teapot. "Fine. Let's go to the pub, and I'll call Pippa."

My boyfriend eyes me. "I would have thought that after a maniac ghost, you'd want to talk to someone sane..."

❧❧❧

Pippa Essen is tall, blonde, so thin she looks as if she'd snap in a good breeze, and has cordially hated me ever since her boyfriend hit on me, found out that I didn't have girl genitals despite my gender, accused me of tricking him and then tried to look like less of an idiot by blaming me. Pippa has long since dumped the boyfriend but kept the dislike. That said, we have a very good working relationship. She's got a nice little business on the shady side of the law, and because her illicit activities occasionally need a human aspect, she hired me.

Well, first she accused me of not being good enough when I offered her my services, so I stole her earrings while she was wearing them and she didn't notice for two hours. When she'd picked her jaw up off the floor and stopped screaming, she hired me.

Anyway. She's the person I call when I need information on a poltergeist.

"*How strong?*" she asks.

"It was throwing paper and, an hour later, computer screens."

"*Nice.*" She pauses, probably to scribble notes. "*Address?*" I give it to her, and get rewarded with a "*Hmmmm.*"

"Notorious?"

"No, surprisingly not. Lincoln's Inn could be any period, though. I don't suppose you got any clues as to age?" Pippa's almost as sarcastic as I am when she wants to be.

"I wasn't wasting my life force checking if there was a simpler option, like getting you to do my work for me."

Luk grins at that. I kick his ankle as Pippa huffs down the phone. *"Fine. I'll research it and call you back."*

She phones me back half an hour later, just as I'm halfway through my pint. *"Murder."*

⁂

Back in the basement office, everything seems to have gone quiet. It's always a bit worrying when that happens.

"Samantha Drew!"

That brings the poltergeist out as if kicked. "Vengeance!"

"Robin Smalls was arrested for your murder and hanged in 1863! Vengeance has been done."

"No!" A wastepaper bin bounces off my shield, shedding paper. "No!"

I glare. "You were buried!" A decent Christian burial often stops potential ghosts, if only because they believe it does. "He got hanged. Case closed."

"No! No!"

"Seriously?" I fold my arms and glare. "What more can you do for vengeance than six feet of hemp rope and a serious neck-ache?"

"Vengeance!"

"Samantha Drew! Samantha Drew! Samantha Drew! I command you to lay your vengeance to rest and to sleep in the land of the dead!"

It doesn't always work, but it usually does something. But this time, she's fighting me. I can see the figure in the centre of the room shrinking, but it's still there.

For a moment, everything's still.

And then the sheets of paper on the floor shift a few inches, and I can see the figure stirring again. It didn't work.

"That's it," I mutter. "I'm calling in the professionals."

⁂

I sit in the hallway outside while the priest does her stuff. I don't entirely see eye to eye with her—mostly because she considers me a sarcastic transgender bitch and I consider her a hide-bound conservative idiot. That said, we're each useful to the other, mostly because she deals with the ghosts that aren't listening to me and vice versa.

Although I do sometimes wonder if she gives me things just because she doesn't want to wander around in the sewers or some such. I get all the fun jobs.

I can hear the thuds and bangs of items moving, along with muffled words. I'm guessing they're decent church-y words rather than swear words—that's something the Reverend also Does Not Approve Of. My reaction to her disapproval possibly doesn't help.

That said, the ghost in that office doesn't appear to be listening to her words any more than it listened to mine. After another ten minutes of bangs, thuds and some louder words, the Reverend comes out, looking quite pale. "It doesn't appear to have been successful."

I stick my head around the office door. Things are still flying everywhere.

I lose my temper.

"What the hell is up with you?" I yell at the apparition in the middle of the room, putting a burst of life into my words. I hate doing it as it takes the strength away from me, but it should give the poltergeist enough strength—and sanity—to actually make sense.

In amongst the screams of vengeance, I hear a laugh. It's the sound of someone enjoying themselves.

Oh, great.

"That's it!" I snap as papers and objects start to whirl around the room again. "I'm calling in the boss."

※ ※ ※

The entrance to the London franchise of the Underworld is in Starbucks on Fleet Street. I know this because I've previously had reason to go there on...let's go for business. That's non-specific enough.

It also means that when I walk in the door, the barista behind the counter goes white.

"Relax," I say. "I'm here to visit the boss."

As I had hoped, he waves me towards the staff entrance without a murmur, I assume hoping that the thugs and traps on the other side will deal with me. Unfortunately for him, I've gained a few new tricks since I last had reason to visit the Land of the Dead.

I step through the door and vanish.

To everyone else, I'm not there. To me, everything goes glassy. Light bends around me, and I grin. That's the hard bit.

The rest of the safeguards simply don't apply. I walk down a set of wide stairs, ignoring the lingering thugs and other assorted nasties, and slide past the dozing three-headed dog. The next thing is the river, which is a bit more of a problem. My tattoo, which gives me my invisibility, doesn't mask my soul...but I do have payment.

Charon gives me a smile as I walk down the dock jutting out into the stinking river. She's dressed as a Venetian gondolier today. "Nice hat," I tell her.

"Thanks! It was in the sale. Didn't you see the picture I posted?" Charon's a friend, surprisingly—or a pen-pal, more likely. She's got a smartphone someplace under that neat suit, and is weirdly good for technology for a thousand-year old psychopomp. Everyone to their own, I guess.

"I've been working today," I say as I step into the boat. "Does it come in purple?"

"I'll check for you. Are you here to pick someone up?" she asks as I tip two coins into her hand.

"Nope, here to see the boss."

She gives me a funny face, sticking her tongue out. "Wow, you're in for it. No-one sees the boss these days."

"Why?"

"She's got lackeys, hasn't she? Too busy to see us minions."

"What happened to personal service?" I moan. "Well, I've got a complaint, so tough."

"Rather you than me! When are we going clubbing again?"

"When's your next evening off?"

Such important matters get us across the river, and I give Charon a wave as she heads back over to the other side. She'll come back to pick me up, or at least she'd better. I don't fancy swimming in that gunk.

The Underworld is actually, once you get past the barriers and the stink-filled Styx, surprisingly light and airy. Most ghosts stay in the earth, sleeping deeper and deeper in the ground as they get older and older, and fading as the years pass. It's only a few who come down here; restless ghosts who won't stay asleep, or disturbed spirits who don't have a place to rest. And the job of collecting those falls to Death.

Who, apparently, has not been doing her job.

I haven't met my local Death yet. As someone who does deal with the Other Side—reluctantly, and with a wide variety of swear words—I have met some of her Collectors. But ideally, the souls of those whose lives have ended should be picked up fairly pronto, and I'd like to know why Samantha Drew hasn't yet been picked up. Two hundred years is long enough for anyone to get around to their to-do list.

The explanation for that is pretty obvious at the point I step into the main room, which has clean walls and a high, glass-domed ceiling. There's a variety of monsters and things...look, that's the best I can do...lounging on chairs at desks. There's a number of hovering screens with a variety of games showing, and one scar-riddled heap of muscle is even reading a book. It's a hive of peace and quiet.

What is not happening is work.

I glance around. There's a large set of double doors at one end, and a large single one with a polished handle the other way. Guess which one I think is Death's office?

I'm not great at illusion, but good enough that I can keep the door 'shut' as I go through it. There's a long white corridor on the other side, and I wait for a moment to check none of the monsters behind me have twigged. When nothing comes after me, I head down the corridor.

The door at the other end has a glass panel in it; very modern. I glance through to see what looks like a standard office and grin to myself.

And I knock. Hey, I can be polite sometimes.

"Come in," a voice calls.

I open the door and let myself in.

There's a woman sitting at the desk; she's got high cheekbones, hair so blonde and fine it looks almost like spider silk, and she's dressed in a black hoodie with Ryuk from *Death Note* on the front. She's also got her elbows on the desk, engrossed in her smartphone.

"Put it there," she says, waving a hand at a stacked in-tray.

"I've got some work for you." I stop in front of the desk.

"Yeah, later." She doesn't look up from her phone. "I'm sorta busy right now."

My fist abruptly winds into her hoodie, and as she looks up from her phone I yank her forward until I'm nose-to-nose across the desk with this angelic vision. "Get un-busy."

"Get off me!"

"Or what?" I ask, my voice low. Much to my annoyance I always revert to my lower register when I'm angry, but in this case the growl seems to be helping. "Skuld hasn't ended my life yet, so you can't collect my soul. What else have you got, lazybones?"

She turns into the Gothic Death, skeletal and grinning. But my fist is still wound around the neck of her shroud, and I'm not fazed by things like skulls. When you've faced down some of the stuff in Faerieland, a skull's easy.

"Try again," I snarl at her. "Or get off your ass and actually collect a soul that's been hanging around for two hundred years waiting for your sorry butt."

She tries one of the Otherworld monsters. I do step back, but only so I can hold it at arm's length. There's only so close you want to be to gunky tentacles and something that smells like sewage.

"This is pissing me off," I inform her. "Either get your butt in gear or get those idiots outside in gear, I don't care. But someone is coming back up with me to collect this soul."

She goes back to the angelic innocence, glaring back at me. "You are rude!"

"You're lazy." I let her hoodie go and she flumps back into the chair. "But I'm not the one causing issues in the real world."

"Ugh, fine!" Death glares at me, picking her smartphone up from the desk with one hand and trying to pat her hair back into some sort of order with the other. "It's not my fault, anyway. I delegate. It means everyone else should be doing it."

"Well, they're not. I don't care if you carry on playing Candy Crush as long as you kick some ass first."

The guilty look on her face says I was right with that hit. She changes it to a glare, then stands up and strides towards the door. "Fine."

The subsequent chewing-out is one of the best that I have ever seen in my entire life. It's possibly the only one which ever involved Death turning into a smartly-dressed business-woman, a dragon, a slime monster and a Demon in short order, and it's certainly the first that used insults so ancient they don't exist in modern language.

At the end, Death turns to me. "There. Please let me know if there are any further concerns."

I turn to the shell-shocked Collectors with a smile forming on my face as the office door slams. "Hi, guys. I know you've got lists, but I want to put someone to the top of one. Who's up for helping?"

☠ ☠ ☠

It's the junior member of the office who draws the short straw: a soul named Darius who is about seven foot tall and almost as wide. He's obviously understood some of the insults—and certainly understood the dragon—as he's very quiet during the journey back to the surface. It's only as we walk towards Lincoln's Inn that he dares to ask, "Who are we collecting?"

"*You're* collecting the spirit of a woman named Samantha Drew, who died in 1863," I inform him. "She's currently being a downright nuisance and we'd like her to leave."

"Yes, ma'am."

"Have you got a direct contact number?" I ask thoughtfully.

"No, ma'am."

"Get a mobile and ask Charon what plan she's on. I want one of you on direct dial for next time I have this issue."

"Uh, the rules say—"

I give him an amused look.

"Yes, ma'am."

As a Collector, he's invisible unless he wants to show himself, and my tattoo means I don't have any visibility problems. We confuse the receptionist with a door that opens by itself but get down into the basement with no problems. I open the door for Darius and step in after him.

He takes in the chaos and then looks at the spirit still hovering in the centre of the room. "Samantha Drew, it is time to sleep."

"No no no—"

I follow my well-tuned survival instinct and step outside the room at that point. Luckily most of the fighting is done in the spirit world, but I still don't need to be hit by anything that does happen to be flying around.

There's thuds. Crashes. Bangs. Two voices raised in argument, one half-mad and the other one taking the opportunity to get a lot of annoyance and frustration out. Well, he has been forced to do his job after however many years of laziness. That's gotta suck.

And then there's silence.

I unfold from the wall and stick my head around the door. The office is still a mess, but there's no longer floating objects, no spirit, and no Darius.

Good. I shut the door behind me and head back outside.

Luk picks up the phone on the third ring. "*Yo.*"

"That was not a 'simple' hundred quid. I want double."

"*I already agreed to it!*"

"Then you can kiss my ass for any future help. I had to talk to Death."

There's a moment of silence from Luk, and then, "*All right. I'll have a chat. All sorted?*"

"She's gone."

"*I bet you could murder a curry, then.*"

I have to smile. He knows me well. "After a day talking to ghosts, priests and Death? A curry is exactly what I need."

THE WORLD DOESN'T END, EVEN WHEN IT SHOULD
by Michelle Ann King

Yes, it was morally ambiguous. Potentially blasphemous, depending on your religious affiliation (although what was Lazarus, really, if not a zombie?), and of course, highly illegal. But since when had any of that stopped anybody?

Lucy wasn't some kind of anarchist—she believed in the need for rules and principles as much as the next civilised person. But it was her dad. What was she supposed to do? It all looks very different when someone you love is at stake.

She met up with Ballard at three in the morning, in the car park of a disused warehouse in Rainham. The whole area was empty, overgrown, and most importantly, not considered worthy of CCTV.

Lucy got out of the car and walked over to Ballard's Jeep. He opened the back and stepped out of the way so that she could inspect the zombie. It was a male, about fifty or so when he'd died by the look of it. He was grey and just starting to flake. A dry, musty smell came off him. Not unpleasant, just a bit stale. Like opening a dark cupboard where you'd kept old, forgotten spices.

"There's a bit of wear and tear," Ballard said. "But he's only done small stuff. Asthma, diabetes, that sort of thing. Nothing major, nothing life-threatening. There's enough juice in him for what you need."

"What's his name?" Lucy asked.

Ballard gave her a look, but pulled a sheet of paper out of his jacket and gave it a cursory glance. "Atkinson."

"His first name."

The look turned to amusement. "He's not going to answer to it, you know."

"Tell me anyway."

He shrugged and checked the form again. "Gilbert."

She wanted to tell Gilbert that she was sorry he was being treated like second-hand goods in a car boot sale, but she didn't want to say it in front of Ballard. So she kept her mouth shut and handed over the money.

Ballard opened the sports bag, rummaged around in the bundles of notes, and zipped it up again. He chucked it on the passenger seat then came back and helped her heave Gilbert out of the Jeep and into the boot of her Volvo. The zombie was purring.

Ballard crossed his arms and looked away. "I wish they wouldn't do that," he said. "It's creepy."

"We're bodysnatchers. I don't think we've got any right to complain about creepy."

She slammed the boot shut, and Ballard went back to his car.

"Pleasure doing business with you, Ma'am." He gave her a quick salute. "Please do think of us again, for all your zombie needs."

"I hope not to have any more," she said, and they both drove away.

⚝⚝⚝

She unloaded Gilbert in the garage and got him to sit with his back against the wall, next to a broken lawnmower. He was very well-behaved.

You heard stories, sometimes, where it all went horribly wrong. But almost always, it turned out that they'd been murder victims. Violent death didn't make for a viable zombie. Which was probably for the best, really.

Lucy liked to think she would never have gone that far, but did anyone ever really know what they were capable of?

Her father was asleep on the sofa when she went to check, the TV still cycling through old *Red Dwarf* repeats. She turned it off and pulled the blanket over his shoulders. He struggled with the stairs these days and slept in the lounge more often than not, but he wouldn't let her officially turn it into a bedroom. As if that would be giving in. Making it real. And Ervin hadn't always enjoyed a fruitful relationship with reality.

Lucy kept a complete set of his novels down there, on the shelf in the alcove. Something else he objected to, something else she ignored his wishes about. He said print books were pointless and old-fashioned. She said he was missing the point—print books weren't for reading. Maybe that was something a writer just couldn't relate to.

It amused her, in a not-really-funny-at-all kind of way, how much of an anti-climax the zombie apocalypse had ended up being. And that her father, of all people, should have been so squeamish about it.

In the early days, a lot of people had phoned the house looking for advice. Mostly fans, but quite a few journalists, too. A couple of police officers. And, she was pretty sure, the Health Secretary.

"But I just made it up," Ervin told them, sounding plaintively bewildered. "They're just stories. It wasn't supposed to be real."

Apparently, the same thing had happened to various people in America, including George Romero and the actor who played the lead role in *The Walking Dead*. Maybe it wasn't that strange, really. When life imitated art, who were you going to turn to?

And some things were consistent with the fiction—decapitation, for example. Head shots. Take out the brain, destroy the zombie. And the initial panic. That had been very similar to what you saw on the shows, in the comics, in the books.

But it hadn't taken long for people to realise that real zombies didn't actually want to eat people. Instead, they healed them. Which had probably turned out to be the most surprising thing of all. Nobody had seen that coming. Not even her father, in as much as a single short story.

⚜⚜⚜

"This isn't right," Ervin said. He backed away from the garage door, his hand covering his mouth. "You shouldn't have done this."

"I know," Lucy said. "But a man who's never smoked shouldn't get lung cancer, either. Things are always happening that shouldn't. That's how life works."

"Where—how—"

"The usual. Money. Connections. More money. It didn't hurt that you're moderately famous. At least two of the middlemen were big fans."

He went to the window and peered out between the slats of the blind, scanning the street.

"Looking for police cars? They won't be coming. They're in on it. You have to know that, don't you?"

Ervin sank down on the sofa and put his head in his hands. "Who is—was—he?"

"His name is Gilbert Atkinson. That's all I know."

"How did he die?"

"I don't know."

"Where did he live?"

"I don't know."

137

"Does he have family?"

"I don't know, Dad. I don't want to know. Nor do you."

"This isn't right."

Lucy said nothing. She went back to the garage door and looked through the glass panel. Gilbert was still sitting where she'd left him. A spider had begun building a web in his hair.

Ervin followed her. "I told you I didn't want this."

She turned around. "You also told me you weren't going to have chemotherapy, either. What was I supposed to do?"

"Respect my wishes?"

"Watch you die, you mean."

Ervin rubbed his hand over his head. "I never wanted you to have to go through anything like this, I really didn't. But when your time's up, it's up."

"Bollocks. I'm sorry, Dad, but bollocks. If that was true, why would we even have hospitals? Why would medicine exist? Leaving the zombies out of it entirely, why would we do any of it? And don't try to give me 'it's unnatural,' either. So are drugs, pacemakers, organ transplants, the lot. All of modern life is unnatural. People who are paralysed can operate computers with their thoughts. How is a zombie any more unnatural than that?"

"It kills them."

"It uses them. You can't kill what's already dead." She yanked open the garage door. The zombie didn't react. "Gilbert, the actual, human Gilbert, is long gone. He's not in there. You're not hurting him. You're not using up his soul, or whatever nonsense it is they're coming out with on the telly these days."

"You don't know that."

"I believe it. That's good enough." She walked over to the zombie and grabbed his arm. It was firm, solid. "Up," she said, and pulled. He got to his feet in a surprisingly fluid, graceful movement.

"Okay, so we don't know why, or how, this is happening. But it is. He can save you, Dad, so why not let him? Maybe this is his purpose. Maybe it's what he's back here to do. Maybe it's how he's going to buy his way into paradise."

The zombie's head turned towards the sound of her voice.

"I don't know whether that's true," she went on, "but I don't know that it isn't, either. And nor do you. So why not believe it? Why not, Dad?"

Ervin had his eyes closed. He shook his head, and a tear gathered under his eyelashes. It slowly slid down his stubbled cheek.

Gilbert's milky eyes tracked its progress.

On first glance, Lucy's room was as neat and ordered as ever. But there were subtle signs. He'd got better at searching it since her teenage years, but she could still tell.

"What were you looking for?" she asked. "It's not like I hide my weed from you anymore."

"Looking for something I didn't find," he said, and she thought of her mother's jewellery box on the cabinet, just a hairsbreadth misaligned.

"Did you sell it all?" he said. "How much, Lucy? How much did it cost you?"

He had his hands on his hips and his angry parent face on, which almost made her smile. That, he definitely hadn't got any better at.

She was supposed to drop her head, be unable to meet his eyes. Be nervous, remorseful. Ashamed.

But she hadn't been any of those things for a long time. She wasn't sure she would remember how.

She lifted her chin and stared at him. "Less than it'll cost me to bury you. Or do I assume you'd rather be cremated?"

His shoulders hunched, and he looked away. "You spent the past thirty years writing about death," she said. "Don't tell me you're going to get skittish about the particulars now. Shall we talk about the music for the service? What clothes you want me to dress you in?"

He winced.

Lucy understood the comforts of denial, of course she did. But the time for comfort was gone.

"Tough love," she said. "You used to think that was a great idea."

❦❦❦

Things Lucy learned from various news sources on the internet:

The zombies were a sign that Judgement Day was imminent, and she should repent in order to save her soul.

The zombies were a satanic inversion of the Rapture brought on by humanity's collective slide into sin, and it was way too late to save anyone's soul.

The zombies were incubators for aliens, the first step in a plan to invade and enslave the human race. Souls were irrelevant.

Drug companies had been trying to find a cure for the ageing process, and it had gone wrong.

The military had been trying to create unkillable soldiers, and it had gone wrong.

The President of the United States had become a zombie, and nobody had noticed.

139

Gilbert Atkinson, Catering and Hospitality Manager, 53, died of a heart attack during a performance of 'We Will Rock You' at the Dominion Theatre. Mr. Atkinson was survived by his wife, Emily, and their two daughters. A service was held at St Michael's in the Field. No flowers. Donations to the British Heart Foundation.

The Health Secretary reminded the nation that so-called 'revivification treatment' was still unregulated and officially unproven and confirmed there were no plans to make it available on the NHS.

The Home Secretary decried reports of a 'zombie shortage' as gross media sensationalism, and hotly denied allegations that the government was colluding in the stockpiling of zombie resources for the sole use of senior politicians, celebrities, and footballers.

The tabloids reported that an unnamed reality TV star was allegedly keeping a 'menagerie' of zombies in the grounds of her Surrey mansion as an organic alternative to plastic surgery. Neighbours were said to be concerned about the effect on property values.

※ ※ ※

Ervin moved out of his bedroom and into the lounge. He didn't speak to Lucy about it. He didn't speak to Lucy about anything.

Lucy received an email from a man in HR advising her that she'd exceeded the company's allowance for compassionate leave. She didn't reply.

Gilbert sat in the garage. Occasionally, he hummed Queen songs quietly to himself.

※ ※ ※

Things Lucy had learned from her father's novels:
Pragmatism gets better results than emotion.
Extreme situations call for extreme solutions.
The end justifies the means.
It's always easier on the dead than the living.
Life goes on: the world doesn't end, even when it should.

※ ※ ※

Last Will and Testament, signed and witnessed. Insurance policies, savings account details, finance agreement for the Volvo. Illegal barbiturates, prescription anti-emetics, cheap alcohol.

Lucy laid these items out on the dining table in neat rows. Ervin stared at them and shook his head, his eyes wide and his face pale.

"It's all about the state of mind," she said. "There's no violence, this way. It's a very peaceful method. Dignified. Plus, I've been meditating regularly. I have no doubt that I will make a highly effective zombie."

"You wouldn't," he said.

"No flowers. Donations to the British Heart Foundation."

"You wouldn't," he said again. It came out in a whisper.

"It's one thing, refusing Gilbert. But would you turn me away too, when I've sacrificed myself to save you? I don't think so. I don't think even you can be that heartless."

"That's—that's—"

She smiled. "I think the phrase you're looking for is emotional blackmail. It's usually quite an effective technique. But if I'm wrong, then you can sell us both. Me and Gilbert. There's a card here for a man called Ballard. He'll get you a good price. Donate the money if you don't want it."

"Lucy—"

"I'll save your life. Or if not, I'll save someone else's. You'll get over it. Or if not, you'll die. It all amounts to the same thing in the end."

Ervin let his head drop. "I've been a bad father."

She put her hand on his shoulder. "Yes. But it doesn't mean I don't love you."

He leaned on the table and coughed, long and harsh. The flecks of blood were bright against the white tissue he held to his mouth.

Lucy picked up the first bottle of pills and flipped off the cap.

"Okay," he said. It sounded broken. "Okay."

⚇⚇⚇

Lucy helped Ervin to the garage and settled him on the mattress. Gilbert was sitting with his legs stretched out and his back against the wall. He was still purring.

STAY DOWN, RUSTY

by Somer Canon

The sound of the ice settling in her glass startled her back into the moment. She drained the remaining iced tea and looked out onto the dusty, grassless yard and the two-lane road chewed up into potholes by the speeding coal trucks.

The secondhand chair creaked and cracked when she stood, and she knew that the piece of junk's days were numbered. She couldn't afford another, not even secondhand, and she'd have to make her tired bones settle onto the concrete porch stairs if she wanted to sit outside.

She looked nervously down at Rusty, who had just come home again. Rusty was her son Mikey's dog. A small rabbit beagle, she assumed, he sat in front of the dirty screen door, blocking her way into the house. Normally, she'd kick the beast, but she dared not do that now.

And she couldn't call Mikey to move him. Mikey was dead. But, Rusty was supposed to be dead too.

When Len ran off and left her all alone with Mikey and a pile of bills, she knew that it was going to be tough. She never graduated high school, had instead been working menial jobs her whole adult life. When Len left, she couldn't afford the rent on the house any longer and had to move to a parked trailer on Gregory's Run Road, her and Mikey and that dog that Len had gotten before he left. She worked as a waitress, at a gas station, and most recently at the grocery store working register. It was all thankless work, lorded over by asshole managers who thought themselves better than the people in her position. She worked full-time on her feet and then had to come home to a boy with no dad. So if she wasn't always at her best, she maybe had good

143

reason for it.

Mikey was ten and starting to hang with a smartass crowd at school. His grades were in the toilet, he caused trouble, and the teachers all stared her down balefully as if it were her fault. When she would confront Mikey about his behavior, she would get a rude reply, or he would go to his room and slam the door. She'd watch television to cool down or eat an entire pizza by herself. Anything to get some comfort in her shit pile of a world.

When Mikey brought home a note from school saying that he had been suspended for fighting, she tried talking to him, tried making him understand that she couldn't afford a babysitter, that she couldn't have him causing so much trouble.

"Shut up, you fat cow!" Mikey had screamed at her.

As if on reflex, she had hit him. Hard enough that he had fallen down. She regretted it immediately, until he started screaming at her, calling her horrible things. There were words coming out of her son's mouth that Len had screamed at her many times in their marriage. Her temper got the best of her, and she reached down and pulled her still young son up by the collar of his shirt and clocked him on the side of the face with a closed fist. His head rocked back and his ranting stopped. Shocked at her own horrible behavior, she released Mikey's shirt and reached out to stroke the side of his face that would surely be sporting a bruise soon.

"I hate you!" Mikey screamed, opening the screen door and running outside.

She was hot on his heels, begging him to come back and apologizing profusely. He ran away from her, down the porch steps, across the dusty yard, and into the road where he hadn't seen the speeding coal truck approaching.

"MIKEY!"

She watched as the truck barreled over her son, his body tossing about beneath the truck, flinging around as if it weighed nothing between the massive tires. The loud brakes on the truck engaged, and all movement stopped. She ran to the truck and looked under it, hoping against hope that she would see movement from Mikey, but there was none. Later, she was thankful that the darkness under the truck had kept her from seeing anything definite. She could tell that Mikey's body was twisted and disjointed, crushed and oozing fluids onto the battered road, but it was mostly shadow.

She got a short break from work to bury her child. Len couldn't be reached, not even by his family, so she did it by herself. There was no peace at home. Rusty would sit by Mikey's bedroom door and paw at it, whining. She tried leaving the door open so that the dog could go in and out as he pleased, but he stayed by the doorway whining, always whining.

Mikey's death was an accident. Rusty's was very much on purpose.

She'd started back to work and was trying to deal with her guilt over Mikey. She was trying to watch television, and Rusty wouldn't shut up. She had gotten up once and kicked the dog, trying to shoo him outside, but he wouldn't go. She had screamed at him to shut up and had huffed her way back to the couch and her bag of Burger King.

He wouldn't stop, and soon he was howling. She had stomped to the dog and kicked it again. Rusty yelped and cowered, and she turned to walk away, and again he whined. She spun and started kicking and stomping the dog. She was still wearing the sturdy sneakers that she wore to work and her foot fell heavily on the dog's body, back and head, with less and less noise coming with each footfall. She didn't realize that she'd been screaming until all was still and she realized that her throat hurt. She went to the sink and spat out a blob of crimson mucus.

Rusty was still breathing, although with great effort, so she took the large cast iron skillet that her grandmother had given her and bashed the dog's head until it was caved in. She buried him in the loose dirt beside the trailer, where she had planned to plant tomatoes someday, finished her Burger King, and went to bed.

It was her most restful night in months.

But the next night, as she was taking the garbage out to the bins, she heard a noise and he was there. Rusty, sitting behind her, staring. He looked dirty but otherwise normal. He didn't appear to be disfigured and beaten like he had when she had buried him.

Afraid to turn her back on the small dog, she backed to the place in the dirt where the dog was supposed to be, and the dirt was as she had left it, the footprint of her work sneaker still indented at the top where she had given a final stomp.

"It's a different dog," she thought.

She walked closer to the dog, and it stood and bared its teeth at her in warning. She put her hands up in a gesture of peace and studied the dog. She had never liked Rusty, thought he smelled bad, and she hated having dog shit dotting her yard, making the whole world stink of it in the warm months, but she knew the dog when she saw him. The dog before her was Rusty, she knew it as surely as she'd have known anybody that she had lived with for four years.

She backed away, the dog following closely. When she opened the door to go inside, the dog darted past her and went in. Instead of going to Mikey's room, the dog sat down beside the couch and stared at her. She sat on the opposite end and stared back at the dog. She tried putting her hand out, like she sometimes did, expecting Rusty to come and lick her hand, but the dog stayed still and stared at her.

She tried to ignore the dog and focus on the television, as she always did when she was stressed. It didn't work. She could feel a weight to the dog's gaze on her. She was frightened, but that fear soon turned to anger.

"Quit looking at me, you damned dog!"

There was no response. The dog kept staring. Her preexisting hatred for the beast sent her over the edge, and in a flash, she was up and stomping the dog again. Its body was much softer this time, much easier to break. When it was still and its eyes stared lifelessly at the floor, she picked it up and carried it to the side yard. She tossed the body to the ground while she got her gardening trowel and again scooped the earth out of the hole. She leapt back and screamed when her digging yielded the original broken body of Rusty, bloodied, head crushed, still in the grave.

She spun on her bottom, looking for the second small, broken body, but there was none. Whatever she had beaten in her living room just a few minutes before was now gone.

When she got home from work the next night, Rusty was sitting on the front porch. She went inside, got a glass of iced tea, and sat down on the porch, wondering why. Why was the dog coming back? Was it a real, physical form or an apparition that gave her the illusion that she was killing it? Would it ever go away?

By the time she had been startled out of her stupor by the ice tinkling in her glass, she was already exhausted, but the dog sat staring at her, not moving.

"Move, Rusty."

It didn't move. Gathering all of her courage, she extended her foot and nudged the dog with her foot. A physical form met her toe, stopping the slight forward momentum. She bent forward and put her hand out, an offering for the dog to sniff. It didn't. Rusty stayed perfectly still, looking up at her with his round, brown eyes. She moved her hand closer, intending to touch him, and the dog bared his teeth, a silent threat.

Huffing, she opened the door and stepped over the small dog. She slammed the door behind her, hoping that she caught the thing, but when she came out of the kitchen with her bag of fast food, it was sitting by the couch again, the same as the night before. She set the food down on the coffee table and went to the bathroom, needing a moment to gather herself. She splashed cold water on her hot and grimy face and stared at herself in the mirror, wondering at the face that had changed so much through the years. Looking away from the hated image, she went back to the living room to find that her food had fallen. When she picked up the bag, it lifted too easily, and she was startled to see that it was empty. She looked for the dog, but it was gone.

"A goddamn ghost dog took my Burger King," she marveled.

Rusty was back the next night, as usual. This time, she was furious. Its presence, and its theft of her previous evening's meal and comfort had gotten on her very last nerve. The dog was sitting by the trailer, in the dirt yard, and she left the gravel path that she was supposed to use to park her car, and she ran over the dog, her car jumping as it rolled over Rusty.

There was no body under her car.

She called in sick the next day, but at four o'clock, she heard the familiar clicking sound of Rusty's paws on the porch. She looked out of the window and there he was, looking at her through the glass. She threw open the door and looked down at the small dog looking up at her.

"Alright, I give. What? What the hell do you want with me, Rusty?"

She stood over the dog, ready to destroy it again, if only for an evening's peace, when it stood and started walking off of the porch. It paused and looked back at her. Understanding, she followed. The dog walked slowly, but with purpose, and she followed silently. A million thoughts were thundering through her head as she followed the dog, not really paying attention to where she was going. Her bare feet trudged through the hot, hard yard, and she realized that she was getting close to the road. She paused, and Rusty, sensing her, turned and looked at her. Scared, she looked down both sides of the road, then back at the dog.

"I hope a truck comes along and runs you over, you mangy sack of crap," she muttered, turning and heading back to the trailer.

"Mom?"

She stopped walking, her heart stopped beating, and all she could hear was Mikey's voice reverberating inside of her skull. A tear rolled down her cheek, and she wrapped her arms around herself. She was too scared to turn around.

A low growl caused her to open her eyes, and she looked down at Rusty standing beside her.

"Get outta here," she said, kicking at him.

"Mommy?"

Her breath caught again, and this time she did turn and fell to her knees. It was Mikey, as solid and clear as his dog, looking at her from the other side of the road. He held his arms out to her, the way he'd done a million times when he was little, wanting his mommy to pick him up. Sobbing, she lurched off of her knees and began walking towards her son, her own arms reaching for him.

She never heard the truck.

147

Olympic Drive

by Eddie Generous

Butterflies square-danced on her guts. Peeking from the corner of an eye, the sight was beautiful. The coral pink sky fell over the mountains far in the horizon. Felicity wanted to express this sentiment. The tongue rubbing against her tongue quieted this urge. Contact was so much better than words. Hands roved in soft exploration.

"Be patient. There's more," whispered Keah.

It was the most romantic date Felicity had ever been on and this despite that it took place on a stainless steel fishing boat. There were rod couplers around the hull and nets stashed in the corners. The orange and red safety jackets made for a soft spot to lie and watch the August sundown in their bathing suits. Bright yellow with navy stripes and lettering. The official colours of the PRU swim team, worn proudly, though neither had taken a class there.

"Enough for me. Come on. You promised. Training's over!" said Felicity, aching for it.

Keah bought into the notion of no fooling around during training. She promised they'd get back to all the good stuff once they'd both made the A-team and not a second sooner. It was never really a question for Keah, her primetime status was a guarantee. She was a star shooting skyward.

The rule helped Felicity take the last spot, bumping off an angry veteran.

What Keah hadn't mentioned was that once the season began, it would be all training. Being less than a second behind the final Olympic spot while still in high school is one hell of a motivator to keep her eyes on Tokyo.

There'd be breaks, short blips, but she lived for one thing and it was not the physical gratification of sex—most nights.

Keah got to her knees and shuffled to the driver's seat. She started the engine. Clunky noise pollution against the otherwise perfect night.

"Now where ya taking me?" Felicity shouted from her seat on the floor, sliding back on a wave of life vests. "Hey, slow down!"

It excited Keah to play a little rough now and then. Felicity was the perfect target. Wound tight, like a stretched elastic band, little things brought the colour up in her cheeks. Blood really pumping, she'd be excited and much more satisfying.

"You'll see!"

"This is amazing. You did this all for me?"

Felicity dripped. Her black hair pressed flat to her scalp, strands hanging over her ivory shoulders. In the soft orange candlelight, she looked almost porcelain.

"No. I brought the candles and wine this morning, but all this stuff is like a tourist hoax. Danny Thole, you know the skinny dude with the shiny head that helps sometimes at the pool? His family runs a scuba business and brings tourists here."

"Oh. Still. It's amazing."

"Yes, and the million-year-dead volcano has a valve under there." Keah pointed to the rocky ring around the steaming pool. Dozens of fat, several hours' dripping, white candles in brass holders lit the scene. "Story is, mutinous pirates hid their treasure down here. They fled when Red Caesar promised all their heads on pikes."

"Wait, his own crew?"

Keah smirked. "Of course. They knew where he'd hidden his treasure."

"Ah, the backstory just makes it hotter." Felicity grinned.

Seeing Keah in her perfect form often was tease enough, but to be only feet away and not touching while the dancing flames sparkled in her deep hazel eyes, against her wet ebony cheeks, was almost painful. Felicity shivered and goose bumps rose.

"Come on," said Keah, holding out her hand and leading Felicity up the rocks.

Wine bottle passed. Suits set aside. Bodies cooked in the hot bath. The wait was over.

The first release was incredible, the second was slightly lesser, and the third was yet to come. Later. There was a second bottle of strawberry wine and still at least half an hour to midnight.

"So what happened to Mr. Caesar?" asked Felicity, afloat, leaning shoulders and back against Keah's breasts.

"Some say Red Caesar died marooned on an island a thousand nautical miles from the coast." Keah adopted a witchy tone. "Others say that he trailed his mutinous traitors to this very cave!" She cackled.

"You goof. But really."

"That's it. Thing he didn't seem to understand was that once he murdered his crew his ship was stuck. One of those mad-with-power situations."

"Be handy to find his treasure. I'm sure there'd be enough to cover tuition," said Felicity.

"I doubt it."

If it wasn't for the partial scholarships and grants, Felicity wouldn't be in university at all. She never asked about Keah's financials. It was unnecessary. If PRU didn't cover her breakfast to bedtime, she'd be someplace else. Still, it was fine to joke about money since everyone else on the team was the daughter of wealth. Most of the school was like that.

"What would you do if you found a treasure, or won a lottery, or whatever? Came into big money?"

Keah thought a moment while gulping down sweet wine from the clear bottle. Felicity let her body float away in search of a seat so that afforded her a sightline to Keah while they spoke.

"The lottery is a gag. It's there to keep folks fantasizing about being Beyoncé without ever working for it."

"All right, what about Red Caesar's treasure?"

"I'd leave that shit alone." Keah wore a serious face for exactly three seconds before busting into a drunken body laugh. "We're dry. Be right back. Dad always has at least a six-pack in the cooler."

Keah had tied the boat to a moor tapped into the rock before they dove down to the entrance of the cave.

"Want me to come with you?" asked Felicity, uncertain how she felt about being in the cave alone, but also knowing that getting up was a pain.

"Stay put and think sexy thoughts. Training starts soon," said Keah, climbing out of the spring pool.

Normally, mention of training would drive Felicity to quiet anger, but she was drunk and horny, and the promise of more fun was enough to abate the grim emotion. Instead of arguing, she watched Keah step away, suit remaining on the rock ledge. The waterproof flashlight clicked alive near the cave's entrance and then quickly disappeared underwater.

Once the sound of another living, breathing soul departed, Felicity recognized the quiet. Only the gentle lapping at the mouth of the cave created a soundtrack. It played alongside the lightly sulphuric smelling bubbles emerging in the pool around her. From somewhere overhead, a gentle breeze wafted through cracks in the stone.

The cave was a corner to a much larger structure. An island of birds and a few bears, though nobody knew exactly how they got there. It would be too far to swim, too far by a goodly sum. They were there nonetheless.

Time alone was time to think. She and Keah weren't officially dating, but neither saw anyone else. And when it came time, if the time ever came, what then?

"You're being ridiculous," Felicity whispered to the thought. What was time, really? Life isn't a board game.

She closed her eyes.

What was taking Keah?

Did they really need the beer?

The sounds around Felicity seemed to sense her budding discomfort, fed it and heightened it. The lapping water increased its activity. The waft became a gust. The bubbles around her quickened.

"Come on, Keah."

Felicity stared at the black hole surrounded by the dripping white candles and imagined the flashlight rising. Over and over, from the dark came the light, if only in her mind.

There was a snap, like a tree felled in a storm, and the life drained from the cave. The lapping stalled, the bubbles ceased, and the whistling gust stilled.

Like sandpaper played over soft vocal folds. "Red is the captain," said a single, quiet voice.

"Keah? Keah, stop it."

A chorus of rusty voices replied with whispers, *"Deed-yay-way."*

"Ha! Ha! Real funny, Keah!"

A little louder: "The lord of blade."

"Creed-yay-way."

"I'm not scared! This is stupid, so you can come out now!"

Light shined dimly from the still waters at the mouth of the cave and Felicity wore a vengeful grin. She'd get her for this.

"Red is the captain."

"Lead-yay-way."

"Ugh, so funny! You're a jerk!" said Felicity waiting for the pirate play to continue.

It was obviously something the scuba leader used to thrill the tourists. The sounds ceased and the light from the mouth breached the surface. Keah rose, a six-pack of Budweiser in one hand and the little flashlight in the other.

"I can't believe you did that!"

Keah climbed out of the water and frowned. Felicity was in no mood to stick around and climbed out, grabbing her suit along the way.

"What's wrong?" Keah asked.

"I know you like to get a rise out of me, but the pirate stuff isn't funny."

"What...no, don't be mad. I didn't mean to take so long. I thought I'd better check our phones and... No, don't get dressed. We're having a good time. I'm sorry I took so long."

"Ha! I don't care about how long you took! You're still trying to trick me! Come on. Lead the way. Back to the boat."

Felicity held out Keah's suit to her. Keah pouted, confused, but accepted the suit.

"I'm not trying to trick you. I'm sorry about going fast in the boat. Is that what this is all about?"

"Nice try!" Felicity had become livid.

"Nice try at what?" Keah screeched back.

Booming, scraping, terrible. "Master of the trade!"

"*Bleed-yay-way!*"

"Red is the captain!"

"*Feed-yay-way!*"

"What the hell is that?" Keah asked, gripping her suit to her chest.

"Yeah right!" Felicity shouted, though not certain there was a game to be had. Not anymore.

The candles fizzled as if drenched by an invisible wave. Pure dark. Felicity reached for Keah's grip and knew then that whatever was upon them was not the doing of a playful lover. Silence reigned in the cave.

"Why did you bring us here?" Felicity carried tears in her voice.

"It's... People come here all the time," Keah whined.

Low, but no less grating, the solitary lead returned to the beginning. "Red is the captain."

"*Deed-yay-way,*" chimed the chorus.

Tiny sparks flashed upon the candlewicks.

"Lord of the blade."

"*Creed-yay-way.*"

The sparks crackled, drying away the seawater.

"Red is the captain."

"*Lead-yay-way.*"

Minute flames flickered.

"Master of the trade."

"*Bleed-yay-way.*"

The flames took hold and gentle light seeped.

"Red is the captain."

"*Feed-yay-way.*"

Oranges, yellows, and reds painted the cave in prismatic glow. Shadows danced behind the two dozen shimmery men packed into the space, backs lining the walls. Unreal, donning the archaic and filthy garb of souls centuries gone. Ghastly grinning mouths rode amid pale beards, beneath deep-socketed eyes, dark and foreboding gazes. Dated felt hats. Hooks for hands. Leather purses. Swords. Daggers. Flintlock pistols.

Felicity screamed. Keah mouthed haplessly like a landed fish.

"Ey, gold ye bade," said the rough whisper of the man stepping toward the lovers.

A walking cliché: black eye-patch riding his pale, deep-red moustachioed face. Sneering lips stretched thinly above a scarred chin. Bald head hidden beneath a scarlet bandanna. A jacket of heavy grey material, red threads holding it together. The ominous man limped as he walked. A long crooked sword bounced against his right thigh. Held between his hands was a small wooden chest.

"Ey, gold ye bade," he whispered again, stopping two feet away. The lid of the chest popped open.

Keah nor Felicity had the nerve to look away. Both knew it was him.

"What do you want?" Felicity managed to say, gripping Keah's toned form against her own.

"Ey, gold ye bade," Red Caesar said again.

The crew began stomping a rhythm.

"What do you want from us?" Felicity screamed, her eyes no longer peering into the empty box. She stared at the captain, stared into his lively long-dead eyes.

"Ey, gold ye bade."

"Keah, dive down. There's no way they can keep up," Felicity whispered, inching back toward the mouth of the cave, that wonderful, inviting hole in the floor.

Keah didn't move, her eyes remained pinned on the chest.

"Ey, gold ye bade."

"Come on, Keah!"

Felicity tried to pull Keah. The lover's gaze remained welded to the chest. Keah's eyes flashed, reflecting a metallic canary flicker.

Red Caesar nodded in agreement.

The chest lid flipped closed and the stomping ceased, the chorus chanted, "*Seed-yay-pay.*"

"Come on, Keah!"

Keah finally turned and said three words she'd never said to another woman before, "I love you." Unfortunately for Felicity, she added, "But I need all the help I can get."

"Wha…?" Felicity said no more.

Heavy, the hands on her throat let only gargling sounds and the high screech of limited air passing through windpipe.

Splashed, down into the dark depths.

Felicity's head struggled to gasp from the surface. The effort was feeble. Keah was always the stronger and more willful. Surprise and terror stole hope, stole her tomorrows.

Keah Burr stared out at the crowd from atop the podium for the third time in three days. The tune "Oh Canada" filled the chlorine-scented poolside. The blue swim lanes streamed before her, beneath her high stance.

Pride swelled her heart.

Relief oozed from her pores.

Guilt fought for inches.

Over the past three years, she thought of that chest and the gold medals within and wondered how she would've fared without the seed payment. The thought made her sick. All that risk was an ugly consideration.

Damn the guilt. Right there as she gazed over the awed eyes, those smiling faces, necks craned to peer at the Canadian hero at the top of her game, she decided that during her first interview back on home soil, she would dedicate her victory to her poor lost friend and swim partner, Felicity Bell.

YOU MUST NOT BE YOURSELF
by Joseph Shelton

Above the door of the Chapel Avenue Bookstore was a Bible quote, a little out of place given the dissident bent of the store and her denizens: "…their idols are borne by beasts of burden. The images that are carried about are burdensome, a burden for the weary – Isaiah, 46:1." Though I am still not sure who put it there, or why, I came to think it had special meaning for the Chapel Avenue Book Club, to whose members, three in particular, it ought to have served as a dire warning.

On Sundays the store was only open from 10 p.m. to five in the morning, a peculiarity which caused a great deal of confusion to the people who came in to get a cookbook, celebrity memoir, or paperback bestseller. But then, the store perplexed most people. They would get lost in its piles of dusty books and winding stacks until, bawling like lambs, one of the employees of the store, perhaps I, would have to find them and lead them to safety—that is, the front door, out of which they spill back out into the sunlight, blinking, disoriented, empty-handed.

At some point after the store opened, the Chapel Avenue Club would begin to arrive, one by one. Some of them arrived on bicycles, some drove, and some even walked. The Chapel Avenue Club was mysterious and ancient, having been formed by persons unknown many years before I ever began to work at the bookstore. Maybe even since the 1970s, when the world was new.

I learned to recognize them by their shape, or their walk, in some cases by what they wore, but only sometimes by their face. Often their costume did not admit a view of their face. But I almost never knew them by their name. Names were strictly forbidden in the Chapel Avenue Club. Or, I suppose it would be more accurate to say that *given* names were not allowed.

For instance, I grew to recognize the woman I called the Cave Bear by her the high pitch of her carnal need and her penchant for furs. Whatever character she was playing that night, she would invariably be decked out in minks and stoats. What she wore under that, I was not privy to, as I never took part in the Club's proceedings, save to facilitate their liaisons by keeping the store open.

The manner by which I came into the job is a long story, and one which is not of interest to the main part of this tale, but suffice it to say that I am more or less unemployable in any other setting. My interests have never overlapped much with those of the world at large, and my degree, expensive though it was, is not likely to secure me any other work.

But it must also be pointed out that I didn't know about the Club when I took the job, nor was I particularly tempted to join in once I was made aware of it. You see, I've always been a bit asexual, and while I do find some things erotic, they are not things which can penetrate or be penetrated, at least not by flesh. I have been moved to near-ecstasy by certain passages in Batailles, and a few phrases of Berlioz, and maybe even by the *idea* of sexual intercourse, but not by the *actual* dynamics of fluid transfer from one soft aperture to another.

But to be a participating member of the Club, one must be caught up in a very specific paraphilic fetish: the intense desire for images and ideas, to actually, physically fuck and suck the bits of literary flotsam and jetsam out of which characters are cobbled.

That night, for instance, the Cave Bear had shown up, dressed in her furs, drunk, as was usual for her, and proclaimed that she was Lady Godiva.

It was early in the evening yet, so her pickings were decidedly slim; a man I knew as Straw Hat was furtively pacing back and forth in the 19th-Century Poetry section, and somewhere in Mid-Century Sci-fi a strange little man wearing a fish-bowl helmet was muttering into the stacks. But Cave Bear was never picky. She went home with Straw Hat within fifteen minutes of arriving. It turned out that Straw Hat was supposed to be the Ancient Mariner, though his head gear was better suited to Walt Whitman, or a Huck Finn gone to seed.

I had heard from David, who you will meet later, that the Cave Bear took them home, but others simply coupled in the store, between shelves, against walls, tucked away in far corners of the shop. Most were sufficiently modest to hide themselves, but a few times they grasped and tangled within sight of my counter. In that case I would try to bury my nose in my paperback and not take notice of their gasping groans.

After the Cave Bear left, I saw *her* for what I thought was the first time. That first night she wore a tattered miniskirt and a t-shirt advertising some rock band. Her hair was cropped short, exposing a long and sinuous neck that reminded me immediately of stone relief depictions of Nefertiti. A large and angular nose which might have dominated someone else's face instead looked quintessential on hers. You might have sliced carrots with her jawbone. She carried a handbag out of which she retrieved a cigarette, already lit as soon as she came in to the store. Of all her many incarnations, this one was particularly striking. She seemed to undulate like a snake.

"Welcome to the Chapel Avenue Bookstore," I said. "Are you a Club member?"

She nodded and took a luxurious drag from her cigarette, which I noticed was a stubby, unfiltered Lucky Strike.

"Thank you. And who are you tonight?" I tapped my pen on the ledger we kept for this purpose. The night being slow, I had thus far only written four or five characters.

"Eurydice."

I nodded and wrote it down in the book, watching as she disappeared, appropriately enough, in the Classical Mythology section.

I knew immediately what David would think of her. David was the only Club member I knew by name. One night in darkest winter, after the Cave Bear had already left, (the Cave Bear who had always been taken with David after they had shared a single night together as, I believe, Dante's beloved Beatrice and Lovecraft's Charles Dexter Ward, an impish concession to David's sometimes macabre taste in literature) David and I struck up a conversation about Victorian erotica and discovered a mutual appreciation for Jessie: *The Confessions of a Fellatrix*. He had, in fact, written a song about it called "Jessie's Delights," for his sometime graduate school band, Bahktin's Carnival.

He asked me how I knew he'd like her.

"She has an insolent bearing, and she looks a little like a boy," I told him. Like most cis males, he prided himself on being outré he was really quite predictable in his tastes.

Now, to be fair, telling David about the woman was breaking one of the rules of the Chapel Avenue Club. In fact, it was breaking the third rule, which said that participants were expected to be sleeping with the character, not the person playing them. I came to understand the Club as a group of people pursuing something like a *reverse exorcism* where the object wasn't to drive out some possessing spirit but to *be* possessed and therefore to drive out one's *self*. In theory, therefore, Eurydice's actual person should have been immaterial. Still, I knew what David liked, and I felt (at the time) there was no harm in making him aware of her.

Of course, I have come to regret telling him all of this. He might still be alive otherwise.

❀❀❀

So it was that the next Sunday David came dressed in a child's Halloween mask, I think it was Shrek, and a wooly sweater under his parka.

"Who?" I asked brusquely, not wishing to let on to the other Club members that we were friends.

"The goblin that walks quietly over the universe." And then, as if by way of explanation, he added, "End to end."

I wrote "Goblin – Howard's End" in the book. Later I added "Chapter 5 – symphony scene," though I will admit that I had to look up the passage to remember its provenance.

It was a relatively busy night. I had already checked in a porcine Duchess of Malfi (Cave Bear), a shy and improbably skinny Leopold Bloom, at least two Esther Greenwoods, and a wiry Hazel Motes dressed in a more-appropriate-than-usual straw hat and clerical collar, not to mention the timid, whey-faced James Bond I had turned away for being, most likely, underage. God knows how he heard about us.

But there was no sign yet of Eurydice.

By 1 a.m. David/Goblin had already defended himself from the pursuit of Cave Bear/Malfi twice, his rebuff leading her drunkenly into the arms of the skinny Bloom.

"Do you think she's coming?" he asked at 1:30.

Once, the bell above the door rang as a confused drunk entered, lured like a moth to the lights. David looked up expectantly. The drunk, seeing the Club members eyeing him from the stacks like cathedral gargoyles, backed out, muttering something about how he "thought it was a fucking bar, not a freak show".

But at 3 a.m., as David was about to give up, a small ginger woman in her mid-forties walked in. She wore a hoodie sweatshirt above a pair of sweatpants and trainers. Her wrists rattled with plastic bangles.

"Who are you," I asked.

"Eurydice."

After I had written down her name and she had settled into the mythology section, David came over and hissed in my ear.

"Not exactly as described."

"That's not her," I said. "At least, I don't think so. Not unless she can transform or something"—later, of course, I discovered this was, in fact, the truth—"Eurydice's a popular character after all. There's nothing like mythic tragedy to get the juices flowing."

After another hour of pacing David resigned himself to the idea that *his* Eurydice (he had already begun to think of her *as* his) wasn't coming. He slinked off to the mythology section to investigate this *other* Eurydice instead.

And as I didn't see him again that evening, I inferred that Eurydice and the Goblin succeeded in crossing time, space, and reams of pages to meet.

⚜⚜⚜

Next Sunday night, I asked David how it had gone.

"It went well. She stayed in character the entire time, so I did too. Do you know how difficult it is to pretend to be a musical, marching Goblin? To try and figure out what one would say as it fucks?"

Perhaps because of those difficulties David had, this week, selected an easier character to inhabit. His Lady Chatterley's lover, Oliver Mellors, consisted mostly of guttural noises delivered in a mock-Scottish accent in addition to a kilt he told he me had found at a Goodwill.

"Has the *real* Eurydice shown up yet?" he asked.

"The *real* one," I grumbled. "Mind the rules. All of the characters are real."

"Yeah, yeah. You know what I mean."

"No, I haven't seen her. But there's another Eurydice."

"*Another one?*"

This time Eurydice was a spectacularly tall African-American woman with a nose ring and dreadlocks and a t-shirt espousing the virtues of the organic co-op. And once again, despite her not being the woman I described to him, David was sufficiently charmed to pursue her. She was reluctant at first, but by the end of the night Eurydice and Oliver Mellors had coupled at least twice in the mythology section, which by virtue of being back to back with the travel section opposite the cash register, allowed me to hear every moment. Were I equipped to be turned on, or alternately, embarrassed, I might have blushed. As it is I simply listened with minor interest as she quietly moaned and he expressed himself in croaking and not-quite-Scottish sounding monosyllables.

The next few weeks proceeded that way, each time with David donning some new persona and each week meeting a new Eurydice. He began, in that way, to collect Eurydices. At the same time, he began to notice certain similarities between them. They all had a fondness for musicians. They were all sad. They all had the same mournful look in their eyes, and all of their eyes were a striking icy blue.

⚜⚜⚜

I present to the reader an excerpt from a paper David wrote as an undergrad when, as he put it, he was a "not yet constrained by grad school groupthink." We shall begin in media res, forgoing the beginning of his

161

argument for the part you may find germane to what followed. He may not have had her pegged, but I do believe it suggests he must have had some idea how it would all turn out for him, or at least a younger David did.

> Plato called Orpheus's journey to retrieve his bride a "coward's quest." He was, Plato wrote, "lack[ing] the the spirit to die as Alcestis did" (ibid, 179d), and therefore unworthy of the "real" Eurydice. The version of his wife which he saw in the depths was no more than a "wraith" of her true self, and Hades had no intention of ever giving her up. His failure of faith in turning to see her go was symptomatic of his cowardice. The second loss of his love and subsequent disembowelment at the hands of the Thracian Maenads* were only "the penalty he deserved" (ibid, 179d). I suggest an alternate reading of Orpheus's failure. He may well have been a coward, unwilling to die for his wife. To this I present no defense. Rather, I posit that Eurydice *herself* appeared as a wraith, and that it was her choice not to accompany him back to the land of the living. She *knew* he would look behind him. Furthermore, I would like to forward the notion that she *enjoyed* being dead. She was tired of dancing along with Orpheus's lyre, tired of being the object of his affections, and tired of being a character in his story. In Hell she could finally be herself. [Plato. *Plato in Twelve Volumes, Vol. 9*, translated by Harold N. Fowler. Cambridge, MA, Harvard University Press; London, William Heinemann Ltd. 1925.]
> (* Maenads – priestesses of Dionysus, known mostly for their drunken, orgiastic worship, which typically ended violently; i.e. in the decapitation of Pentheus by his own mother, who thought he was a lion.)

At the end of that paragraph someone—I assume his professor—had scrawled "BACK UP WITH EVIDENCE FROM THE TEXT!!!" in red pen. I noticed that his grade for the paper had been a C+.

He showed this paper to me after some weeks of liaising with Eurydices. He handed it to me sheepishly and asked me what I thought. I told him that he was maybe starting to love the character herself, no matter who played her, and he agreed.

☙❧☙❧☙❧

One Sunday near the end of winter Eurydice became a Lebanese man in a muscle t-shirt. Though personal appearances (costumes notwithstanding) were strictly to be ignored, I rather thought he looked more like an Odysseus than a Eurydice. Even so, I could not fail to notice that he had a pair of very striking, ice-blue eyes. I cannot speculate on the amount or intensity of David's homosexual experiences prior to that night, but I can confirm that he did leave with that evening's Eurydice. He was too bashful to talk about it much afterwards, but what little he did say made it apparent that he now believed that all of his Eurydices were, in some fashion, the same person.

I was skeptical. Even so, I played along. "How do you think all of this will end, David?" I asked him. "You'll recall it didn't end so well for Orpheus. Listen, if he, she, *they* really are this figure of classical mythology, what are they doing here? Not just at the store, but on Earth? And if all those people really are Eurydice, wouldn't they have a hell of a laundry bill? Why does she switch bodies? Have you asked them any of this?"

At this he looked shocked, even incensed. "No, of course not. That's against the rules of the Club. You don't ask someone who they really are. The first rule is —"

"I know what it is," I snapped.

David had been a casual member of the Club for a few years now, but I would never have said that he made much of a display of following the Chapel Avenue Club's rules. He had, about a year before, flogged them by dating another Club member, a very pale young woman with a penchant for quilting and bondage, for some six weeks.

"Ok, when you leave here with Eurydice, where do you go? Do you go to a house? Hotel room?"

"No, never. We usually just go to the alley behind the store," he admitted bashfully.

He rubbed his temples. He looked tired, as if he had stayed up all night for a week. His Radiohead t-shirt was dirty, dotted with leopard spots of spilled coffee.

❀❀❀

After that it is difficult to establish the series of events that led to David's death. I only saw what I could from my vantage at the counter of the Chapel Avenue Book Store, and as the action of the story now shifts outside of the store I can only reconstruct them through informed conjecture. Those moved to check this account against the official findings from the police investigation will see that my recollection of these events does not jive with theirs, but the reason for this should be obvious; the police do not often attribute supernatural causes to crimes, even ones in which someone (not just someone, a good friend of mine) is disemboweled and disarticulated by someone seemingly overtaken by a spirit from ancient Greece.

Nevertheless, I can personally attest to certain parts of the story. First, several more Sundays passed much as they had. Someone, usually but not always a woman, registered in the Club's ledger as Eurydice. Second, during that time, the Cave Bear became increasingly aggressive in her unsuccessful pursuit of David. More and more she was drunk on her arrival and somehow drunker upon leaving. Somewhere under her furs she must have kept a flask. It remains unknown, at least to me, whether she knew David was falling in love with someone else, especially whether or not she knew that he was falling in love with multiple people sharing one identity. I can confirm, however, that on the night of David's death she came in to the Chapel Avenue Book Store wearing what appeared to be the skins of fauns and a crown of laurel. She also carried a long staff enwrapped in ivy and tipped with a large pine cone.

"Who?" I asked.

"Agave. The Maenad." She smelled strongly of some kind of cheap cocktail, most probably a couple of liters of Harvey Wallbangers.

Though I tried to hide it, writing it down in the ledger like any other identity, I blanched. I tried to catch David's eye but, as we shall see, he was distracted.

Third, I know that at some point in the intervening weeks he had resolved to talk to Eurydice, and to maybe ask her on a real date. I warned him this was strictly against the rules of the Chapel Avenue Club. We might surmise he intended to ask her that night.

Finally, I can attest that when Eurydice appeared near 4 a.m. she was "dressed" in the body in which I first saw her, the slightly androgynous punky girl that I knew would destroy David. It is to be a perfect storm then, thought I.

That evening David was Cyranno De Bergerac, whose affect he effected through the use of a large plastic nose strapped around his face and a Tudor ruff around his neck. Though tempted, I did not chastise him on the slight anachronism achieved thereby. He also carried a mandolin, a touch of traditional hipster that I think would have embarrassed him in any other context.

All the rest is speculation.

※⁂※

When he saw Eurydice he knew at once it was her. He walked over to her and took her hand. "Madame," he might have said.

I never saw her smile, at least not at my remove, but I imagine she smiled at this.

Once in the alley outside, he played some sweetly sophomoric song he had written her, plucking the chords of the Andalusian Cadence, another anachronism he would have thought might have sounded mythological to her. I imagine she likewise smiled at this.

In the midst of their lovemaking, limbs entangled like vines crawling up a Doric column, the Cave Bear, perhaps eating a shank of raw goat meat, entered the alley. She waited there, in the dark, until they were done and Eurydice gone. Somewhere in there he must have gathered up his courage and asked her.

David, perhaps heartbroken, perhaps elated, headed towards his bicycle. There the Maenad Agave struck him, repeatedly, with the staff (forensic evidence bears this out, as there were bits of conifer pine under the skin of his cheek), and in a holy fury, possessed by the God Dionysus and driven mad by some frenzied lute which only she could hear, she tore him limb from limb.

The policeman who told me about the scene said he was scattered about the alley like streamers at a birthday party.

When the police arrested the Cave Bear the next week, (I imagine) she was dragged away raving something about the west wind, and how there were lions all around her.

❧❧❧

I only saw Eurydice one more time after that, on a Sunday months later, as spring turned to summer. The night was cold but muggy, and she wore the ill-fitting body of a sad old man, eyes wet, sniffling and dabbing at a veiny nose with a wadded handkerchief.

"Who?"

"Eurydice," the old man said quietly, as if in anticipation of my response.

I settled back in my chair and looked at him over the frames of my glasses for a long time.

"I'm sorry, but you're not allowed here anymore."

He nodded, but still he asked, "Why?"

"Because you have broken the rules of the Club. I have too. I used to bend them for a friend, but now that friend is gone. I miss him, and now I realize now why the rules of the Chapel Avenue Club are inviolate. "

The old man bent her head low, looking chastened.

I continued. "You know something about rules, I think. If my friend had followed them, he might still be alive. *If your* friend had followed them, you might have left Hades. Do you understand?"

He nodded. "I told him, you know. I told both of them."

"Maybe you did. Maybe it wasn't your fault what happened. But nevertheless, you broke the most important rule, and so you can't come back."

Eurydice cocked his head as if to ask: which?

"The Chapel Avenue Club is only for pretending, for seeing yourself as someone else in someone else's eyes. It doesn't matter who you choose to be, but you can't come as yourself. The first rule is 'You must not be yourself'."

At this Eurydice nodded once more and turned towards the exit. Then, before she left, she turned back and looked at me through those ancient, watery eyes. She opened this body's mouth to speak but said nothing, only stepped back out into the night, her Hades.

I could hear the old man's shuffling steps on the sidewalk after the bell above the door stopped ringing.

That night, driven by some spirit I dared not name, I decided, for the first time, to try out the Club. I didn't do it out of desire, exactly, certainly not the desire to fornicate. Instead, I did it to be the living expression of a principal. I did it, that first night, to demonstrate to gods and humankind alike that proper observance of the Chapel Avenue Book Club's rules was possible, if only one went about it dispassionately, reverently, even chastely. Finally, I did it to atone.

Who, I asked myself. It was not a decision to be entered into lightly. My pen hovered over the ledger for a long while before I wrote anything down.

WAKING UP

by Deb Jannerson

Milo awoke on his tenth birthday to learn that his cousin had died.

He sat at the breakfast table, shocked still, while his special pancakes grew cold. His dads stared at him, at a loss about what to say. Alissa had been one of Milo's closest friends, and they were almost as upset as he was.

"How did it happen?" Milo whispered finally.

His parents exchanged a look. Bob cleared his throat. "The police are looking into it, but they're not sure yet. They found her in the cemetery late last night. She had no visible wounds."

"So she was sick or something?" Milo felt the first tears fall down his face.

"Maybe." His other father, Liam, gave him a careful look. "But Milo, if Alissa was involved with something she shouldn't have been, or if someone wanted to hurt her...please tell us."

A flash of anger ran through Milo's body. "You think *she* did something wrong? Or that *I* did? How can you say that?"

"No!" Liam assured him. "Not at all. But, you see, they found this next to her body." He lifted a small machine off of the floor: Milo's old cassette player that he and Alissa had traded back and forth. "They released it to us this morning, once the investigators determined that there was nothing of interest on the tape."

The tape? Milo hadn't loaned her anything lately.

He hit the Eject button, and an old-looking cassette popped out. Milo picked it up and looked at the label. Alissa had written one word on it in her big, uneven handwriting: "MILO."

Milo pushed back from the table, ran into his room, and slammed the door, crying as he clutched the cassette tape and player.

His fathers stared at the place where their son had been and wondered what to do next. Both had the feeling that he was hiding something.

They were right.

Alissa had called Milo just before their bedtimes the night before. "I just found the coolest thing for your birthday!"

"Yeah?" Milo had felt a flutter of excitement in his stomach. "Just now? Hmm... Who's even open this late?"

"That's the best part! It's not some garbage from a store. It's something one-of-a-kind. It was Lea's."

Whoa, he had thought. Lea, Alissa's much-older sister, had vanished years before. Everyone assumed she had run away with her boyfriend, who had disappeared on the same night, and her family had never heard from her again. The whole thing had seemed sad, but not mysterious, until Alissa and Milo found Lea's journal when they were eight. There was very little in it about the boyfriend and a lot about Lea's obsession with ghosts. Lea had actually written that she had found a way to communicate with the dead. Since then, everything about Lea had taken on an exciting air.

Alissa had never shown her parents the journal. Lea was a sore subject with them. They had never recovered from losing a daughter.

And now they had lost two.

Milo wiped his eyes and looked at the tape again. He still had trouble believing that Alissa was gone when she had sounded so much like her usual self the night before.

Alissa hadn't told him what possession of Lea's she had found. "It's your birthday surprise!" she had insisted. "You don't get it until tomorrow...unless you want to meet me you-know-where tonight! I have to go to make sure it's as cool as I think it is, anyway."

Milo had known where Alissa wanted to meet: the graveyard. The place where they often went to talk about music, Lea, and creatures of the night, and feel a morbid thrill. The place where Alissa's body had been found.

Milo, of course, had not gone. He had never been as good at sneaking out as Alissa had. Now, he wondered if he could have prevented whatever had happened to her.

Plus, he wondered if this tape was Alissa's gift to him.

Milo stayed in his bedroom until dinnertime. His dads came to see him briefly, and they left him water and a sandwich, but he had no appetite. He sat on his bed for hours without moving, just listening to Alissa's—Lea's?—tape and remembering the fun he had had with his now-deceased cousin.

The tape had only one long song on it. The song had no words, and its instruments seemed to go back and forth between rock 'n' roll and melodic New Age music. He had never heard it before and could see why Alissa had thought he might like it. It was unique, eerie and beautiful, but what Milo really wanted from the cassette was an explanation for Alissa's death. No matter how many times he played the music, it never gave him that.

Milo came to the table for his supper and birthday cake, but it certainly didn't feel like his birthday. He knew that his fathers would do everything they could to make him feel better, but Milo did not want their help. He was planning a tribute for Alissa, and this time, he would be as sneaky as she had always been.

⚙☙⚙☙⚙

Late that night, Milo crept outside. He kept to the shadows as he passed the cemetery, where cops were still inspecting the area where Alissa had been found. At some point, he wanted to hang out there himself, but for now, he would settle for his cousin's second-favorite creepy spot: Old Man Tim's.

According to neighborhood lore, Old Man Tim had been a ruthless killer. He had died of old age the year before, but no one had moved into his ancient house or fixed it up in any way. People said that he had left it to his family in his will but that no one could find any of the members of his family. As it was, Old Man Tim's ancient home was now a classic "haunted house": dilapidated, creepy, and easy for kids to break into.

Milo pried open a window in the way that Alissa had taught him. He dropped his tape player inside before he climbed in after it. Sitting in the dusty dark, in a place Alissa had loved, Milo felt closer to her than he had all day. "Alissa," he whispered, "I'm sorry I didn't come out last night. I'm really, really sorry. I wish I could have listened to this with you." He hit Play.

Music filled the air. Milo hoped that the nearest families, who lived a good block away, couldn't hear it, but he hardly cared anymore. He closed his eyes and felt almost peaceful for the first time since he had heard the awful news.

Then he heard a *clack*.

Milo sat up and looked around. *There's nobody here*, he told himself. *Old houses make noise; that's all.* But then he felt the floor rumbling beneath him.

Before Milo could scramble to his feet, a figure burst from the floorboards. Bits of wood flew all over the room. The figure was shaped like a person, but its skin looked shriveled and rotten. It stretched. Bones showed through on its limbs and ribs, and goo dribbled from its desiccated skin onto the shattered floor. Then the creature turned its bare, protruding eyeballs onto Milo.

He picked up his cassette player and ran.

On his way down the hall, Milo heard crashing and crackling in other rooms of the large house. One by one, other creatures rose from the floors and began to stalk after him, each more terrifying than the last. The scariest part, Milo realized as he gained speed, was not that they were monstrous. The scariest part was that he knew, instinctively, what they were.

They were humans, dead humans, who had been buried underneath the floorboards.

One of the dead people sprung up between Milo and the front door, but he charged through it, screaming and wielding the tape player like a weapon. He had run almost a block before he realized that the creature's arm had come off and was sticking to his shirt. Milo shoved it off of him and made a beeline for the cemetery, his heart pounding in his ears. If anyone could protect him now, he figured, it would be the police.

The people in suits noticed Milo long before he ran through the gates. He realized the music in his hand was still playing, which was probably drawing even more attention to him, but he didn't care. The last thing he wanted was to be alone right now with a group of dead things following him.

Milo finally stopped, panting, in front of a group of police. "You've got to help! I was—I was in—"

Then the screaming began. Milo spun around, expecting to see the monsters from Old Man Tim's, but new monsters were rising from the dirt all around him. Grave by grave seemed to explode. Some of the dead people were fresh enough to almost look human still; some nearly crumbled into dust with each step. All had their eyes on Milo, and all looked angry.

The adults Milo had been speaking to were now fleeing at top speed. Maybe no one could protect him after all. He ran toward the other end of the graveyard, where the ground looked undisturbed, but as soon as he got near its graves, dead figures burst out in quick succession. Milo ran back out onto the street.

Gasping for breath, he looked at the tape player in his hand. The dead were waking everywhere he went, ever since... The music. It was the music.

Though it tore his heart to give up his link to Alissa, Milo knew what he had to do. He hit Stop and then threw the device, with all his strength. As he ran, he heard it break into pieces behind him.

Milo looked back for only a second, hoping that the dead would have disappeared, but they were still there, still following and looking angry. With his head still turned backward, Milo collided with someone.

He looked into a familiar face. Its skin had begun to peel away, but its creepy eyes were unforgettable: Old Man Tim.

"Did you really think it would be that easy?" the dead man rasped. Reaching a skinless hand into the air, the dead man caught an object that another creature must have thrown him.Milo told his exhausted body to keep running, but before he could, Old Man Tim grabbed his throat.

Milo felt the dead fingers dig into his neck, through his skin, and scratch around inside him. The dead man removed his hand quickly, but Milo continued to feel searing pain. His throat seemed to be tearing itself apart and weaving itself back together. He tried to scream but could not, and finally, he passed out.

When he came to, the dead creatures were nowhere in sight, but Milo still felt the worst pain of his life. He ran toward the nearest house, crying "Help! Help!"—but the words would not come out. Indeed, the only sound coming from his mouth was music, a complex and haunting instrumental song.

Once again, the dead in the graveyard began to awaken behind him. Milo ran down the street, trying to call for help, but every attempted word produced more music. A long-dead squirrel climbed out from the nearest sewer grate and joined the angry, eager crowd forming behind Milo as he played the tape fused to his voice box.

Until There's Nothing Left
by J.A.W. McCarthy

Her hands are warmer than I'd thought they would be; even though I knew better, I had feared spindly fingers that might even snap and crumble at my touch, like that seance scene in *Beetlejuice* when Adam grabs Barbara's hand and it disintegrates. We used to watch *Beetlejuice* together when we were kids. We would dare each other to say his name three times, and she would slap her hand over my mouth on the last one, between *Beetle* and *juice*. She always waited until the last second, even though she claimed it would be awful if it really happened. She said she hoped the afterlife was like that, that she was looking forward to haunting people. I said I would be her Lydia.

I think about that movie often, about how I'm supposed to take care of her and how I might fail. We're supposed to watch it together—"first thing," she said—under a blanket on the couch, in our sweats with the lights out. "I'll need a drink," she would remind me. "And you'll have to tell me everything I missed."

☠☠☠

It's not all spells and chants and animal sacrifices and trading souls— it's just something I can do. The first time I was six or seven. I saw a possum get hit by a car on the road in front of our house. I watched its body fly up and land at the end of the driveway, scattering gravel into the street. I'd never seen anything bigger than a sparrow dead before. There was a little blood smeared along the possum's mouth, but it didn't look too bad. I poked the animal with the long stick that was supposed to be my sword. I sat down on

173

the driveway and dared myself to touch its grey and white fur. I loved animals, even the ugly ones, even the ones that rooted through our garbage and scared our cats at night. For what must have been at least twenty minutes, I just sat and stared at that poor dead animal. Then, just as I was standing up to get the shovel, the possum rose to its feet, hissed at me, and ran off across the street.

So maybe that possum wasn't really dead. *It was just playing possum*, my father said, laughing at his own joke. But my grandmother wasn't playing possum. I saw her in her casket. She wasn't getting up from that one.

I was twelve then. My first funeral. My mother cried the whole time. She hadn't eaten or slept since the hospital, and I just wanted to fix that; I wanted everything to go back to the way it was. That night after the service, while my father slept and my mother stared vacantly at the TV, I snuck out to the cemetery and sat at my grandmother's grave. I thought about my mother's ashen face, her permanently red eyes, the way she had stopped hearing me when I called for her. I thought about what I was sure I had done with the possum. An hour later, riding my bike home, I saw my grandmother in her 1950s wedding dress sitting on the sidewalk in front of Sears. She asked me why no one had given her shoes.

By sixteen I had brought back one possum, two cats, one dog, my grandmother, a boy from my literature class who had been hit by a truck while skateboarding, and six people I'd never seen before in my life. The six people came back from the same cemetery after the boy from my class. I guess I had a lot of feelings about the quiet boy who sat in the back, reading Hunter S. Thompson when we were supposed to be discussing Shakespeare.

It took years to control it, years to pinpoint and specify and not bring up every creature buried in the vicinity. There was a time when I thought I would quit all together, stop working against nature because I know now that what I can do is wrong and selfish and causes more pain than just leaving them in the ground. With her, though, I have to try. And this time—the last time—I have to get it right.

※ ※ ※

She doesn't come back craving brains or human blood; I don't have to give her rabbits then goats then high school bullies in order to keep her human. Right away she is herself, and she eats saltines, and she is quiet. She knows me, she remembers me, and she remembers her home.

She remembers *Beetlejuice* too. I help her out of the stiff black lace dress our parents had chosen and get her into her favorite Huskies sweats that always sit neatly folded at the end of her bed in the apartment we haven't yet cleaned out. I make her favorite drink: a Manhattan with two cherries. She

174

drinks it all at once, but doesn't say anything. I arrange the blanket over her, making sure the edges are tucked under her feet like she likes. I ask her if she wants more saltines. She still won't say anything.

I keep wondering why she doesn't have any questions. If I'd been gone for ten days, I would want to know if anyone had touched my stuff and who was still crying over me and if the embarrassing potty training photos came out after the service. I would want to tell her about all the things I saw, what it's like on the other side.

During the movie I catch myself eyeing the dent in the side of her head. It doesn't look too bad; her hair covers most of it. "You haven't missed much," I tell her.

☠☠☠

She knew about the woods first. Being two years older than me, she knew about everything first. Kids from the high school went there to drink and smoke and fuck, but they never went in much deeper than where the trees start to knit together and the moss overtakes your shoes. There were overturned logs to sit on and a little firepit someone's parents had probably made back when they were our age. You almost had to be invited there; the oldest kids, the coolest kids, controlled who got to drink forties under the broken branches.

Once she finally got invited, she was going almost every weekend. She got her first kiss in those woods, smoked her first joint there, lost her virginity and countless earrings there. She started letting me tag along when I was a sophomore. We sat around the firepit with her friends, all these worldly girls with shiny hair and skin that glowed with vitality instead of French fry grease under the moonlight. While they talked about college prospects and sneaking backstage and who got a boob job, I tried my best to keep up, to prove that I was as worthy as she told them I was. I threw up malt liquor for the first time in those woods, got rejected by my crush there, held in lungfuls of smoke as my throat burned and my friends kept asking me if I was okay. I lost earrings there too, lighters, keys, CDs, everything that meant something to me so far.

If we had a little brother or sister, they wouldn't go to those woods now. Even back when we were kids, before we started hanging out there, people were talking about the crying woman with the big red hole in the middle of her chest. Some said she was a witch, others a ghost. There were stories of kids going just a little deeper into the trees for some privacy and feeling boney fingers along their backs as they made out. The woman would grab a bare shoulder or a fistful of hair and wail or mumble something unintelligible. She plucked keys and quarters from pockets and kept anything

175

you dropped. Even up front, around the firepit, you could sometimes hear her crying in the distance.

It got worse by my junior year, and by the time I graduated no one was going to the woods anymore; the risk of getting caught drinking or fucking was better than getting groped by a sobbing witch. When I went I was usually too drunk or preoccupied by some boy to notice the figures rustling behind us, but I did hear the crying once. I had let a boy lure me deeper into the trees than I had ever gone, and when I heard the woman's wails rise and pour towards us, I took off running towards the firelight, leaving my date holding my bra as he called my name.

I've been a few times since high school, but it isn't because of nostalgia or trying to relive all those blustery firsts. Now just thinking about those woods fills me with nausea and sadness and regret. I avoid going anywhere near that part of town, and even knowing all those dense, mysterious acres are in the distance drives me to take the long way despite the waste of time and gas. I was going to leave this town, but she didn't want to go. If she wants to see those woods again, I won't let her. It's the one thing I won't do for her.

※ ※ ※

The first night goes okay. After the movie, all she says is "tired" and it makes sense and I help her into bed and she seems to fall asleep right away. I settle on the couch with a blanket and pillow so I have a view of her open bedroom door. My eyes grow heavy thinking about the things I want to ask her, the things the others never answered, like if she was in heaven or if it was like being under anesthesia, like you're awake one moment then suddenly you're not and all you have is the vague ache of what happened in between. Did she slip in and out of rooms, trying to communicate with us? Did she sit in on her own funeral counting tears and ex-boyfriends? Was she worried that I wouldn't bring her back?

Just before dawn I am awakened by someone standing over me. There is blood, shiny and dark, slicked over her lips and down her chin, a little splatter on the collar of her grey Huskies sweatshirt. Right away I think about how irritated she'll be that she got a stain on her clothes. She's staring at me, unblinking, and holding out her palm between us. She is offering me a molar and an incisor, and I'm afraid that how badly I wanted it didn't change anything, that nothing has changed this time.

※ ※ ※

He followed me home, the boy from my literature class. Even though

I didn't really know him, I went to his memorial service. I sat in the back row with our school's vice principal and who I would later learn were four of his cousins. I was the only one there from our class.

I didn't sneak out to his grave at night or cry over him or make any wishes, but I did think about him. I had seen him in the woods a few times, alone with a book when there weren't many people around the firepit, then drinking beers far off with his friends when it started to get crowded. I had even seen him go deep into the trees with a stoner girl once, and I remember not being able to keep up with the conversation because I kept watching for him to come back out. Sometimes I would see him skating with his friends in the quad at lunch. One time he saw me reading a Barbara Gowdy short story collection and he asked me about it, then I saw him reading it himself the next day.

He showed up at my house two days after the funeral. She saw him first, standing in our backyard after our parents had gone to bed, and she came to my room and said, "You did it again, didn't you?"

I didn't know what to do with him. In the dark of my bedroom he immediately began to peel off the suit his family had buried him in, tugging at the pants and shirt as if he didn't remember how to unzip zippers and unbutton buttons. He ended up tightening his tie until he was choking. I tried to get him back into his shirt and pants, but he kept shedding them as quickly as I could get them on him. From the little bit of moonlight that leaked through my window, I could see dark red hollows under his ribs and streaked up to the center of his chest, the edges stippled purple and black.

For the next three days he stayed in my room wearing my bathrobe and pajama pants while I faked sick so I could stay home from school. I brought him water and trail mix and carefully explained to him that he could never leave my room without me as if he was a puppy I was hiding from my parents. I snuck him leftovers from dinner, but he wouldn't touch them. The only thing he ate was saltines.

She said I couldn't keep him and I got mad at her because it wasn't my fault—not this time—and he'd already made it one day longer than our grandmother, so I thought maybe I had a shot at finally getting it right. I figured once I got him talking and close to normal again I could take him to his family and leave it to them to figure out what to do next. He was good and he was quiet and he read every book in my room and he never slept. He got in my closet without prompting whenever he heard footsteps outside my door. On the third night she even suggested that I bring him downstairs to watch TV while our parents were at a movie. He sat between us on the couch and he even laughed a couple of times during *Beetlejuice*, and in that moment, I believed it really was going to work out this time. I found myself imagining him back at school, reading in the back of lit, skateboarding with his friends, smiling at me from across the firepit.

Then that night, when everyone was asleep, I came back from the bathroom to find him sitting on my bed, his fingers and face wet with blood. In the saltines box I found six teeth, four fingernails, and multiple plaits of thick brown hair, the ends sticky and anchored by pink bits of scalp.

❈❈❈

We're pretending it didn't happen. Because unlike the boy from my literature class, she's started talking and she sleeps a little, and she even ate half of the steak that I made for her. She ate it normally, too—fork and knife, no bare hands—and her missing teeth don't seem to be bothering her. She brushes her long, dark hair in the morning just like she used to, the only difference being that she now has to be careful to arrange it over the dent. She dresses herself and keeps all her clothes on.

When I stand next to her in the bathroom, all elbows and knocked shoulders like when we were teens jockeying over the shared mirror, I breathe her in and I am reassured. No graveyard moss or musty crypts or the sickly-sweet smell of rotten fruit that I imagined I might encounter. Our grandmother had smelled like a mixture of the perfume she always wore and those plastic dry-cleaning bags at first, then the damp, sour odor moved in quickly, in a matter of hours. The boy from my class had smelled of wet laundry left overnight, then an earthy, peaty smell that got stronger and stronger every time he came back. But she is different: perfume sunk into her hair, faded but lingering, and the same cucumber lotion she used to smooth onto her face every night before bed. I tell myself that she's different from them because I got it right this time.

"You know the place where you buried the teeth?" she begins one morning, leaning into her reflection. When she pulls on her lower lip, I cringe. I am reminded that it can happen at any time, right after she starts to forget the things we did together.

"Yeah, the back corner of the yard. Remember when mom started talking about planting gardenias back there? I nearly puked."

She smiles like she remembers, a small relief. "Are my teeth there?"

"I haven't done anything with them yet," I answer, though I'm thinking, *I won't bury them with the others. Not yet.*

She nods at the mirror, runs her fingers gently over her lips. "Good," she says. "I think I want to keep them anyway."

It's only been two teeth so far, so a week later when she says she's ready to go out, I agree. She seems to enjoy getting ready, sliding into her favorite skinny jeans and leather jacket, blotting and powdering her lips between coats of lipstick like she taught me to do in high school ("kiss-proof

178

and other-things-proof," she had promised with a wink). I drive us to a bar two towns over where we won't know anyone. It's dark with the worn sexiness of red velvet curtains and loners sipping bourbon to Bill Callahan songs. Three guys at different tables look up from their drinks and their dates the minute we walk in. I suggest a table in the back corner, but she is already striding to the bar, buoyed by all of the eyes that follow her across the room.

It doesn't take long before she's flirting with the bartender. Openly, shamelessly—worse than she would've done just a few weeks ago. The more agitated I get, the more she giggles and preens, and I start thinking about how the boy from my class didn't speak at all, how the only times our grandmother spoke were to ask questions I couldn't answer. I wanted her back more than anyone ever before, and that is why it worked this time. *It's going to be okay*, I reassure myself as I watch her. I start drinking my gin and tonics a little faster, letting the warm bite settle my limbs.

The bartender is young and cute and he flirts back, leaning across the bar to whisper into her ear as the place gets louder. He even brings us a plate of stuffed dates on the house, and I notice him watching her as she delicately pulls each bite between her lips. One bite and I've got bacon and blue cheese all over my chin. She downs four Manhattans in a row and mouths to me, *I feel nothing*. She keeps drinking until the bartender cuts us both off.

I haven't been more than fifteen feet from her since she came back, but the alcohol and my new sense of optimism have convinced me to allow myself a smoke. Outside, staring across the street at the other bars and restaurants full of people talking and laughing and doing the same normal things she is doing right now, right behind me, I start to imagine what will happen next. For now I can keep her in her apartment and keep everyone else out. We have privacy and time, things I didn't have before. Once I know she's fine and not like the boy and not like our grandmother, I'll be able to tell our parents. I'm picturing the looks on their faces when I go back inside and find that both she and the bartender are gone.

I scan the room, panic tightening my jaw when I don't see her face among the diminishing crowd. She's done this before—run off with some guy she just met—but at least she would always tell me where she was going. And besides, this time is different and she knows she can't just leave. I go back to our seats at the bar in case I somehow missed her. I finish the remnants of gin and ice in my drink and wait for her to come back. My cocktail napkin is soaked through, leaving little bits of red paper on my fingertips as I pick at it and wad it up and flick it behind the bar. A different bartender comes and asks me if I want another. I tell myself that she is in the bathroom and the cute bartender's shift is over.

After paying the tab, I head for the bathrooms in the very back of the bar where there are no tables and it's obvious where you are going. Outside the women's room I pause when I hear feet shuffling behind the door. She's about to come out, I think, freshly lipsticked and chiding me for worrying so much. But I don't want to open that door. The image of my grandmother in her wedding dress floods my mind, her fingers clawing at her chest, nails tearing through fabric and digging out little chunks of flesh. I had screamed for her to stop, but I didn't actually try to stop her because I was scared and I didn't know what to do and I didn't want to touch her. I stood there crying and watching as she busted through her brittle ribcage and pulled out her shriveled heart. I remember how she held it out to me, her palms filling up with blood even though her heart wasn't moving, wasn't beating. It was just dead and leaking, a slowly deflating balloon.

But now, I have to open this bathroom door. The first thing I see as I push forward is the bartender backed up against the sink, blood smeared all over his mouth and chin. She's right in front of him, blood all over her mouth too, but unlike him, she looks more confused than scared. She's peering over his shoulder at the mirror, examining her reflection. She touches her chin and looks at her fingers in surprise. When she opens her mouth, more blood dribbles out.

The bartender turns to me, his eyes huge. I can't tell if he's injured, if it's all his blood or hers or both. "She's crazy. You gotta do something about her. She's fucking crazy!" he exclaims. Then he's pushing past me and back out into the bar.

"Are you okay?" I ask her once we are alone. She shakes her head then starts to cry. The tears streak tracks through the blood, diluting what rolls onto her shirt. In the sink I see what looks like half of a tongue.

☠☠☠

I took the boy from my class back to his house. She went with me the first time, in the middle of the night, and held my hand as I begged him to go inside. He regarded the narrow, white two-story as if he couldn't quite place it, then stared at me over his shoulder as I offered encouragements. "It's okay. They want you back. They can help you," I kept saying, though I knew that wasn't true. I cried on the drive home, thinking of him in his crumpled suit, hand on the doorknob as she whispered to me that I was doing the right thing.

Two hours later, he was in my bedroom again. Having found him in our backyard without his jacket and shoes just before dawn, she brought him to my room and the three of us sat there on the end of my bed watching the sky turn from black to navy to orange.

When I got home from school that day, I found him in my closet picking at his remaining fingernails. He had spent the day reading the entire

Narnia series and filling my coat pockets with his blood-streaked teeth. She drove us to his house again that night and we didn't leave until we saw him go inside.

He didn't come back until the next night, shirtless and covered in dirt and tiny scratches as I hurried him in from the backyard. In my room, I picked out of his remaining hair bits of grass and leaves as crumbly as the saltines he ate while staring out my window at the flickering streetlight down the block. I put him in one of my father's sweatshirts and did everything I could to convince him to go home. I told him he couldn't keep coming here because she was leaving for college in the fall and I couldn't do this without her.

The following afternoon, when he tore through his forearm down to the bone as she and I stood there watching, she told me she would do whatever it took to help me make this right. "This can't be like grandma," she said, drawing her arm around me. We watched him chew his own flesh in the pocket of his right cheek where he still had his top and bottom teeth, blood seeping from between his sunken lips with a comical sort of squeak. She helped me clean him up and tie his hands behind his back. He never struggled, not even when we loaded him into the car for the last time.

⁂

I'm following her. She knows it even though she never once looks back. The first time I followed her in my car, driving extra slowly while begging her to get in as if we were quarreling lovers. Then the next night, when I saw her get out of bed, I let her have a head start before following on foot. She kept looking over her shoulder and motioning for me to go back. She even grabbed my arms and shook me and started to cry. Tonight, though, she knows it's not worth trying to stop me.

When we get to the edge of the woods, I let her make it to the firepit before I take her hand and we sit on one of the overturned logs. There are still beer bottles sunk into the dirt and peeking out from the grass, Rainier and Coors Light and others I remember drinking, and I wonder if any of them are mine. She stares into the firepit with me, assessing the dead leaves and other debris that have gathered there, what little we can see in the dark. We sit like this for a long time because I don't know what to say that won't end in crying or begging. I'm just glad she's sitting with me. I'm glad that we're alone.

"You can't give up now," I finally say, and I am struck by the cliché, though I've never said these words before. "You've done better than the others. You're doing better. You don't belong here."

She looks down at her hand still in mine and shakes her head.

"Listen to me. It's okay. It's going to take time, but you've already proved—We'll get there, okay? You're not like them."

She pulls her hand from mine. Then, as if to demonstrate just how wrong I am, she starts to pick at one of her six remaining fingers, unraveling a ribbon of skin into her lap.

"Are you worried about the bartender?" I try. "You didn't hurt him. You know that, right? He's fine. You haven't hurt anyone. Maybe we went out too soon, but we have lots of time to get there, okay? We have plenty of time."

She doesn't say anything, just continues to pull meat from bone. I watch the blood snake down her wrist, another sleeve ruined.

"I'll come here every night if I have to," I swear. "I'm not giving up on you."

I imagine every night spent like this, the long trek to the woods like it's our after-dinner constitutional or something. She's staring into the trees now, somehow even thicker than when we used to come here as teens, shapes outlined in what little moonlight penetrates. She'll go deeper and deeper every night because I will never be able to convince her, because she knows that I am wrong. And when I fall behind, there will be pieces of her for me to follow. Teeth, fingernails, hair, like she's shedding until there's nothing left for me to hold onto.

Because we are here, I have failed.

"Please…"

Shaking her head again, she stands up and turns towards the trees.

Even though I am right behind her, she doesn't run. The trees are getting closer and closer together, but she walks confidently while I stumble through the darkness. Every time I grab her arm or shoulder she pushes me back. I lose a shoe and scream her name and fall on my ass. I have to run to catch up. When I start to cry, she finally stops and turns around and wraps her arms around me.

"Please," I hear, soft and round and broken against my ear.

I cry into her hair. I try to memorize how this feels, the rise and fall of her chest, the imprint of her fingers on my back then in my jacket pocket as she takes my lighter. Unlike our grandmother now just ahead of us, her heart will stay in its place. Unlike the boy from my class, she has come here on her own and she won't return to me. They'll take her and the stories will continue and I will never do this again.

"I'm sorry," I say when she releases me. This time I stay where I am as I watch her walk deeper into the woods, towards everyone who is waiting for her.

WE ARE GOLDEN

by Adrean Messmer

"There is no such thing as love," Kostya said, standing in the center of the room and turning slowly, making eye contact with everyone in turn. In front of people like this—strangers— he played up his rolling accent. It made the girls smile.

Nico leaned back to watch Kostya rant and wondered if they would have time for him to finish before sunrise. The audience—the hangers-on, the ones that didn't leave after the afterparty—watched Kostya with drunken interest.

Julie, an American girl—Nico had to remind himself they were almost all American girls now—sat up, leaning with her elbows on her knees. She was pretty in a way that Nico hadn't seen back home—all sun-kissed skin, fawn colored hair, and grey eyes.

"That isn't true," she said.

Kostya stopped to face her. He bent down until his nose almost touched hers. Nico knew that if she weren't drunk and if Kostya hadn't *accidentally* spilled a tray of shots all over himself, she would have smelled the rot.

"What is love, Love?" Kostya purred at her.

She laughed. It was a delicate sound, like tiny bells. "Love is," she paused, pawing at the air like she could pluck the words from it. "Love is when you care more about someone else's happiness than your own."

Kostya smiled and rubbed his hand through his short, dark hair. "That isn't love. That's stupidity."

Julie shot him a glare. "That's not true. Love is amazing. Love…love is so powerful that it only takes one second and people know."

"Lies." Kostya gave an exaggerated shrug. "No one falls in love at first sight. They fall in lust. Look at all of the people who have love at first sight. They all, they are all pretty, yes? Ugly people don't fall in love. Ugly people settle."

Julie pushed him away. "You're awful."

Kostya stumbled back with practiced clumsiness. "Love is mutual Stockholm Syndrome."

Nico watched Julie roll her eyes and tried to remember what girls smelled like. First, there'd be the scent of alcohol. Then smoke. The tang of sweat. Hairspray. Underneath all that, maybe raspberry body spray. The mint of her gum. He forced his ruined lungs to inhale, hoping to catch a whiff of something. But, like always, there was nothing.

The alarm on his watch chimed. It took him too long to realize the noise was coming from him. By the time he did, the others sitting on the ratty couch with him were searching for the sound too. He gave a wobbly smile, hoped it looked drunk enough, and dug his nail into the impossible-to-press button to silence the alarm. His nail polish was chipping. Cracks ran through the black lacquer, and a jagged piece was missing on his thumb. Dark blood, almost the same color as the polish but lacking the shine, showed through his nail. He told himself not to forget to fix that.

"Kostya." He had to repeat his friend's name a few times before Kostya finally looked at him. Nico pointed to his watch. "We have to go."

"*Uzhe?*"

Nico nodded and started for the door. He could feel the others watching him as he put on his coat. He tried to tell himself it was because he was famous—half the reason these people were there. Not because anyone knew the coat was for show. That he had no idea if it was cold outside, just that other people were wearing coats, so he thought he should as well. He'd been looking forward to the weather in America. To the sun shining golden and warm. But he couldn't feel it now. He hadn't even seen the sun.

"Do you like American music?" Kostya leaned into Nico, but the question wasn't really for him.

Nico put his arm around Kostya, pretending to hold him up as they both stumbled to the door. "You know I do."

Kostya pulled them both to a stop: to grin at a skinny, cadaverous girl, inviting her to impress him the way he always did when the girls looked desperate enough.

She lolled her head to the side to look at him and brought a crooked cigarette to her lips. "What's to like? It's all noise."

"Shut your mouth," Kostya pushed the girl's face away. "You don't know anything."

She giggled, and her arm dropped to the side. She had the marks on her arm. Crocodile bites is what he would have called them back home, but these were smaller. Less angry and violent-looking. Heroin. Nico scratched at his own arm, trying not to think about the sting of the needle and the euphoria after.

"And what do you know? You're not American. You don't play American music." Her voice was slow and lazily insulting.

Kostya's eyes went wide. "Of course we do!"

"You're," she repeated, emphasizing the individual words like sentences, "not American."

Kostya opened his mouth, but Nico pushed him towards the door again.

"Let's just go," Nico whispered.

A gust of wind battered them as they stepped outside. Nico pulled his jacket tighter, and they made their way back the motel. Not a cheap one like where they used to stay, sleeping with their hands gripped around the necks of their guitars, worried they would be stolen. No, this was a penthouse. Top floor. The elevator ride was long enough that Nico had to pop his ears twice.

Kostya, giving up the act now that they were alone, dropped himself on the overstuffed, white couch.

"I'm hungry. We should have eaten."

"Too many people. We'll eat tomorrow." Nico drew the shades tight, pausing to look at the streak of bright blue on the horizon. "The sun's coming up."

"Good for it. Get those curtains closed."

"I did." Nico made his way to the bed. He could never remember sleeping on it when he woke. He felt the same after a night on it as he did sleeping on the bench seats in the bus or leaned against Kostya on a plane. But at least he got to feel the weightlessness of a good mattress and fluffy comforter for the few moments before sleep—or death—overtook him.

❧❧❧

Consciousness came with difficulty, slower with each waking. Like sleep was some monster sitting on his chest, getting heavier as it supped at his soul. Every night, it sat for a little longer, more reticent to leave. He wanted to ask Kostya if he felt the same, but Kostya never wanted to talk about serious things.

Slowly, Nico became aware of a banging coming from somewhere. He sat up, feeling his fingers tingle. The first time he'd felt that, he'd been excited. It was something; the first physical sensation since *that* night. But it never went away. Just got worse. Then he'd realized it was decay. The tingle of cells dying. He would have thrown up, but without eating, he'd had nothing to vomit and just dry-heaved for several minutes. Kostya, usually so ready with a biting comment, had stayed silent and put a comforting hand on his back.

The banging, he realized when a voice rang out in accompaniment, was coming from the door.

"Nico! Kostya! You're late for the soundcheck!" The door rattled, and Nico could picture Roger out there in his hipster glasses and high-water pants, pulling on the antique knob.

Nico stumbled out of bed and into the big living area.

Kostya was still sprawled on the couch, but he glared at the door. Without getting up, he shouted, "I told you we wouldn't be there until seven!"

"It's eight-thirty!" Roger's shout was muffled by the door.

Kostya turned to the oddly out-of-date-and-place digital clock under the TV. "*Der'mo.*"

Nico crossed the room, tripping over Kostya's shoes and coat, and let Roger in.

"You're not even ready. That's the same thing you wore yesterday."

Nico nodded dimly. "I'll go get dressed."

"No. There isn't time." Roger went to the closet. Neither of them had ever gotten further than just tossing their suitcases in there. Roger rifled through them, grabbing a few things while Kostya and Nico put on their jackets.

Kostya trudged over and sat on the floor, putting on his shoes like a dejected toddler.

"Jesus, you guys. We've talked about this. You can't just get trashed every night."

Kostya laughed and wiped his nose. His hand came away with a streak of dark red. Thicker and blacker than a standard nosebleed. "What exactly do you expect from us? We're not choir boys."

"I expect some modicum of professionalism."

"We're a punk band," Nico slid into his jacket. "I think you might be in the wrong line of work."

⁂

The venue was a square, brick building. Tall enough to be two stories, but the second was just the balcony seating. A line of people in winter coats wound around the structure. They cupped their hands and breathed hot air into their fingers. Groups of them huddled together, talking and laughing, tiny white clouds forming at their moving mouths. They tripped over each other's feet as they moved forward. At the front, a set of double, glass doors were guarded by a man tearing tickets. On the other side, the people shed their coats like skin as they made their way to the waiting theater.

"Why are they still outside?" Kostya's breath frosted the window glass.

Roger sighed like being alive—right now, in this moment—was the hardest thing he'd ever done. "Because you guys weren't here."

Kostya smirked. "Then why are they letting them in now?"

Nico flinched at Kostya's callousness. "It's cold outside. I'm glad they're letting them in."

"At least one of you has a heart." Roger said it with one hand already on the door handle, ready to push them out of the car.

Kostya's smirk turned into a smile. "I wouldn't bet on that."

Nico was amazed by how honest a person could be. It wasn't the first time Kostya had hinted to Roger about their condition. When they were first offered a record deal, Kostya read over it and asked if cadavers could still be legally bound by a signature. Roger hadn't laughed. The man knew everything about their afterlife and either didn't care or thought it was a joke. Nico liked to believe that if Roger thought the story was even moderately true, he would have felt obligated to do something.

They parked behind the building, and Roger led them in through the back. He all but held their hands, treating them both like children who couldn't be trusted to cross the street.

"The openers did your soundcheck already, so you'll have to live with it. There's food in the back. Go get dressed and," he sniffed at them, "brush your teeth or something. Take a shower when you get home. You two smell like death."

Nico tried to not laugh. Kostya didn't bother.

They changed quickly, honoring their practiced tradition of neither looking at the mirror nor each other. In the wings behind the stage, standing next to the tables of catered food, Nico could hear the music of whatever local band they'd found to open. It was distorted and discordant, echoing through the halls. He looked at the plates of bread and meat and inhaled. His dry lungs crackled, and he put his hand to his chest, as if to mute the sound.

"Did you eat?" Roger's voice startled him.

"I had a sandwich," Nico lied.

"And Kostya?"

"I made him one too." Nico closed his lips around a laugh. Even when he was lying, it seemed like too much of a stretch to say Kostya had done something as mundane as making a sandwich.

"Good." Roger patted him on the shoulder. "You're a good kid."

Nico let the laugh out as the music came to a cacophonous end.

Roger nodded and pushed off the wall. "All right. Go. Get your shit together. Show time."

⚘⚘⚘

The lights warmed Nico's skin like the sun. It was his favorite part of being on stage—more than the applause and the people, more than praises and professions of love, more than anything. The spotlights were the closest he'd ever get to the sun now, and even with them, it was half-imagination. Like with everything else, he only knew the warmth for its secondary and tertiary effects on him. The smell, for one.

Not anything *he* smelled. No, it was all in the faces of the hired band. The way they turned slightly away when he got too close. The furrowing of brows. The tightening of lips. The almost hidden looks of pity, like they thought he didn't know. The fill-in members never lasted long.

The strings cut into the tips of his fingers, leaving them bloodlessly torn open, the rotting flesh too soft to handle being dragged across the metal.

But he could lose himself on stage. If he just stood at the edge, facing the lights and the people and ignored everyone behind him that could tell he wasn't quite right, he could forget everything and just get lost in the music.

But he always found himself again after the encore. He followed Kostya off the stage as the house lights came up. Kostya went out the back doors, stopping only to set his guitar down by the dressing room.

Back in Moscow, when they hadn't had any money, they'd wait near the back. They could hear the music through the walls. The people inside, they had money and friends and family. They had phones with GPS and tagged their location on social media.

Kostya was the one who'd thought to look out back for food.

Because the ones outside in the cold, the ones that couldn't afford to be inside, they were invisible. Even if one of them was missed, it wasn't as likely to be reported that they'd been at the show. It was safer. And, Nico thought, a little cannibalistic.

A boy and a girl sat on the ground, huddled in jackets that were too thin for the weather. They both smiled and stood up. Nico tried not to hear it when they introduced themselves. Or when they talked about how the much the music meant to them. How it had saved their lives. He watched Kostya smile and play the part of the flattered celebrity. In Nico's lies, he was the one making sandwiches for Kostya, but in reality, it was Kostya taking care of them.

"Cat and Miles," Kostya said, forcing Nico to pay attention. He pointed at the couple and ducked his head, making eye contact with Nico. "They're going to help."

"Help with what?" Nico was suddenly very self-conscientiously aware of how slow his voice sounded.

Kostya smiled, raising both eyebrows and giving Nico a look like he were dumb. "Come on."

"Oh." Nico gave a dead-eyed smile. "Awesome."

The two led them to a house that looked the same way Nico felt—threadbare and worn down. In the living room, a single bulb hung from a cord snaking out of a hole in the ceiling. People littered the house, seen through holes in the walls like rats, lying like death across stained mattresses, and staring with glassy eyes at the dirty carpet. Five of them sat around a table soaking weed in clear vials of formaldehyde and giggling.

In the room furthest back, sitting in an oversized chair like a king, they met JT. Nico thought it interesting that, even across the world, drug dealers were all the same. Not exactly in looks, though they all did seem to have greasy hair and eyes that darted around like fish when they weren't staring through his skin, into the trembling mass of his soul. Not in clothes, though they did always seem to have the most expensive name brand of whatever was in style in the nearest trailer park. And not in demeanor, though they all liked to speak too loudly and use big, thesaurused words slightly incorrectly. And though it was none of those things, it was a little bit of all of them.

JT had milky, dark skin and baggy clothes. A baseball cap, the brim straight and crisp, sat crookedly on his head, still sporting the shiny sticker declaring its brand. His shoes seemed oversized and so bright white that Nico wondered if he'd ever even worn them outside.

He'd managed not to think about how hungry he was until he found himself in that small room with three perfectly alive people. He wasn't sure if it was his imagination or if he was actually hearing the sound of their hearts beating. Each one rhythmic, but slightly off-beat from the others. It was so loud he could, if he wanted to—and he did want to—make himself believe it was his own heart, manic with anticipation. Every beat jarred him. Made his skull vibrate. He closed his eyes to keep his balance.

When he opened them again, Kostya was grabbing his wrist and leading him out of the small, master bedroom, down the hall, and into a smaller guest room with Cat and Miles following behind. Kostya closed the door behind them and locked it. They didn't seem to notice.

Nico sat on the bed, at the head, and leaned against the wall. The others crowded on, Kostya so close his arm brushed Nico's. They watched as Cat dropped little chunks of white-gold powder into a burned spoon, spat into it, and let it dissolve in the heat of a cheap, plastic lighter. She used the same needle in Miles's arm that she used in hers. He winced, she didn't. She had to catch him as he leaned back, seeming to forget he was perched on the edge of the bed. They kissed.

There was a click, and Kostya lurched across the bed. A splash of red sprayed the dirty mattress as his switchblade found Cat's throat. Miles stood up, eyes wide and dull, and stumbled back from Cat's convulsing body. He looked at Kostya dimly. Kostya shrugged, smiled, and mumbled an apology before burying the knife somewhere between Miles's ribs. Nico felt like his hearing was going bad. No screams, no whimpers—it was like the heroin had stolen their voices.

He knew Kostya would want the girl, so Nico moved to sit on the floor next to Miles. Miles's brown eyes scanned the ceiling, not focusing on anything. Just back and forth like the pendulum on a clock. Nico touched the growing pool of red and brought his fingers to his lips. The blood coated his mouth and went down warm. Like whiskey.

He always told himself it would be different this time. That he'd be gentle and apologize. He'd respect the dead. But he never could. His face was down, teeth tearing at the ragged edges of the knife wound on Miles's belly. Nico might have heard a whimper, a nightmare-quiet scream as Miles tried to call out for help. He couldn't be sure, though. His own heart, jumpstarted by the borrowed arterial blood, began to pound in his ears. The tingling in his fingertips turned to a buzz then an itch as the rotting tissue stitched itself back together. As his skin warmed and his nerve endings sparked back to life, he felt the dry, hot air from the vents try to combat the cold all around him. The stagnant scent of the moldering carpet almost overtook the tang of blood.

Slowly, like molasses, as he cracked Miles's ribs to get at the barely beating muscle inside, he felt his own muscles relax. The fist his brain had clenched itself into loosened, and his vision grew hazy. He breathed in, the dank smell of the house no longer bothering him, and relished in the feeling of air filling his lungs. He was glad Kostya had convinced them to see JT first. The heroin in Miles's blood turned the aftermath into an afterglow.

He grabbed a handful of what he'd come to assume was the heart and crushed it between his teeth. Blood sluiced down his throat like the pulp of exotic wild berries. He started to let himself fall into it, just relax and sleep like it wanted him to, but Kostya was pulling him to his feet.

"*Otpuskayet.* There are people out there. We're short on time." Kostya wiped at Nico's face with the stained sheet on the bed. He frowned, shaking his head. "You're a mess."

Giddy, Nico leaned forward, falling against Kostya's chest. His lips brushed Kostya's cheek. The warmth sent a shiver through Nico's body.

Kostya gently pushed him back, one hand on his chest, the other around his shoulders to catch him.

"*Otpuskayet,*" Kostya repeated and pulled Nico to the door.

Nico winced. The high always made him forget his better judgment. "*Izvini.*" He whispered the apology as they left the house. Nico looked to the people as they passed, careful not to make eye contact, but worried they would see the blood on his sleeves and running down his shirt.

"We're going to get changed. Then we're going out," Kostya said.

Nico nodded dimly.

He could barely keep track of himself. Time sped up and slowed. The trip back to their room took place in seconds, but it took him days to change his clothes. He felt the individual threads of his shirt like links of chain as they passed over his face.

The club was loud and full of colors. The smell of cigarettes, sweat, and cheap liquor made his vision swim. He found himself dancing with a pretty boy that sparkled under the shifting lights. His skin was damp and hot, and his breath smelled like something sweet. The guy bought him a drink, and Nico gulped down the icy syrup. He wanted to sober up, but more than that, he wanted to keep feeling everything. Even the way the liquor made the floor seem uneven and the nausea it brought.

Kostya found Nico hunched over a toilet. He helped him to his feet and out into the early morning light. The sky was bruised blue and lightening on the horizon. Even that little bit of sun made Nico wince.

Back in their room, Nico vomited again in the trashcan while Kostya took the toilet. Their undead stomachs, losing the borrowed life, rejected the last of the night's fun.

❀❀❀

Nico only dreamed after eating. He guessed his brain was too dead the rest of the time. The dreams were always memories, rehashed and remixed. It was like he couldn't think of anything new.

He dreamt of *that* night. He remembered looking up at the sky and watching the snow fall. He'd come out of the club he shouldn't have been in. The glitter was still caught in his hair and stuck to his skin. He wiped his nose with his sleeve and started back home. In the deep recesses of his coat, his phone sang out Kostya's ringtone.

"Hey, are you coming home?" he asked.

"On my way." Nico glanced behind him. A group of people were smoking in the shadows between buildings.

"Get some food, yeah? I'm starving."

"There's some—"

"No, no, Nico. I don't want to make something. I just want warm food to suddenly be in front of me. Bring me the magic of a cheeseburger."

Nico smiled. "Fine, fine. I only have enough for two things." A sound behind him caught his attention. "So, do you want a drink or fries?" The group in the alley; they were falling in line behind him.

"Ahh, Nico." Kostya's voice was forced through his teeth, the way he did when he was annoyed.

"It's all I've got. I'll get you fries. Drinks are cold and hard to carry anyway."

He turned a corner. The people, gaining on him now, turned too. Nico tightened his fingers around the phone. Had they seen him leave that place alone?

"Kostya," he whispered.

"Hey," someone yelled.

"But I want a coke," Kostya whined.

"Hey!" they repeated.

Nico spun around, walking backwards.

One of them grinned and raised his chin.

"Kostya," Nico whispered again, "I think I need help."

Kostya's tone turned serious. "Tell me where you are."

Nico faced forward again, trying to ignore the group as he explained his route. He heard the sound of Kostya locking the door to their studio apartment. The squeak of the termite-infested stairs as Kostya jumped down them, only hitting every fourth one the way he always did when he was in a hurry. By the time the sound of the cracked glass door slamming shut came through the phone, someone was grabbing Nico from behind.

He dropped the phone as they slammed him against the wall. He threw a few wild punches. Felt the skin of his knuckles tear against someone's teeth. Then, the dream always turned a hazy red. Maybe it was the blood in his eyes or how the crack in his skull sounded when he was thrown to the pavement that caused it. He wasn't sure. He couldn't count the pairs of hands pulling and hitting him. The shoes that came at him.

From somewhere very far away, he heard Kostya shout. Nico's knees smacked into the frozen pavement as the fists suddenly withdrew. He doubled over, catching himself on his hands, feeling the cold bits of rock dig into his palms. He couldn't breathe. Something tightened around his chest when he tried. His mouth filled with blood.

Barely audible over his ragged breaths were the sounds of shouting. Something like a fist against flesh. Nico dragged himself into the alley. He collapsed on the ground—shivering, or shaking, he wasn't sure—as he ached and went numb in the snow. Whimpering with the effort, he rolled himself over to look up at the sky.

The stars were falling. None left in the perfect, pitch black sky. Softly, they came down all around him and melted into his cooling skin.

Then, hot hands hoisted him up. Kostya said words that didn't make any sense. Nico rested his head against Kostya's chest.

That was where Nico wished the dream would end. He wanted to wake up and not remember the rest. Or just not wake up at all. Let that have been the last thing that happened.

But this was the price he paid for feeling alive again.

He ripped at Kostya with his teeth. Kostya screamed and tried to push him away.

Nico woke up with a start. The sweat was already drying on his skin. He took a few deep breaths, felt the stiffness of his lungs. Death was coming back faster and faster every time.

※※※

Kostya was sitting on the couch, flipping through channels. He smiled at Nico over his shoulder.

"*Izvini*," Nico said, recoiling.

Kostya shook his head. "Don't."

Nico sat down on the couch with him, watching but not-watching the television.

"Roger called. Said we should pack up. Heading out tonight."

"When?"

Kostya looked at his watch. "Half-an-hour."

"Oh." Nico watched as the girl on TV manically tried to sell him a car. "Why didn't you wake me?"

"I thought it'd be more fun to be late and watch that vein in his neck pop out."

Nico smiled. "*Ya lyublyu tebya.*"

"I know."

They took their time. Kostya meandered in the hot steam of the bathroom. Nico sat outside the door, soaking up the overly sweet smells of hotel soap. By the time Roger arrived, they'd done almost nothing to be ready.

"If we're ever on time, he'll start thinking he can expect us even earlier," Kostya explained.

Roger huffed and checked his watch. Then, he ushered them out the door and onto the elevator, where he scolded them like children all the way to the bus then to the city limits sign.

In the morning, they hid from the sun in the back, cut off from the rest of the bus with thick, black curtains and tinfoil on the windows. They claimed hangovers and light sensitivities and occasionally even told Roger that the light made it feel like their eyes were melting inside their sockets and quickened the rotting. He laughed when he was in a good mood and clucked his tongue when he had no patience left for their antics.

The cities blurred together. They needed more blood—or meat. If Nico was honest, he wasn't sure what the necessary ingredient was. But the usual dose hardly lasted through the night anymore, and the death was quick

195

to return, rotting them from edges to core.

Sometime between two desperate, dead groupie girls and a club suggested by the show's promoter, Kostya leaned out over the edge of the overpass. He took a breath and closed his eyes. Only the tips of his toes touched the ground as he barely balanced on the wall. The wind blew his hair around his face like a halo. The sound of the cars passing underneath them was a rhythmic whisper. They were somewhere warm with the smell of salt and water blowing in from the east.

Nico watched him for a while, until he could understand the look on his face. It almost looked like a smile, but it wasn't really.

"Are we done?" Nico fought back the urge to pull his friend away from the edge.

Kostya opened his eyes slowly, a cat waking up from a sunny nap. "Done?"

Nico nodded. "Done. Yeah."

Kostya turned his back to the noise and long fall. "Are you?"

Nico swallowed. His own spit tasted sour as it went down. Even though they'd just eaten, he could feel his heart starting to skip beats. "I think we're running out of time."

Kostya put out his hand. "*Otpuskayet.*"

Nico took it.

They walked until they found another bridge, this one quiet, cracked, and mostly forgotten. Nico fished a pack of cigarettes out of his pocket. It was old, and the red packaging was feathered white around the corners and edges. Kostya smiled when he saw it. They each took one. Nico let the box go and watched it float down until he couldn't see it anymore. He imagined he could hear the smallest of splashes as it hit the water below. The smoke burned Nico's throat. He held it in his lungs, waiting to need to breathe, but it didn't happen. He let it out in a sob.

Kostya moved his hand over Nico's and smiled.

"Watch this."

Kostya blew the smoke out in a series of perfect rings. He raised his eyebrows the way he did after telling a joke that no one was laughing at, so Nico laughed.

The bruised blue of the sky lightened. The stars faded. On the horizon, a slash of red appeared, bleeding across the water, staining the clouds. Kostya's hand tightened on Nico's.

"It's okay," Nico moved closer to him. "I'm not angry this time."

The stars disappeared as the golden light of the sun chased away the red. Nico tried not to, but he had to close his eyes. It was too much. Too much light, too many things sparkling. Flashes went off behind his eyelids like an electrical storm. He felt his hand melt into Kostya's and wondered if

Icarus felt like this just before he fell.

DELILAH'S HOME

by Jeremy Megargee

This box is my home. It's old and crumbling, but it is mine. It is not spacious, but I've never been a woman of considerable wealth, and it suits me just fine. The red velveteen that lines the walls used to be soft, vibrant, but time has stolen away some of that rose-tinted color. It's a dull shade now, dirty maroon, and portions of the cloth hang down in tatters. I've been here a long time. Friends visit me sometimes for dinner, but they are not talkative, and often I am alone.

I'd like a window, but the architecture of my home would not be suitable for a window. I long for a view beyond these walls, just a glimpse of something memorable. A garden. A moonlit sky. A lonely tree on an equally lonely hill. I'm not picky, and I'd find beauty in whatever might wait behind the glass. I cannot hope for sunshine again, not now, not ever, but a window would be nice all the same.

I am a homebody, but most people in this community are homebodies. It's always quiet here and there's never much excitement. Sometimes I hear lawnmowers churning and robins singing, but they're distant sounds, far away. I'd open my door to those sounds, but the clasp is rusted and broken, and I'm too withered and weak to lift my hands high enough to try. I don't let it get me down. Sometimes I hum in my home, creating my own music, putting together tidbits of songs that I used to know, stitching the melodies into something entirely new. The memories are fragmentary, and they often fade, but I can catch one or two sometimes when I'm extra vigilant.

My dress was white, pristine and silken, and how I used to twirl in this dress. My days of twirling have ended, but you never forget how it feels, the whole world spinning, just a kaleidoscope of colors and laughing faces. Braun laughed loudest of all, the sound emerging from his barrel chest like the rumbling of a jovial steam engine.

He was bearded with a dark, vulgar humor that made some turn their nose up at him, but it only endeared him to me more. He was a bear, a gentle bear, capable of great kindness and throaty ballads whenever he was full to the brim with spirits. I was just a girl, a flower just learning how to bloom, but Braun tended the soil of my heart, he found me beautiful…and he helped me to grow. I opened the petals of myself to him, and in meadows, forests, and cool streams beneath pinprick stars, we intertwined ourselves together, that bear of a man and me. Love sneaks up on you, a refreshing breeze, and you don't truly understand the feeling until it caresses the back of your neck. I found love in Braun's hazel eyes. I found love in a grove of weeping willows with crows cawing out their approval far above us. I found love in humble places, and I suppose those places are the best kind.

His ballads were reserved for his friends in the bar when his belly was swirling with mead, but he saved his poems for me. He kept most of them in his head, but a special few he carved with his pocketknife on circles of oak. He'd give them to me, these words whittled into wood, and I keep my favorite clutched to my chest even now.

I remember how he whispered it to me one cold night with winter howling at the door, his strong arms encircling me, holding me close. His breath was hot across my cheek, the scent of the wilderness seeming to emanate from his skin, a lumberjack that had trodden past all the oldest trees—his rough hand sometimes reaching out to touch the bark and feel that age beneath his palm, thanking the tree before he took the axe to it.

He held me then in the same way that he touched the oaks before he felled them. He spoke in the night hours with all the candles unlit and our bodies huddled together for warmth.

"Love has roots just like a tree, and even when the soil takes us, I'll come find thee."

I still hold that circle of oak. My fingers have grown frail, and my dress is ragged, black with mildew, and I wish I could wash it in the river before Braun comes for me. I'd like to look pretty for him. My hair was marigold yellow once, and the ringlets bounced when I walked across the cobblestone streets. Sometimes Braun would lift me high up onto a stone wall and we'd watch the carriages rumble by. The horse's hooves went *clickety-clack,* and I miss that sound. I miss all sounds. I miss the things that I left behind. This place is lonely, sad, and silent. Even if I could open the door, there's a big stone up there above me and it would fall forward and crush my head if I tried to get past it.

My life changed when I reached twenty years of age. The cough came first, a deep cough, and sometimes it felt endless. I began to wake with blood rubies decorating my pillow, and sometimes my lips were stained red when I gazed into the looking glass. I knew what it was. I knew what it meant for me. They called it many things in the town. The robber of youth. The graveyard cough. All the names were the same, and all the names spelled death.

I remember candlelight and sweat on my brow on that last night. I remember Braun holding my little hand, rubbing at the flesh, willing it to become strong again. I wanted to be strong for him. I remember wanting to whisper something to him, something memorable just like the poems that he carved into the oak for me.

The darkness came before that whisper ever left my lips.

I died of consumption on October 29th 1827.

I went to sleep in a deathbed, and I woke in a deathbox.

There is nothing but eternity in this casket that is my home, and even when my friends visit for dinner, they only eat of my rotten flesh, and never stay long enough to keep me company. The earthworms, the rodents, and the beetles with the glossy black shells—all of them selfish, not willing to stay long after they've taken bits and pieces from what remains of my body. My skin is tight and taut, gray instead of pink, and soon there will only be bones, nothing much left at all. Can bones still love? Can bones wait patiently for a promise carved into a circle of oak? I do not know, but I hope they can.

Something is burrowing through the dirt to my left, seeking that splintered hole where the moles sometimes enter. Just more vermin to take what little is left of me. My heart is a shriveled thing, just a little husk under a sinking rib cage, but the beetles haven't eaten all of it yet. It doesn't beat, but it still yearns.

The soil sifts as something pushes through that splintered hole in the side of my casket.

I would gasp, but my lungs are deflated balloons, home to cobwebs and nesting spiders instead of the breath that once circulated through them.

There is a hand reaching through the hole. It is decayed like my own, but big, burly, the knuckles so familiar. I should know. The memory of that hand caressing my cheek is sometimes lost in my broken brain, but now I find it, and it is the sweetest memory of all.

The hand falls on the circle of oak that I hold above the remnants of my heart.

His voice comes from beyond the wall of my pine box, gruff and choked with dirt, but steadfast all the same, a voice made for tavern ballads and whispers reserved just for me.

"Delilah…"

I strain to hear him with my dried eardrums. I summon all that I have, a withered, skeletal limb rising, the fingers of my hand finding his and interlocking with them. Little pieces of dead, mummified skin flake off and float in the box that is my home, but to me, here and now, they are as beautiful as dust motes drifting in the sunlight.

"*Love has roots just like a tree, and even when the soil takes us, I'll come find thee.*"

I smile, my lips eaten away by time and insects, only the teeth remaining, little enamel gardens covered in moss. True darkness finds me now. It's not the darkness of a pine box, but the darkness of night in a forest with great, old oaks that reach towards constellations that shine in the sky.

A bearded lumberjack with an axe slung across his shoulder waits for me in a moonlit clearing. I go to him. I cling to him. We've found each other, and we've left the soil and the pine boxes behind. Our roots run deep, and now we grow again.

About the Storytellers

Everyone knows that a gathering of crows is called a murder, but they're also called a storytelling. As writers, we aim to tell our stories, murdering those errors and fears that hold us back.

Please help us by reviewing this book. Whether you liked it or not, authors need your feedback and validation. It's like air.

To learn more about any of the authors or projects, visit www.amurderofstorytellers.com.

CPSIA information can be obtained
at www.ICGtesting.com
Printed in the USA
BVHW07s0313050718
520783BV00016B/1028/P

9 780998 651286